139    4

# THE HOMECOMING

*Also by Anna Smith*

Spit Against the Wind

# THE HOMECOMING

Anna Smith

review

First published in 2004
by HEADLINE BOOK PUBLISHING

A REVIEW hardback

10 9 8 7 6 5 4 3 2 1

Cataloguing in Publication Data is
available from the British Library

ISBN 0 7553 2112 X

Typeset in Minion by Palimpsest Book Production Limited,
Polmont, Stirlingshire
Printed and bound in Great Britain by
Mackays of Chatham plc, Chatham, Kent

Headline's policy is to use papers that are natural, renewable and
recyclable products and made from wood grown in sustainable
forests. The logging and manufacturing processes are expected
to conform to the environmental regulations of the country of origin.

HEADLINE BOOK PUBLISHING
A division of Hodder Headline PLC
338 Euston Road
London NW1 3BH
www.reviewbooks.co.uk
www.hodderheadline.com

For Sadie

I would like to thank Marion Donaldson and Jane Heller for their invaluable assistance and support. My agent Ger Nichol for all her encouragement and continued faith. All my family and close friends who mean more to me than they will ever know.

Out of his eyes I saw the last light glide.
Here among the light of the lording sky
An old man is with me where I go

Walking in the meadows of his son's eye
On whom a world of ills came down like snow.

Dylan Thomas, 'Elegy'

Back then, the world was swaying to a whole new beat. You could feel the change, the sense of adventure. If you walked down the street you could hear the music drifting from the open windows on a summer's day. There were 'Strawberry Fields Forever' and 'Marmalade Skies', and all you needed was love. Nobody really understood any of it, but it was easy to be swept away. And when the sun split the pavements in the hottest July in years, teenagers picked flowers from gardens and wore them in their hair, just like the song about going to San Francisco.

Bad things were happening all over the world. American soldiers were dying in Vietnam, there were race riots across the USA, and the Rolling Stones got busted for drugs.

But in a little corner called Westerbank, life was more predictable. *Sunday Night at the London Palladium* was on television every Sunday night, and the Tiller Girls on the carousel at the end of the show gave a shape to your life, a kind of comfortable certainty. For Westerbank was a place with no shadows and no secrets. It was a safe place to come home to. Or so it seemed.

# Chapter One

A t first Maggie wasn't sure what it was. It looked like a bag of clothes that somebody had dumped. But when she squinted against the glare, she could see a glint of sunlight on a balding forehead. She looked again, more closely this time, from the head down, and sure enough there were shoes attached to the bottom of the trousers. It was a man.

Instinctively, she swiftly looked straight behind her up the path to the farmhouse where the smoke was swirling out of the chimney as her mum prepared breakfast. She would be safe there if she ran, if he tried to attack her. But she knew she couldn't run because of the choking tightness in her chest from the asthma. No. If she wanted to get back home safe, she would have to go now, walk fast, so that she didn't get out of breath. But she was curious to see more, and found herself taking a couple of short steps towards the figure lying still in the ditch. She stopped just a few feet away from him and squatted down to get a better look.

It was definitely a man, and he was sound asleep, his head resting on what looked like a rolled-up coat. She watched quietly, hardly breathing, in case her wheezing woke him. She watched him breathe out every two or three seconds, and in the silence she could hear a whistling noise coming from the tiny gap where his lips parted just a little. He looked peaceful, his pale face smooth, but his thinning hair made him seem older than her dad, whose hair was blond and thick. Maggie smiled to herself, scanning him from top to toe, observing his grey trousers, frayed at the bottom, and shoes with holes in the soles. He must be a tramp, she thought.

2

The ones she had seen before were always lying drunk at fairs or in the streets on the few occasions she had visited the city with her parents. One always stuck in her mind: he had been lying asleep over an iron grille on the pavement outside the train station in Glasgow. Steam was coming up through the metal and Maggie's mum had told her that would keep him warm. She told Maggie to pray for him, because he was somebody's son. The tramps she had seen always looked grubby and smelled of stale drink and cigarettes. Now she leaned closer and sniffed. This one didn't. She had never been this close to one before and she was fascinated.

The silence was shattered by the loud, low rasping of a magpie that had landed on the fence post above the man's head. The noise startled him out of his slumber and he woke, his eyes wide as though he was surprised to find himself there.

Maggie fell back onto her backside with the fright, but scrambled to her feet immediately and stood over him. She stepped back as he made to sit up. She was ready to bolt, if she had the puff.

'You better not try to murder me,' she said, walking backwards. 'My dad's just up at the house and he'll kill you if you touch me. And you'd better watch my brother too. He's only thirteen, but he does judo and he could kill you easy. I'm nine. And you'll never catch me because I can run really fast,' she lied, standing with her hands on her hips, a safe distance from him, trying to look brash. She hoped she could make it to the house without collapsing if he made a grab for her.

The man sat up, rubbed his eyes and looked straight at her. His face broke into a smile. He raised a hand as if to signal to her that he wouldn't harm her. Then he raised two hands together and spread them out in a pleading way as if to tell her to calm down, everything was fine.

'Who are you?' Maggie said, thinking now he was probably not a murderer.

The tramp said nothing but smiled at her, raising his eyebrows. There were tiny wrinkles at the side of his eyes.

'What's your name? Have you got a name?' she persisted, moving a little closer to him.

He made no response, but began to get to his feet. He put out his hand again in a calming motion as Maggie moved back a step or two. She stood her ground.

'You must have a name. Are you foreign? Do you not understand me? Listen. Me, Maggie. Me, Maggie. You?' She made exaggerated gestures pointing at herself, then to the tramp, the way she remembered the story of Robinson Crusoe when he met Man Friday.

He laughed and shrugged his shoulders. When he stood up, Maggie noticed he looked quite thin, as if he needed a good feed. He dusted the grass off his trousers and jacket, then rubbed his chin, and sniffed in the morning air as he looked across the wide open fields where the Flahertys' black and white heifers had come closer to the fence and now grazed peacefully, watching the scene.

'Can you not talk?' Maggie said, a bit exasperated. 'Are you deaf?'

The tramp shook his head.

'Can you hear me?' she said.

The tramp nodded.

'But you can't speak?' Maggie said, enjoying the excitement of her find.

The tramp nodded.

'So you can't speak but you can hear?' Maggie said.

The tramp nodded, smiling. He put his hand in his pocket and brought out a tiny shiny pebble and handed it to her. She was hesitant at first, but took the smooth stone in her hand and examined the bright rust and blue colours that ran through it.

'Are you hungry?' she said, rubbing her stomach, forgetting that he wasn't deaf.

He nodded, rubbing his stomach and smiling.

'Come with me. I'll ask my mum and dad if you can get something to eat at our house. My mum's making the breakfast. It's

French toast. Do you like French toast?' she asked, walking backwards as he followed her.

The tramp smiled and walked alongside her as they headed up the pathway to the farmhouse.

Through the kitchen window, Kate Flaherty looked out across the farmyard and down the lane edged blood-red with the fuchsia bushes in full bloom. She loved this sight on a warm summer's morning when the rays rising across the fields signalled a scorcher of a day ahead. It had been like this for more than a week now and she was praying every day that the weather wouldn't break so they could bring in the hay, unlike last year when torrential rain ruined all the crops, leaving them with barely enough hay for the animals. She and Frankie were still counting the cost.

In the distance, she caught a glimpse of someone walking towards the farmyard with Maggie. Kate was drying her hands on a tea towel and peered out of the window, wondering who it was that had come to visit at this time on a Saturday morning. She turned the ring of the cooker down and went out to the door to greet them, still with the towel in her hands.

'Who's this now, Maggie?' she said, not recognising the man, and a little suspicious of the gaunt, shabby figure who walked a step behind her daughter.

'Mum. Mum. Look. It's a tramp. He was lying sleeping in the ditch at the bottom of the path. He's all right though. He's friendly. But he can't speak. He can hear though,' Maggie blurted out, her voice beginning to wheeze from the excitement and the short, brisk walk from the end of the path.

Noticing her breathlessness, Kate went towards her and automatically looked for any signs of distress. She lived in dread of Maggie collapsing from the asthma that had plagued her since she was a toddler. She touched her daughter's pink cheek with the back of her hand.

'I'm fine, Mum,' Maggie said, touching her mother's hand, anxious not to be fussed over in front of her new friend.

Kate felt awkward but she managed to smile at the stranger before turning towards the byre and calling for her husband.

From the darkness of the byre, a cow made a tired moaning noise as if it was in distress. Kate knew one of their cows was calving and Frankie and their son PJ had been up since daybreak with her.

'Bit of a problem with the calf,' she said to the stranger who looked towards the byre from where Frankie and PJ emerged, squinting in the sunlight.

'This is getting really serious. We're going to have to get the v—' Frankie broke off when he saw the stranger in his farmyard. He squared his shoulders and quickenend his step. Kate knew he didn't have time for visitors today. If he didn't get the calf out soon he could lose it, as well as the mother who was one of the best cows in the prize herd he had been breeding for years.

'What's all this then? What's going on? Who's this?' Frankie sounded impatient and aggressive, and Kate could see how exhausted and frustrated he was. He wiped drips of perspiration from his brow with his forearm. His shirt was drenched in sweat and his hands and dungarees were caked with blood and gunge from the exertion of trying to pull the calf out of its mother. PJ stood at his side, picking bloodied skin from his hands. Kate reached out and took her son's hand, examining what she recognised as rope burn.

'I'd better get you something for that,' she said.

Frankie looked from Maggie, to Kate, then to the stranger in front of him.

'What's going on?' he said again.

'He's a tramp.' Maggie gave them the news and described how she had communicated with him. She smiled at the tramp who stood with his hands by his side, looking slightly afraid.

Everyone looked at him. The Border collies came out from where they had been lying drowsing below the tractor and circled the tramp. They sniffed around him, then sat down at his side.

6

'See,' Maggie said, happy that the dogs liked her new friend. 'Molly and Rex like him. He must be all right.'

The tramp reached out a hand to one of the dogs and stroked its head.

'Jesus wept, Maggie!' Frankie said. 'What have we told you about talking to strangers?' He looked with exasperation at his daughter. 'Have you a name?' Frankie asked the stranger briskly. 'What are you doing here? Where are you from? Listen, pal, I'm a bit busy for visitors.'

The tramp stood quietly. He touched his lips with his finger and shook his head.

'I don't think he can talk, Frankie,' Kate whispered. 'I think he's a mute. Maggie says he can hear.' She put her hand over her mouth. 'Is he maybe from the asylum?' she whispered, thinking of the huge mental hospital which housed in locked wards all the psychiatric patients from the surrounding area. For as long as she could remember, Calvin Hospital, the grim, grey sandstone building just a few miles away, had always been there, and wild rumours about the asylum had conjured up images of fear among the locals for generations. People who had ventured there, either to visit or work, told stories of inmates locked up and tied to beds. Others spoke of electric shock treatment and rooms where mentally ill patients paced up and down all day long or sat rocking to and fro. Inmates who didn't appear to have too much wrong with them stood at windows, gazing into the grounds and forests beyond. Sometimes people escaped and were caught, and villagers in Westerbank could terrorise their children at night with the threat that they had better get to bed because a loony had escaped from the asylum and was headed up their street.

'Maybe we should just tell him to get on his way,' Frankie whispered back. 'We don't know who he is or where he's been. And I've a cow in there that might die if I don't get that calf out in the next half-hour. I don't have time for social calls.'

Maggie's face fell. The stranger shifted on his feet. They all stood in awkward silence. The tramp walked towards the barn. Frankie and PJ looked at each other.

'Maybe he can help us, Da. An extra pair of hands would be good right now. Get the calf out,' PJ said as the two of them walked after him.

'Listen, pal,' Frankie said, quickening so he was in front and facing the tramp. 'Do you know anything about farm animals? Do you know anything about cows? The calf's coming out hind legs first.'

The tramp nodded and touched his chest. He stuck his thumbs up.

'I think that means he does know about animals, Da,' PJ said.

Frankie looked at the tramp who was smiling enthusiastically at him. 'Would you be able to give us a hand? The cow's a bit old and she's having real trouble. If we don't get the calf out soon we'll lose both of them. Can you help?'

The stranger nodded his head and shrugged his shoulders.

Maggie followed them to the barn and stood in the doorway, watching.

Inside, the brown and white cow stood unsteadily on her feet. Steam rose from her nose and her breath came in short gasps. The stranger rolled the sleeves of his blue and grey checked shirt, went forward to the cow and put his arms round its neck. She flinched, but he leaned into her and seemed to make gentle shushing noises with his head close to hers. The cow appeared to settle. He softly ran his hands across her back until he was behind her. Then he pushed his arm gently inside her up to his shoulder. Frankie and PJ stood watching silently, the rope in their hands. Suddenly the stranger looked at them, his eyes wide.

'Have you got him?' Frankie said. 'Have you got hold of its legs?'

The stranger nodded.

'Quick, PJ. The rope.'

They handed him the rope with the loop and watched anxiously as he pushed it inside the cow and yanked it tight. Frankie raised his eyes to PJ, both thinking the same thought. Whoever this man was, he had done this time and again. All three of them pulled on the rope, gently at first then with more pressure. Finally the small creamy hooves emerged, then the black and white spindly legs. The cow gave one last groan as the calf slipped out covered in slime and dropped onto the straw. Frankie was on his knees quickly to make sure it was alive.

He looked up, his face beaming.

'It's fine. It's a girl, PJ. You're an auntie again,' he joked, smiling. 'And you know, you could just as easy have been an uncle.' He sat back and watched as the calf teetered to its feet after two attempts and nuzzled into its mother. While a bullock would have fetched more at the market, the new heifer would be a welcome addition to his breeding herd, or could be sold off along with some others as a yearling.

In the gloom, Frankie looked into the stranger's pale face. Their eyes met and Frankie sensed that whoever this drifter was, he was harmless. He noted how rake-thin he was, then reached out and shook him warmly by the hand.

'You look as though you could do with a good feed,' he said.

The tramp nodded and smiled. Maggie's face lit up.

'Come on. Let's get washed up and get some breakfast inside us. I don't know about you, pal, but it's been a long day so far and it isn't even noon.'

Everyone filed into the house.

'You're a nutcase, our Maggie,' PJ said as he shooed away the dogs. 'Picking up strays. What if he's escaped from the asylum?' He ruffled his sister's hair. 'But I'll tell you this. He saved that cow in there just now. No doubt.'

'No. He can't be from the asylum,' Maggie whispered. 'He's not mental. He can hear. I'm going to ask if he can stay.'

After they had eaten, Kate and Frankie watched out of the window as PJ, stripped to the waist, chopped logs with the long axe while Maggie and the tramp stood by. The muscles in PJ's lean, adolescent frame rippled under the straps of his dungarees.

Maggie smiled proudly to the tramp at the strength of her big brother.

'He was half starved,' Kate said, lifting plates from the table. 'Did you see the way he wolfed down that food? Maybe he's not eaten for days. Who do you think he is, Frankie? Is he maybe one of those gypsies from the caravans that landed in the village a few years ago? I hope not. Because once they get the road to the house you can't get rid of them. I was glad when the lot of them finally went.'

'I don't know,' Frankie said, studying him from the window. 'He doesn't look like a gypsy. He seems a peaceful type. Harmless. I don't think he's from the asylum. But you never know. Do they not sometimes let people out if they're older? I'll tell you this though, he's been around cattle before, that's for sure. He was inside that cow and pulling the calf out like an old hand. Had that cow calmed down like he'd known her all his life.' As he spoke, he suddenly felt concerned as the tramp hitched up his trousers, which were held up with a piece of rope, and motioned to PJ to let him chop some logs. PJ looked across the yard to the window before he handed over the axe.

'For God's sake. There he's handed an axe to a total stranger,' Kate said, ready to move to the door.

'Calm down, woman. Let's just watch for a second.' Frankie touched her arm gently.

The tramp raised the axe above his head and chopped clean through a fat log. It split and fell beside the small pile that was building up. The tramp smiled to Maggie and PJ who once again looked back at the kitchen window. Maggie waved, and gave a thumbs-up. The tramp placed another log and split it in half. He kept going, chopping the pile of logs effortlessly despite his scrawny frame.

'He's wiry enough anyway,' Frankie said, stroking his chin. 'Could do with some help like that around here, with the hay to be brought in and stuff.'

'Oh, Frankie. You don't even know where he came from. He

could be anybody,' Kate said. She knew they needed help but couldn't afford to pay farmhands after the miserable crop last year left them with huge losses. But she was wary of taking on a total stranger, especially one who couldn't even tell them where he came from.

The door opened and Maggie came in full of excitement.

'Do you see how strong he is, Dad? Look at the logs he's chopped. I think he's brilliant. He'd be great helping with the hay. Can he stay?' Maggie looked from her mum to her dad, her eyes pleading.

'We don't even know his name, Maggie,' Kate said. 'I mean, where did he come from?'

'It doesn't matter. Who needs a name?' Maggie said. 'I think he maybe fell from the sky. Why don't we just call him Sky? That's it. Sky. That's what we'll call him.' She was smiling with delight at her logic. 'Wait till I tell PJ,' and she ran out of the door and across the yard.

'I think we'll keep him on. For a few days anyway. He can sleep in the caravan. It's only lying there empty anyway. What do you think, Kate?' Frankie said, knowing the decision was made.

'Well, at least he won't make a lot of noise.' Kate smiled. 'All right. We'll let him stay and see how it works out. But we'll need to keep an eye on him. Just in case.'

Through the open window they could hear Maggie telling the tramp that since she didn't know his name, she would call him Sky. She looked up to the sky and pointed. He smiled as though he was quite happy with the name.

As Frankie walked out of the house, his nearest neighbour Tom McBride pulled into the yard in his battered old blue Ford Cortina. Maggie spotted him and sprinted across to jump into his outstretched arms.

'Uncle Tom! Uncle Tom!' she screeched as if she was seeing him for the first time in years, even though they met nearly every day.

Smiling, Tom scooped her up and held her upside down.

'There she is, my best girl! How's every single bit of you?' Tom pulled her towards him and held her up in mid-air as though she was a doll. Maggie giggled, her legs kicking wildly. He stood her down and pulled a paper bag out of his trouser pocket.

'Sweets for my sweet,' he said, shaking the bag in front of her. Maggie thrust a sticky pink sweet into her mouth immediately.

'Look, Uncle Tom,' she said through bulging cheek. 'We've got a new worker. I found him. He's my friend. He can't speak, but he can hear.'

Frankie walked towards Tom, smiling at the way his daughter worshipped his friend. He delighted in how close they were because he would trust Tom with his life. Often on a summer's night he and Kate would walk down to Tom's farm and they would sit at the table in the farmyard with a drink or they would stroll down to the village for a pint to hear the latest gossip. Tom had been a great friend to Frankie when Kate was trying to settle into the role of a farmer's wife, getting used to the quieter, slower way of life after years of working as a teacher in a primary school in the town a few miles away. An educated man, Tom would bring books for Kate to read, and slowly Frankie had also begun to read and enjoy glimpses of a world beyond the hard graft he had been used to growing up on the farm. And Tom had been a tower of strength when they lost their first baby, Emily, after just a few weeks.

Frankie saw Tom glance curiously towards Sky and PJ.

'Who's Mr Universe?' Tom said, jerking his thumb in the direction of Sky who stopped chopping and smiled towards him.

'He's some guy who I'm going to take on for the hay. Seems fit enough,' Frankie said. He didn't want to admit that he had no idea where his new worker came from. He told Tom he was just passing through and wasn't able to speak. Frankie said it matter-of-factly as if mutes came in and out of his farmyard every day.

They both stood watching as Sky methodically chopped, while PJ piled up the logs into a wheelbarrow.

'Our Joe's coming home from America.' Tom looked at the ground as he spoke, then at Frankie.

Frankie had hoped never to hear those words. He felt his stomach tense and his hands begin to sweat inside the pockets of his dungarees.

'Is he?' he said finally. He didn't really know what to say. Joe McBride was coming home.

Frankie looked out across the field and saw himself twenty years ago on a rain-soaked October morning, gazing down the hillside to McBride's farm as Joe was spirited away from Westerbank. Since the day he left, Frankie had lived with the secret and the shame of what they had done, believing – hoping – he would never see Joe again. Now the friend he had grown up with since they were five years old was coming back, and bringing with him memories that had haunted him for a lifetime.

'He's coming back to sort some stuff out,' Tom said. 'You know. Now that Ma's gone. There's a bit of money and things. He says he might stay the summer.'

Frankie could see the darkness in Tom's eyes. He himself knew the monster Joe could be. The smaller, sensitive Tom had borne the brunt of it many times when they were kids. Joe, four years older, was the bigger, stronger, favoured son who, it seemed, could do no wrong in his mother's eyes. Frankie had always been the peacemaker between them. Joe was his own age and the two were like blood brothers, but there was an edge to Joe, an element of danger. He would always push everything that bit further, and Frankie knew that sometimes it was just to antagonise his younger, weaker brother. In the past years, with Joe out of the picture, it was Tom who had become Frankie's closest friend. They were always there for each other in a way that was not possible with Joe. Frankie had always been slightly in awe of his bold, uncompromising friend and whenever Joe got into trouble he only had to flash a knowing glance at Frankie to be assured he would cover for him. And Frankie always did it, right down to that one last time.

Now he was coming home, and Frankie was terrified that the world he had built for himself would come tumbling down. From the moment he knew that Kate was the only woman he wanted for the rest of his life, he had lived in dread that she would find out about the secret only he and Joe shared. So many times in the early days of their relationship he had tried to find a way to tell her what had happened, in the hope that she would understand, but he was afraid of losing her. So he kept it to himself and as the years went on, the enormity of what they had done somehow diminished. It drifted and settled somewhere in the back of his mind so that he never had to deal with it. But now everything could change. The thought made him feel slightly sick.

'It's been a long time, Tom,' he said. 'I didn't think Joe would ever come back. I suppose we're in for an interesting few weeks. You know how Joe always sets the heather on fire wherever he is.' Frankie tried to sound light-hearted.

'I know, Frankie. But I tell you one thing. I'm not the man he left. I'll not be browbeaten or pushed around. I don't care how much piggin' money he's made over there. I don't care if he's shitting fivers. I'm my own man now, Frankie. My own man,' Tom said, his blue eyes hard.

'Sure you are, Tom,' Frankie said, knowing that Tom was trying to convince himself. 'Come and meet my new helper.' He pulled Tom towards Sky. He wasn't ready to deal with a conversation about Joe.

'It was me who found Sky,' Maggie said proudly, slipping her hand into Tom's.

'Sky? What kind of name's that?' Tom said, bemused.

'Christ knows. Don't ask,' Frankie said, shaking his head. 'You've done a right turn there,' he said to Sky. 'There's a job here for you for the summer if you fancy it.' He ruffled Maggie's hair. 'I hear this one's got a name for you – Sky. What do you think?'

The tramp's pale eyes lit up and his thin downturned mouth broke into a smile. He gave them the thumbs-up.

'Yesss!' Maggie punched the air, and looked up at her new friend. 'It'll be great, Sky. You can stay in the caravan. It's just like having your own house.' Maggie pointed across the yard to the rickety old caravan they used mostly for storage. 'We'll help you clean it out. Won't we, PJ?' She turned to her brother, waiting for his approval.

'Yeah. OK. Suppose so.' PJ tried to sound uninterested but in truth he was just as fascinated by Sky as Maggie was. He had never met anybody before who couldn't speak. There had been a deaf lad at school who used to wear two hearing aids and whose voice came out in a kind of yodelling shriek when he spoke. PJ remembered how the boy was taunted in the school playground and was always in tears.

Sky looked across at the caravan and smiled to all around him and shook Frankie's hand vigorously. Then he shook Tom's hand and smiled at Maggie and PJ.

'That one's got you right round her little finger,' Tom whispered to Frankie.

'Oh yeah! That's good coming from you. She's got you jumping through hoops.'

They both laughed and walked towards the house where Kate waved them inside for tea. The radio was blaring Tom Jones singing 'I'll Never Fall In Love Again'.

# Chapter Two

The setting sun threw shafts of sunlight onto the table where Tom pored over papers from the box he had taken from beneath his mother's bed. Even now, going into her bedroom, he half expected to hear her voice, demanding, criticising. Her prayer book still lay on the lace cloth that covered the dark mahogany table beside her bed. In the two months since his cousin, the undertaker Marty O'Hare, coffined his mother from the big brass bed where she lay cold and stiff, Tom had moved nothing in the room. It was as though by closing the door he could blot out the misery. He had only gone in now because he had to retrieve the big box.

He sat at the kitchen table with his mug of tea, deftly lifting out sheafs of dusty, yellowing paper. He blew on them and watched absently as tiny specks of dust danced in the light. His birth certificate. Joe's baptism certificate. A fading first Holy Communion certificate with his name on it and a date that seemed a lifetime ago. It conjured up a flash of childhood images.

He could see Joe and Frankie swinging across the burn from a length of rope that hung from the old oak tree. Then he saw Joe ridiculing him from the far bank because he was afraid to get on the rope and follow the pair of them on the daring leap.

He lifted out a bundle of papers tied with a red ribbon, and saw the name of the insurance firm, and he remembered his mother handing over the book every week to the tall, sickly looking insurance man who called at their house every Thursday afternoon. Tom put the papers to one side and rummaged around in the box.

He took out the black picture frame that was lying face down, and even before he turned it over he knew what it was. He smiled to himself as he looked at the young, fresh-faced black and white snap of himself in his uniform the first year he started at the seminary. He was wearing a dark blazer and grey flannels, his hair slicked into a perfect parting and combed to one side. His younger self was smiling broadly from the picture, looking just like an older man cut down. His mother had been so proud of him that day. This was her gift from God, her own boy chosen to be a priest by the man himself. She had prayed for it all her life, knowing full well that Joe, even though she couldn't help loving him more, could never aspire to be a priest. But Tom would give her the respectability that would set her apart from the others in Westerbank. Her boy would be the best priest there ever was. Sure with his gentle nature, he was made for it, she used to say. Tom put the picture down and sat back, watching the sun slip behind the hillside.

He heard Frankie's car pull up in the yard and put the picture inside the box and moved it to the floor. He stood up and tried to shake himself out of the melancholy that had washed over him in the last hour. He went to the door, just as Frankie gave it two knocks and walked in.

'Frankie,' Tom said. 'How're you doin'?' He noticed that Frankie looked fresh and washed, and he guessed he was calling to see if he wanted to go to the pub.

'Hiya, Tom. Goin' for a pint? Loughran's has got new owners. Some couple from the Borders. I think their name's Delaney or Mulvanney or something. Thought we'd go down and see the cut of them,' Frankie said, standing with his hands in his pockets. His eyes roamed around the tiny living room where he, Joe and Tom had spent so much of their childhood locked in boys' games. He had always loved the smell inside the old cottage, with its low wooden beams and the crooked windows set into the thick stone walls more than a hundred years ago, fashioned by Tom's great-grandfather. The ashes from last night's fire still lay in the hearth,

17

but the rest of the room was neat for a man who lived on his own. Much neater, Frankie thought, than he would have been had he not Kate to pick up and lift for him at every turn. It must have been that early discipline of the seminary where boys kept every-thing in neat little bundles, from their clothes to their emotions. Never let anything get out of control. That was when the Devil would move in, he remembered Tom telling him one night when too much drink had been taken.

'Mulranney, their name is,' Tom said, remembering what he had been told earlier in the day when he had been in the butcher's. 'His wife's a Protestant. It's a mixed marriage.'

'As long as they can serve a good, cold pint, I don't give a shite if they're Jehovah's Witnesses. Do you?' Frankie said. He was a Catholic, but despised the bigotry among Catholics and Protestants that was a way of life in the west of Scotland. He knew there were certain pubs in the village that were locally accepted as having Catholic customers, and others that were frequented mainly by Protestants. Even though they worked together in farms, pits and factories, and were friends, the bigotry still bubbled beneath the surface.

'No. Not really. But there's some eejits that will. You know, with Loughran being a big Catholic and stuff. Anyway, I'll just give my face a shine and be right with you,' Tom said and went into the bedroom.

They drove down to the village in Frankie's car, passing the caravan site at the edge of the river that wound its way from Westerbank all the way to the sea ten miles away. The caravan site covered the length of one farmer's field and belonged to big Alex Hardie who rented it out for caravans and tents every summer. He didn't care who stayed there, whether it was gypsies or hippies smoking funny cigarettes and singing all night long, as long as they paid their rent. Frankie and Tom could make out children jumping into the river from the side and screaming when they hit the cold water. There were already twelve or fourteen cara-vans of all shapes and sizes parked, and various people unpacking things from their cars. A football was kicked high up into the sky and several children and young teenagers jostled each other, screeching and laughing on a stretch of grass, waiting for the ball to come down. Two or three dogs barked, excited to be free after being cooped up in cars for whatever journey they had made. The holidaymakers who travelled every year from their various little corners were busy making a home for themselves in their new surroundings. Tables and chairs were being unfolded and placed outside caravans for the coming days and nights of eating and drinking in the open air. Strangers waved to their new neighbours and chatted at caravan doors, delighted that the evening sky was burning with an amber glow that was sure to bring the sunshine tomorrow – unlike last year, when they stayed inside steamed-up caravans with squabbling, frustrated children, listening to the rain battering on the roofs, while the caravan park turned into a muddy quagmire outside.

'I see the white settlers have arrived. The wagons are in a circle. God knows what kind of headers we'll be stuck with this summer,' Tom said as they slowed down on the way past, remembering some of the antics of last year's batch.

'Look, there's our Maggie and PJ down there already in case they miss anything. They've got that Sky fella as well,' Frankie said. Maggie and PJ were sitting on the fence surveying the caravans. 'God knows what she'll be dragging home before the week's out.' He shook his head, knowing that whatever his daughter did, he could never in a month of Sundays scold her with any conviction.

At the corner of the village, just across from Mulranney's pub, half a dozen men stood passing the time of day, exchanging gossip and adding on their own little strands. The corner, as it was known, was the focal point for any of the men in the village who had time on their hands and nothing to do with it. Every evening as the night closed in they would stand there smoking their pipes and puffing fags, telling stories and jokes that had been handed down for generations. And it was there at the corner that they passed judgement on everything from the price of coal to the size of the breasts on the new young Irish wife of Baldy Cassidy, the widowed baker who had just recently remarried a woman years younger than himself and was the envy of every healthy man in Westerbank. As Frankie and Tom drove past, the men gave them the traditional country greeting among people who were comfortable with each other, which involved as little movement as possible: they blinked, touched their caps with just one finger, or gave half a nod.

Inside the pub a fug of smoke hung in the air and clung to the wood-panelled walls yellowed from years of pipe and cigarette smoke. In the small snug at the far corner, a couple sat close together, the stained-glass window above the swing door disguising their shape and making them look mysterious. Wooden shelves all around the bar were cluttered with the bric-a-brac gathered from generations of village life. Old football trophies. Darts shields. Faded pictures of young men in ancient football shirts who had gone on to greater things with Celtic or Rangers. A miner's lamp, always polished, stood by a framed black and white picture of grinning teenagers, most of whom had perished in the disaster of 1948. Six men and five teenage boys had died after a beam collapsed in the colliery, crushing them under tons of rubble. But even as their bodies were brought out, the men continued in shifts to try to dig out three men still unaccounted for. The story had entered Westerbank folklore, because after the third night, as everyone sat in the pub, shellshocked, the door opened and the missing men staggered in. They had been trapped in an air pocket and amazingly managed to free themselves when everyone else had given them up for dead.

Frankie and Tom nodded to a group of farmers they knew who were listening to a story one of them was relating. They all burst into lusty guffaws at the punchline.

The barman, who they guessed must be Mulranney, pulled the two pints of beer Tom requested and shoved them across the bar to them.

'On the house,' he said as Tom was about to hand him a five pound note.

Tom and Frankie looked at each other, surprised, almost suspicious.

'Cheers!' Frankie lifted his pint. 'If Loughran had given anybody a free drink we'd have thought we were about to get measured for a wooden waistcoat!' he said with a smile.

'Just getting to know my customers,' Mulranney said, his grin showing a gap between his two front teeth that gave him a rakish look. 'Everybody I meet for the first time is getting a free pint. Just the one, mind.'

'Best of luck to you. Cheers, pal,' Tom said, lifting his pint to his lips. 'You'd better watch the Badger Ryan over in the corner there. He'll be in here with half a dozen disguises on for the next two weeks to get as much free drink as he can,' Tom joked, loud enough for the Badger to hear.

'Kiss my arse, McBride!' the Badger said. 'Mr Mulranney here has become a personal friend of mine. And I've put him straight about some of the miserable shites that stoat in and out of here. You know, I might even have mentioned your name.' The Badger was sarcastic, his words slightly slurred. But he seemed to be taking the ribbing in good part.

Tom and Frankie laughed to Mulranney who winked back as though he had already got the measure of Mickey Ryan. It was easy to see why he was nicknamed the Badger. A silver streak of hair ran from the front of his fringe to the crown, and a pinched face and pointed nose gave him the distinct look of a badger. Ryan was the equivalent of the local newspaper who could tell you everything that moved in and around Westerbank. He was nearly sixty now, and though his face showed the deep lines of a man who had spent most of his life working outside in all weathers, he still looked fresh. His cheeks, though lean, were ruddy from years of drinking, because he had nobody at home to keep him in check since his mother died ten years ago, leaving him to run the small farm on his own. The Badger Ryan was an expert on who was buying what and how much for, and he was always ready to whisper the details of who was cutting whose grass, the local expression for illicit sexual liaisons.

Tom always felt a little sorry for him because he was the butt of everyone's humour, and he used to think the Badger had the look sometimes of a lonely man who had seemed to arrive at middle age without ever having any joy in his life. Now and again he cooked dinner for him, but he could never keep going to him with drink. And he couldn't understand why, when he was the worse for drink, the Badger would rant about Joe and how Westerbank was well rid of him. When Tom pressed him further, he just looked bitter and wouldn't say any more. Tom had too much on his own plate to be interested in the gossip that was dreamed up in Westerbank. His father had always said you could never trust the Badger and that his eggs were always double-yolked.

As the evening wore on and the men in the pub continued to drink, the noise level rose. The older men, dressed in much the same sort of clothing they had been wearing for years, sniggered at the style of a group of younger men in the latest flower power fashion with long hair and sideburns, tight bell-bottom trousers and open-necked garishly floral shirts. The lads gulped their pints fast, slagged each other off about girls and boasted about what a success they would be at the dancing in a couple of hours.

In the far corner a domino match between four old men almost came to blows.

'You're looking at my hand, ya cheatin' bastard!' said the fat old man with the crimson face.

'Away and give us peace! Play your domino, ya eejit!' his lantern-jawed companion said. 'All you've done is moan all night!'

The third man sat studying his dominoes, moving his bottom set of false teeth in and out of his mouth while he concentrated.

'Are you going to stop doing that with your bastardin' teeth? You're giving me the boak!' the fourth man said, screwing up his face in disgust.

'Shut up! I'm trying to think!' the man with the false teeth said.

The Badger peered through the window of the pub and piped up from his seat at the bar, 'Look who's coming in. Love's young dream.'

All eyes turned to the door as in walked Baldy Cassidy with the voluptuous Breige, the woman he had managed to make his wife. Baldy held the door open for her and touched her arm proprietorially as he led her to a seat by the window. People had remarked that since Cassidy married Breige four months ago, just nine months after his wife passed away, there was a glow about him that had never been there when his wife was alive. His face was scrubbed until it positively shone as much as the completely hairless head he had been inflicted with since the age of twenty-four.

'How's it goin', gents?' he said by way of a general greeting. 'Tom. Frankie,' he added with a sideways glance as he stood beside them at the bar to order his drink. The whiff of aftershave nearly knocked them over, and Frankie could barely keep a straight face.

'How's tricks, Baldy?' he asked, feeling he had to say something.

'Tricks, Frankie, could not be better.' Cassidy licked his lips and rolled up the sleeves of his shiny black Bry-nylon shirt, baring hairy, muscled forearms. Frankie and Tom knew exactly what he meant. Since he'd married Breige, who was only twenty-three, in a quiet church ceremony twenty miles away, he had been making less than subtle remarks about how explosive his life was in the bedroom. The Badger said he had hinted to him that he was barely able to get out of bed to bake the rolls in the morning because he was up half the night doing things he'd only ever read about in the kind of magazines you got sent in brown envelopes.

'Out on the tiles, is it, Cassidy?' Tom said, sipping his fresh pint.

'No.' Baldy gave them both a considered look as he took his change off Mulranney. 'Actually we've just had a lovely meal and decided to drop in for a quick drink before we go home. You know. For an early night.' He winked.

Tom and Frankie smiled broadly. Then Baldy leaned towards

them and whispered, 'That chicken Maryland up at the hotel. Must be an aphrodisiac. Jumpin' out her skin, she is.' He glanced across at raven-haired Breige who was sitting cross-legged, her tight, short, black skirt revealing ripe, sturdy thighs.

'On yourself, Baldy,' Frankie said. 'As they say in the best of bakeries, I hope your doughnuts turn out like Fanny's – Craddock, that is.'

Tom spluttered into his beer. Baldy tutted and shook his head. He lifted his whisky and a double Bacardi and lemonade and almost shimmied towards the table where Breige sat smiling like a predatory cat.

By the fourth pint, Frankie and Tom had covered almost every bit of small talk they could, from the hay to the markets, from Tom's mother's funeral to the weather. Now and then they brought Mulranney into the conversation. He seemed a pleasant enough man, keen to be part of the community. There was no sign of the wife yet, Tom remarked to Frankie, quietly. Both of them wondered who was going to be first to bring up the subject of Joe's homecoming. Feeling more relaxed with the drink, Frankie ventured first.

'So when's Joe coming, Tom?' he said.

Tom took a swig of his beer and wiped his mouth. 'Next Thursday.'

The word was that Joe had made a lot of money in the building trade since he went to New York. He lived in some fancy house now, somewhere in Long Island. Frankie had no phone, so he had not heard Joe's voice since the day before he left for America. But the occasional letters he had written to his mother and the two or three to him made it sound like a fantastic life. The only knowledge Frankie had of America was from what he had seen on his black and white television. He liked to watch *The Untouchables* on a Sunday night or *Bonanza* and he loved the confident swagger of the Yanks in some of the films he and Kate would see on their rare visits to the cinema in Ayr.

The furthest Frankie had been was to Blackpool for a week's

holiday and that was seven years ago. He was beginning to feel that his old pal would see him as a failure who had never really achieved much. Sometimes he thought he was a failure. The way Joe had described it to Tom, he had his own building company and about thirty workers, mostly Irish and Scots out to America to make their fortune. Frankie wondered how Joe had made his money. Knowing him, he probably just took what he wanted.

Frankie looked at the four old men playing dominoes, suddenly seeing himself in twenty years. That's how it was. Everyone turned into their parents. Joe's life in America seemed exotic. Maybe he would be sneering at them all when he got home. Maybe he had managed to put everything behind him and was coming home as if nothing had ever happened. That would be typical of Joe.

'Funny how he never got married,' Frankie said. He remembered how successful handsome Joe had been with the girls when they were teenagers.

'I think he's had more women than hot dinners. Or so he tells me,' Tom said. 'He told me once on the phone when he was drunk that he'd shagged every nationality from Brooklyn to Bombay. I'm surprised his knob hasn't fallen off by now,' he added drily.

Frankie laughed, recalling how Joe had always bragged about his prowess with girls. Somewhere inside him there was a hankering for the great days they had had as teenagers before everything changed.

'I'm looking forward to seeing him, Tom,' Frankie said. He didn't want to tell Tom how edgy he was about Joe's return. He wondered how Westerbank would react to Joe's return after everything that was said when he suddenly went away. He wondered what Joe would think of Kate and if she would be impressed by his wealth and good looks. That would be too much to bear. Down the years he had amused Kate with stories of their antics as they grew up. He painted Joe as some kind of exotic, daring dreamboat who had every girl in the area swooning over him. But that was all right as long as he was thousands of miles away in America.

Tom leaned towards Frankie and spoke softly. 'To tell you the truth, I was glad he went to America, even if I've always kind of wondered why. I didn't really care. What was important was that he wasn't here. I hate to say that, but that's how I felt for a while. I can handle it better now though. I hope.'

Frankie didn't want to be drawn into the reasons behind Joe's sudden departure. He looked at his watch and finished the dregs of his pint. 'I think we'd better make tracks.'

'Yeah,' Tom said, smiling. 'You never know, if you don't hurry back, that Sky fella might be climbing in beside Kate. And the thing is, he's that quiet she'd never know he was there till it was too late.'

'No fear of that, Tom. There was no chicken Maryland on our menu tonight.' He laughed and slapped Tom on the back. They waved to Mulranney and headed for the door.

# Chapter Three

Tom's back was aching, and he was glad to see there were only two more stretches of fence to whitewash. He was beginning to get blisters on his hand where he held the shaft of the brush, but he pushed on, driven to get the place into shape for Joe's arrival in two days' time.

He seemed to have been working flat out for the last five days, taking advantage of the good spell of weather to get the hay in and do lots of outside work around the farm. He didn't want his brother coming home after twenty years and remarking that the place had gone to rack and ruin.

Eventually he went into the house out of the sun and sat at the table drinking cold orange barley water. He had sorted out most of his mother's financial affairs and the insurance matters were all being dealt with. He looked at the picture of himself at the seminary and smiled at the boy smiling back at him. When he really thought of himself on that day, he recalled that he had been truly happy. He wished it could have stayed that way.

He lifted more papers from his mother's box and then stopped dead. On a rolled-up bundle of papers there was handwriting that he thought he recognised. The way it flowed, the curling loops. His heart jumped. It couldn't be. He took a deep breath, but it wouldn't come. He reached in and fingered the bundle, which was tied with a faded blue silk ribbon. He noticed that his hands were trembling, and he sat back, afraid to lift the papers out. His mouth was dry and he gulped more barley water, spilling some out of the side of his mouth. He got up and walked around, looking at the box from every angle of the room as though it was a bomb waiting to go off. He was sure it was her handwriting. But why would her letters be here? His head was swimming.

He heard PJ's voice calling him and he swiftly tried to compose himself. He took a deep breath and walked to the door.

'Hiya, Uncle Tom.' PJ was standing in the yard, smiling. Sky was with him and gave Tom a kind of shy wave when he came out of the door.

'Hi, PJ,' Tom said, trying to sound casual. 'Hello, Sky.'

'Mum says can you come down for dinner tonight?' PJ said. 'Da's got some steaks from the butcher for a job he did and Mum's going to cook them.' PJ smiled. 'He says you and him deserve a few beers now that the hay's nearly all in.'

'Yeah. That'd be great. I don't think I've the strength to cook for myself. I'll definitely be there, PJ. I'll bring a few cans down and we can have a good blether. I haven't talked to Kate in ages. Great stuff.' Tom was genuinely enthusiastic. He had a feeling he would need some company tonight, and he loved talking to Kate who was like the sister he never had. He was anxious to get back to the letters, but he felt he should ask PJ and Sky if they wanted a drink. He was glad when they declined.

'How're you settling into your new home, Sky?' Tom asked. 'That's some tree house you're building there. A man of many talents, eh?'

Sky nodded and then pointed to the part of the fence that was still to be painted. He seemed to be offering to do the job.

'That's really good of you, Sky,' Tom said. 'But another hour will do that and then I'm for a bath. But don't worry, if you're looking for extra work, I'll find it for you.'

PJ said they had to get back down to invite their new friends from the caravan site up for dinner, and Tom watched as he and Sky disappeared down the road. Then he went back inside and locked the front door. He sat at the table and lifted out the bundle of letters.

There was no mistaking the fine lines of her handwriting, the generous way it flowed and looped and the little flurry she seemed to do at the end. The familiar signing off. 'With all my love, always and for ever, Maria.' The 'y' was underscored with a loop that made it look almost musical. Even with the letters in his hand, Tom's head was still confused. Somewhere in a leather bag among his possessions he thought he had every letter that Maria had ever written to him. He had read them every day for the first year as if by reading them he could believe she was still there and they could relive their time together. Through tears and choking grief, he had scanned them line by line, searching for a reason why she had suddenly stopped writing. All the promises. All the nights in the seminary in Rome where he had become adept at leading a double life, hiding his love affair while he struggled with his vocation. In time, he realised she must have found someone else. He even talked himself into understanding it. But it took much longer for her face to cease to haunt his dreams, and for her gentle laughter to fall silent in his thoughts.

As he read the first letter, his face paled and his stomach began to churn; now at last he understood.

He could hear her voice as he read: 'I am trying so very hard, my darling, to understand and accept that this is the only way you are able to deal with this. Perhaps it would have been too painful to meet and finally to part for ever.' Even as he read the words, Tom could scarcely believe them. He read on.

'Maybe it is better that I remember you as you were, happy and smiling, while we believed we could be together. How naive we were. What fools, that we did not walk away long ago when we still could.'

Tom felt tears coming to his eyes.

'Your silence has made me understand how truly impossible our dreams were. I hope you will be happy, Tom, and will make a great priest. I will never forget you, and I will love you every day of my life. With all my love, always and for ever, Maria.'

The tears streamed down Tom's face as he sat with the letter in his hand. He put it down on the table and his head sank into his hands. In the stillness of the room, he could hear himself breathe. He wiped his tears with the back of his hand, then folded the letters and put them away.

Up in the Flahertys' farmyard, Maggie and her new friends from the caravan site were carrying bowls and plates from the kitchen to the huge wooden table that sat outside, below the living-room window. The dogs jumped up and down after them, excited by the activity.

Marty and Jess McKay had been inseparable from Maggie and PJ for a week now. The McKays were down from Glasgow on holiday with their caravan which stood out on the site because it was falling to bits. Maggie and PJ couldn't believe there were four of them living in the cramped, dingy caravan, with its sheet of polythene taped over one of the broken windows. When Jess and Marty teamed up with Maggie and PJ after a football game on the grass with the other kids, they had become instant friends. But they could sense the embarrassment as, later on, they walked their new friends home. Their dad was nicknamed Gunboats, and Marty said it was because he was in some kind of secret squad in the army and went on special missions. When they saw him for the first time he was sitting outside in his vest, his arms and shoulders covered in tattoos. He was swigging from a can of beer and smoking. Their mum was sitting puffing her fag with pinched, pale cheeks. Jess and Marty's high spirits disappeared as they approached their caravan and PJ and Maggie didn't wait around.

It was Maggie who had insisted that their new friends be invited up for dinner, though Kate drew the line at asking the parents, until she had at least met them in person. But she did agree to allow Marty and Jess to sleep over for the night.

'We've got raspberry jelly for afters. And cream,' Maggie said proudly to Jess who raised her eyebrows and licked her lips.

'My granny used to make that for us on a Saturday night when she watched us,' Jess said, placing a bowl of salad on the table. 'We used to help her stir in the jelly squares then wait for it to set and on Sundays we would have it after Mass with our dinner. Not any more though.' Jess looked sad.

'Why not?' Maggie said, her eyes questioning.

'She died,' Jess said, pushing her hands into her pockets.

Maggie nodded knowingly. She was an expert on death since old Mrs McBride had died in her bed a couple of months ago.

'Did you see your granny?' Maggie asked. 'Did you see her dead? I've seen a dead person.'

Jess looked pensive. 'I was in the bed beside her when she woke up dead. Well. I mean, she didn't wake up. I woke up and she was dead beside me.' Her face was pale.

Maggie's eyes nearly popped out of her head. She and PJ had sneaked into Tom's house during one of the quiet moments because they were desperate to see what old Nora McBride looked like now that she was dead. They had recoiled when they saw the waxy, wrinkled face and thin lips lying in the coffin, her body wrapped in a white silk shroud. But to wake up next to a dead person was really something. Maggie was agog as Jess told her how her granny was warm but wasn't breathing when she woke up and she ran out of the house in her pyjamas to get her mum and dad in the next tenement.

They stood in silence for a moment, Maggie studying her friend with a new respect. 'That's amazing,' she said finally. Jess shrugged her shoulders and they went back into the kitchen.

Outside the barn, Sky sat with PJ and Jess's thirteen-year-old brother Marty. Sky was carving some kind of animal from a piece of wood and the boys watched him intently.

In the kitchen Kate was slapping steaks and link sausages onto the grill. Frankie took some glasses out of the dresser.

'These do?' he asked, lifting them up to show Kate.

'Yeah. They're great. But give the kids the plastic ones.'

Kate lifted the lid from the bubbling pot of potatoes. Her face was flushed from the heat of the kitchen, and she blew her fringe out of her eyes. Frankie watched her from where he stood at the edge of the fireplace, thinking how lovely she looked in her yellow cotton dress. To him, she hadn't aged a day in the sixteen years they had been married and he loved to see her face every morning now just as much as he had the day after their wedding. But sometimes he felt she could have done so much better for herself if she hadn't married him and given up her job teaching art. Life as a farmer's wife was a daily grind of hard work and counting the pennies. They lived for PJ and Maggie, both more precious than ever because their firstborn had died of meningitis when she was just four weeks old. They had christened her Emily two days before she was struck down with the fever and she was dead within twelve agonising hours. Frankie had never known such pain. He had never known he could feel so deeply about anything. His first thought was that he was being punished by God. He woke every morning with a choking tightness in his throat, but he had to hide his tears as he comforted Kate who cried for a whole year after they buried their baby. They never believed people when they said that time would heal, but finally it did and the darkness began to lift when Kate became pregnant with PJ. When Maggie came along their joy was marred when they discovered she had chronic asthma; and she almost died during an attack when she was two. They lived in fear that they would lose her the way they had lost Emily.

In Frankie's darker moments he felt he was a failure and that Kate deserved so much more, but she always told him not to be stupid, that nobody could love her more than he did and that was all that mattered to her.

'Well, that's everything just about ready. When Tom comes we can have a drink outside then eat in a little while,' she said, pushing her wispy red hair back from her face.

When they went outside they could see Tom's figure in the distance walking across his field in the setting sun.

Tom saw them at the door and waved. Maggie was making for the field to come and greet him. He took a deep breath and smiled, hoping his face didn't show any sign of the distress he had been in only a couple of hours ago. His eyes still felt tight and he blinked once or twice to ease them. His insides felt as though someone had punched him, but he knew he had to keep his feelings to himself. He could never discuss with anyone what he had just discovered. The timing of it couldn't have been worse. He was edgy enough about Joe coming as it was, without now finding out that the path of his whole life had been decided for him by his mother. He could hardly get his head around it. He had lain in the bath until the water was cold, staring at the wall, trying to come to terms with it all. What had happened to Maria?

He had fallen in love with her on the Spanish Steps in Rome. He had looked up from the book he was studying and was instantly captivated by the dark-haired girl taking a picture of her two friends. From her looks and chatter, he assumed she was Italian. But when he offered to take a picture of all of them together, she answered him in a broad Scottish accent. By the end of the evening they had walked and talked themselves into exhaustion and Tom knew his life would never be the same. They arranged to meet the following day, when Tom resolved to tell her he was studying for the priesthood. And so he did. But by that time it was too late for both of them.

Where had she gone? Where was she now? The questions swirled in his mind, tormenting him, but he had to put them away for now. He drew on all his years of self-control and denial at the seminary. He could push this out of his mind. He had to.

'There she is.' He put out his arms as Maggie ran towards him with a wide smile. His spirits were lifted. He pulled her up and threw her onto his back, then continued down the field and into the Flahertys' farmyard.

After they had eaten they all sat around the table feeling relaxed. Tom and Frankie sipped beer, but Sky politely refused their offer and stuck to orange squash along with Kate and the children. Night had begun to fall and the light from the oil lamps cast shadows across the farmyard. The radio in the kitchen was turned down low but they could hear the strains of Petula Clark singing 'Don't Sleep In The Subway Darling' playing in the background.

'That was brilliant,' Jess said, wiping her mouth with the back of her hand. 'I wish we got dinners like this every day, don't you, Marty?' She looked enthusiastically at her brother who glowered back.

Kate changed the subject. 'Maggie, why don't you and Jess help me clear this stuff away then you can have the rest of the cream that's left over.'

'Brilliant,' Jess said, starting to pile plates on top of each other.

'C'mon,' PJ said, nudging Marty. 'That's girls' stuff. We'll play at keepy-upy before it gets too dark.' Marty got up from the table and followed PJ across the yard.

Tom glanced at Frankie fleetingly, both of them feeling slightly awkward because neither of them knew how to converse with Sky.

'Enjoy that, Sky? Good food, eh?' Frankie said, louder than he needed to.

Sky smiled and gave him the thumbs-up. Tom gave Frankie a look, hoping to convey to him that he didn't have to shout because Sky was mute. Frankie seemed to take it on board. They sat in silence, wondering what to say next. Sky seemed perfectly comfortable.

'I wonder if he can communicate by writing,' Frankie said. 'You know, we've never asked if he can write. Should we ask?' He spoke softly to Tom, but Sky overheard and shook his head when they both looked at him.

'What about drawing, Sky? Can you draw? Like a picture?' Tom said, making a picture frame with his hands.

Sky nodded his head eagerly. Frankie and Tom looked at each other, surprised. Frankie got to his feet and went into the kitchen where Kate was piling dishes into the sink.

'Kate, Sky seems to be able to draw. I think we should give him a pen and a bit of paper. See if we can learn any more about him,' Frankie said, rummaging through a drawer.

'Really?' Kate said. 'That's great. How come none of us thought of that before?' She opened the drawer next to the one Frankie was searching in and handed him a notepad she used for sketching and a pencil. 'There. See what he does with that.'

Outside, Frankie handed Sky the pad. Tom sat forward with interest.

'Right,' said Frankie. 'We'll keep it basic. Where did you come from, Sky?'

Sky stared at both of them for a few seconds before looking at the notepad, then back at them.

'It's OK, Sky. It doesn't matter where you came from. You're a good man. We trust you.' Frankie's voice was encouraging.

Sky smiled and started to sketch. Frankie and Tom tried to make it out upside down. It looked like a baby. In a couple of minutes Sky was finished and turned the notepad towards them.

On it was a quite skilful drawing of a baby wrapped in a shawl inside a basket of some description. There was a drawing of a woman with her hands outstretched towards the baby, and another of a woman who seemed to be taking the baby.

'What do you think?' Frankie said to Tom.

Tom studied the drawing. Kate had joined them and stood behind them, also looking at the sketch.

'Well, it's obviously a baby,' Tom said. 'The first woman looks as if she's trying to reach it.'

'Or maybe she's giving it away,' Kate said.

Sky nodded his head furiously, indicating that Kate was correct. All three looked at each other, intrigued.

'Someone gave you away?' Kate said.

Sky nodded.

'Your mother, Sky?' Kate bit her lip.

Sky nodded again, his eyes bright.

'Jesus!' said Tom, suddenly filled with emotion as he looked at the slightly forlorn figure of Sky, eager to please his new friends.

'So what brought you here, Sky? Where have you been for most of your life?' Frankie said.

Sky turned a page on the notebook and started to draw furiously, his brow furrowed in concentration.

'Maybe we shouldn't be prying,' Kate said.

But Sky looked up and waved his hand as though to indicate he wanted to do it.

They watched him fill the page, shading and sketching. They could make out a couple of animals and a small field. Then some houses, and then a seemingly endless building with hundreds of windows, which looked familiar.

Frankie, Kate and Tom all seemed to recognise it at once: Calvin Hospital, the asylum they had only ever driven past or seen in pictures. They glanced at each other.

'You lived there? All your life?' Frankie asked.

Sky turned the page and pointed to the baby in the basket.

'Your mother gave you away to another woman? And she gave you over to that place? Is that what you mean, Sky? Is that what you're saying?' Tom said almost in disbelief.

Sky put out his hand and hovered it above the ground.

'When you were a young boy?' Kate said.

Sky nodded.

'Because you couldn't speak?' Tom asked, looking into Sky's pale eyes.

Sky nodded.

They sat in silence for a while. They had all heard that this kind of thing used to happen many years ago. There were stories of people who had been locked up in that place who suffered from nothing more than epilepsy. And there were even worse stories about people being abandoned by families because they had some physical disability or were merely a bit slow-witted. They had always thought these stories had been embellished over time. Until now.

Sky finished his orange squash and sat back, wringing his hands. He looked suddenly uneasy, as if he was nervous of what he had told them.

'He's worried we're going to get rid of him now. Tell him it's OK, Frankie,' Kate said to her husband. Sky's eyes darted from one to the other.

'Don't worry, Sky. Everything's fine. Nobody's going to harm you or send you away. You're safe here,' Frankie said, reaching over and touching Sky's hand. He looked as though he was about to cry.

Tom shook his head. He thought of what his own mother had done to him, of how her only consideration was herself and her selfish ambitions for her son. That was bad enough, but it was unthinkable that people could do things like this to their own flesh and blood.

Sky got up and shook Frankie's hand. Then he put both his hands to the side of his head, indicating that he wanted to sleep, and walked away from them across to the caravan that had become his home.

Frankie, Kate and Tom sat watching him as he opened the door and went inside.

'How can people do that to each other?' Kate said. 'I mean, if he's telling the truth, then it's such a sad story. Poor man.'

Frankie poured a glass of whisky for himself and Tom.

'Yeah,' he said. 'But that's how things were back just after the war. People were ashamed of disability. They still are, a lot of them.'

'But imagine a mother giving her baby away,' Tom said.

'Yes, Tom,' Kate said, 'but you don't know the mother's circumstances. Perhaps she was unmarried. Maybe she was just a young girl. You can imagine the scandal in these parts, the attitude of the priests, not to mention her family.'

'I know, Kate, but it's no excuse for the way people just make decisions about other people's lives like that. They have no right to. No right at all,' Tom said fiercely, thinking again of his own mother's cruelty.

Nobody spoke for a few moments, and they could hear the sound of a football being kicked and the laughter of Maggie and Jess in the kitchen.

Kate got up and touched Tom's shoulder affectionately as she passed him on her way to the kitchen. Frankie and Tom sat on in silence. Then Tom threw back his whisky and stood up.

'Right. I'd better get back down the road. Getting late.' He smiled and stretched.

'You all right?' Frankie said.

'Right as rain, Frankie. Fine,' Tom replied.

Kate came out of the kitchen with Maggie and Jess. Maggie hugged Tom.

'Night, Uncle Tom. Sleep tight,' she said as he ruffled the top of her head which reached his waist.

Kate handed him a torch. 'Here, Tom. You'll need this.'

'Cheers,' he said, and turned and walked across the farmyard. He climbed over the wooden fence into the field and disappeared into the night, only the faint glow from the torch indicating he was there at all.

'He seemed a bit emotional. He's worried about Joe coming, is that it?' Kate said.

Frankie shook his head. 'No, I don't think it's just that. There's something more. He'll tell us, in his own time.'

'Are you looking forward to seeing Joe?' Kate asked, looking straight at Frankie.

'Course,' he said. He finished his whisky and placed the glass on the table.

'It's just that you've seemed a bit edgy the last few days.'

'No. I'm looking forward to seeing him. But it's been a long time and I wonder what he'll make of us all.'

Kate slid her arms round his waist. 'Well, Frankie, I for one don't give a damn what he makes of us all. If he's made the big time in America, good for him. He won't have what we have. That much I'm sure of.' She kissed Frankie on the lips and he wrapped his arms round her, pulling her close as he tried his best to blot out the memories.

# Chapter Four

PJ and Marty were inside the tree house. They could hear music blaring from the direction of the two tents that had been pitched the night before by a group of long-haired teenagers. Smoke swirled from the fire the teenagers had lit and they were clowning around it, swaying to the music with drinks in their hands. PJ could see Marty's dad standing in his string vest with his hands on his hips, glaring at the gang who seemed to be disturbing him – he'd been drowsing in a deckchair earlier. PJ and Marty watched through the small tree-house window as a girl with long stringy hair and pink-tinted heart-shaped sunglasses and a tall skinny boy danced to the song 'Light My Fire'. Other girls lay around the grass, some wearing long kaftans with psyche-delic patterns. They had glassy-eyed expressions and giggled among themselves.

'Do you think they're hippies?' PJ asked Marty.

'I'd say they are,' Marty said. 'I think they're smoking reefers. You know. Hash or something. My pal's big brother does it. He used to be quite sound, but now he's running about saying peace and love all the time. He painted flowers all over the walls of the close. Headcase.' Marty shook his head.

PJ watched as Gunboats drank from a can of beer then crushed it in his hand. He threw it across at the crowd who were only about ten feet away from his caravan.

'I'll light your fire for you, ya bunch of wasters,' he shouted at them. 'Away and work.'

A stocky teenager with long hair and a beard like a nanny goat, wearing a bright red military-style jacket with gold braid unbuttoned to reveal his bare chest, staggered over to the radio and turned up the volume.

'Hey, cool it, man,' he shouted back to Gunboats, a fat cigarette in his right hand.

PJ watched as Gunboats clenched his fists and went across to the crowd.

'Look, Marty,' he said. 'I think there's going to be trouble.'

'Gunboats will waste them,' Marty said. 'He's crazy when he starts. He was raging last night because they played music all night long and we couldn't sleep.' Marty left the window and sat at the other side of the room. But PJ stayed to watch. He couldn't believe his eyes as Gunboats marched over to where the gang were lying around. They all smiled up at him with dazed looks as he stood over them. Then, to PJ's amazement, Gunboats lifted the radio, bent the arial and threw it into the fire.

'Does that light your fuckin' fire, son?' he spat at the stocky boy who stood with his mouth open. Everybody stood around in shocked silence, watching the radio melt in the flames.

'There's no need for that, man.' A tall, thin boy took a step towards Gunboats.

'And what are you going to do about it, ya skinny bastard?' Gunboats leaned into him so they were face to face.

The boy said nothing and all that could be heard was the crackling of the fire.

'I'm sick of listening to your racket,' Gunboats said to everyone. 'Let me tell you this. If you're planning on sticking around here, then don't think anybody on this campsite is going to listen to you or your shite music all night long. Now if you're smart, you'll fold up your tents and get to fuck.' He turned to walk away, then stopped and turned back. 'Oh. Peace and love, by the way. Up yours!' He gave them a two-fingered salute.

PJ sniggered. He had never seen anybody confront a crowd like that. Marty had told him that his dad was a former soldier and a real hard man, but he had never expected anything like this. He looked down and saw that Maggie and Jess were about to climb the wooden ladder Sky had made for them to get in and out of the tree house.

PJ thought Marty looked a bit worried and couldn't think why since it must be great having a tough guy for a dad.

'C'mon, Marty,' he said. 'Let's go down and go for a walk. Your da's brilliant. I bet he's some fighter.'

'Yeah,' Marty said, looking away from PJ. 'Some fighter.'

Maggie and Jess joined them as they walked along the edge of the caravan site, down towards the river and along the narrow path at the river's edge. When they got further along, the trees started to thicken, signalling the start of Beggar's Wood.

'We're not supposed to go in here by ourselves. Dad says,' Maggie said to PJ.

'It's OK. We'll just go in a wee bit, then we'll be back,' PJ said, leading the way.

When they had walked in a few yards, they heard a man and woman talking and they stopped in their tracks.

'Sssh,' said PJ, signalling to everyone to get behind him.

They walked further in until they could see an opening in the trees. A woman was handing something in a bag to the man. PJ was thinking that the woman looked like the Irish woman called Breige who had married Baldy Cassidy. Yes, he thought, peering at her. It was definitely that Breige woman. She had served him in the baker's only last week when he went in for his dad.

'Who is it?' Maggie said, pulling back a branch. 'Oh. It's that Breige wom—'

PJ put his hand over her mouth. 'Sssh. Let's just watch them.'

They saw the dark-haired man, who was about thirty, take what looked like a wad of notes out of the bag and stuff them into the pockets of his leather jacket. Then he began to touch Breige's hair. The children watched, dumbfounded, as he pulled her towards him and kissed her. Her hair was swept up in a solid beehive and didn't move as he held her tight.

PJ immediately turned round and shooed everyone away.

'Quick. Quick. Out of here now.' He pushed them on. 'Before they see us, or we'll be in real trouble. We'd better never tell anybody about this.'

Maggie quickened her step to keep up with the others, but she kept looking back towards the woods. She couldn't for the life of her understand why the Breige woman would be doing that with a man in the woods when her husband Baldy Cassidy was in the house all by himself. And she was giving him money. PJ had a worried look on his face as he quickened his step back towards the farm.

# Chapter Five

The morning was bright and clear and full of promise. Tom threw open the windows of his bedroom and breathed in the freshness of the new day. Not a cloud in the sky. His eyes scanned the rolling fields, the caravan site where nobody stirred, and down the road to the village where he could just see the start of the houses. The chapel with its ancient bell dominated the landscape. This was the day. And Tom was ready for it, delighted and a little surprised at the rush of good feeling he had woken with.

When he left the priesthood just two years after he was ordained, Tom had struggled for a long time with his faith. But in recent years he had found himself turning to God more and more when he was lonely, or when he was just trying to cope with the thankless task of looking after his domineering, uncompromising mother.

Last night he had prayed to God to help him understand and live with what his mother had done. He prayed for help to get through these next few difficult weeks with Joe, and to try and put Maria to the back of his mind. His prayers seemed to have been answered because this morning he felt ready for anything.

He whistled as he went about his early chores on the farm, brushing the yard, tidying things around the barn. With his dogs trotting at his heels, he opened the gate into the field where his cows were and walked briskly across to check out the two new calves that had been born three days ago. They were in great shape and lay basking in the early sunshine next to their mothers. In the distance he could see Frankie up in one of his fields in the tractor. Another early bird. He knew Frankie would be looking forward to seeing Joe and guessed that was why he, too, was up an hour before either of them normally surfaced.

Towards midday Tom began preparing a pot of stew for the steak pie he was making for Joe. He peeled potatoes, rolled ready-made pastry, sliced runner beans from his garden. He stood, leaning on the sink, and looked around the place. It was spotlessly clean, the way his mother kept it, but different. He took a deep breath and smiled to himself. Somehow there was a freedom, a sense of release about the place that had been transferred from him to the house, now that his mother was gone. Part of him chided himself for feeling like this, but in truth he had felt relief and something close to happiness when she died, long before he knew about the letters. He had been his own counsellor for most of his life and had talked himself in and out of lots of problems, and he told himself now that it was no sin to feel the way he did about his mother. In fact, it was good that he had finally admitted to himself that he couldn't stand her.

After some time he left the pot simmering away and went out into the yard to do some work on his car. He looked at his watch. Joe would have landed by now and would be arriving soon in his hired car. Tom was looking forward to it.

With his head inside the bonnet of his car, he hummed to the songs on the radio as he cleaned the spark plugs vigorously with a wire brush. Frank Sinatra was singing 'You Make Me Feel So Young' and Tom sang along happily. Suddenly the music seemed to come from some distant place – a dance floor teeming with couples gliding around to the band playing the Frank Sinatra hit. He held Maria, his arm round her waist as they danced. She looked up at him and sang along to the lyrics. Tom could still hear her voice, and saw his own face smiling back at her. He couldn't believe his luck. There he was, a shy, sheltered 22-year-old seminarian, dancing with the most beautiful girl in Rome.

During Maria's two months with her cousins in Rome, Tom had seen her every day. Even after he confessed to her that he was a seminarian, she still took him to meet her cousins, telling them he was a philosophy student spending the summer in Rome. When she went back to Scotland, they wrote long, loving letters to each other every week and when Tom came home, he had to lie constantly to his mother while they met in secret. They made love only once, in the sand dunes on a late summer's evening. It had been an intense, unstoppable passion, and afterwards as Maria lay in his arms, he brushed her tears away as she told him she never wanted to grow old unless they could lie together like this. He promised her they would, his heart and mind in turmoil as he prepared to go back to the seminary the next day.

The sound of a car engine brought him back and he bumped his head on the raised bonnet as he jerked himself up. It was a taxi. Tom's stomach turned over and his mouth went dry. He wiped his hands on the oily rag that was hanging out of his jeans pocket. He took a step back from his car and stared at the taxi, waiting. He had been waiting for twenty years.

The door of the taxi opened and a tall, slender figure got out and stretched. It was Joe. He pulled a huge case from the boot and dumped it in the yard. Then he waved at the taxi driver who turned the car and drove off.

The two of them stood, face to face, like two old gunslingers. So many years lay between them. So often as a child and teenager Tom had felt anger and resentment towards his brother as he watched his mother openly favour him, only for Joe to pack up and leave him behind, trapped on the farm, with nobody to share his heartache. And now here he was, the brother he felt he hardly knew, who had abandoned him with barely a backward glance. They could find no words between as they stood, studying each other. Tom wiped his oily hands on the rag and took the first steps towards him. Joe stood where he was, his head erect in the defiant pose that Tom remembered so well. But as he got closer, he could see something in Joe's eyes he had never seen before. It looked like fear. But it couldn't be, not Joe. Then suddenly, Joe's eyes filled with tears. Automatically, Tom reached out and wrapped his arms round him, feeling Joe squeeze the wind out of him as he whispered, 'I'm sorry, Tom. I'm sorry for all the hurt I ever caused you.'

'Sssh. Don't be, Joe. You're home now.' Tom felt tears spill out of his own eyes. They stood like that for a long time, until they could safely pull away without breaking down. When Tom finally stepped back, he was quick enough to catch Joe's attempt to punch him in the solar plexus the way he used to years ago.

'Not quick enough these days, Joey boy. Not quick enough. America's made you soft,' Tom said, grabbing his fist and grinning.

'I'll show you soft, Father McBride,' Joe said, and he caught his brother with a playful right hand to the chin.

They both laughed, their eyes searching each other's faces, recognising the lines, remembering the laughter but not the pain.

'Look at the state of this place. It's falling to bits,' Joe joked as he gazed around the pristine farmyard and freshly painted fences.

'Kiss my arse,' Tom said and lifted his brother's case, striding effortlessly across the yard.

He pushed open the door of the house and stepped inside to the kitchen. He put Joe's case down on the floor and turned to see his brother walking through the doorway behind him. He watched as Joe looked around the old kitchen which had barely changed since the day he left. The pots and pans hung from a wooden pulley stretched across the middle of the room, above the solid oak table where they had sat as children and teenagers while their mother dealt out massive dinners for her growing boys.

'You know, Tom, I can still see you there at that table with your head in your books, writing and studying,' Joe said.

'A lot of good it did me,' Tom said, moving towards the cooker to check the pots. 'I'm still working like a navvy from dawn till dusk.'

'I don't think I ever did a day's homework in my life, Tom. I hardly lifted a book,' Joe said, sounding as though he regretted it.

'I don't see it mattered a damn. Look what you've done with your life. You've made your money and you've probably had more experiences in a week in the States than most people pack into a lifetime here.'

'It might seem that way, Tom. But it's like everything else. There's always things you wish you had done.'

'Listen to you,' Tom said, stirring a pot. 'You're sounding like you're about to peg out. Christ, you're only forty. You can start reading now.' Tom threw a packet at Joe, who caught it with one hand. 'There. Read me the instructions for that rhubarb crumble mix. I'm going to make us an old-fashioned dessert, but I'm not sure what to do.' He winked at Joe who smiled back as he sat down at the table, and studied the back of the packet.

'Makes no sense to me,' he said after a moment. He got to his feet, picked up his case and went into the living room.

'Your old room's all set for you, Joe. Just get your stuff in there and relax,' Tom called after him.

Joe stood looking around the living room. He ran his hands over the fireplace and then went to the window to look out at the fields. Tom watched him drag his case into the bedroom with something of an effort. He thought he must be tired from the trip.

Joe seemed more mellow, somehow, he thought. As though the stuffing had been knocked out of him. He still looked the same, the square shoulders and the swagger in his walk, but he seemed different, not as threatening as Tom always remembered him.

When Joe came back into the kitchen and sat down, Tom put a mug of tea in front of him and sat at the table opposite him. They seemed stuck for words, then Joe looked his brother in the eye and spoke.

'Tom,' he said, 'why did you leave the priesthood? I mean, you never really told me. I always wondered.'

Tom looked at Joe, then at the table, then beyond him. He didn't speak. He couldn't find the words.

'It has to be a woman,' Joe said, his dark eyebrows raised. 'It has to be.'

47

Tom half smiled and sighed. He shook his head. 'Another time, Joe,' he said, pushing his chair back and standing up. 'Another time.' He tried to make his voice light as he said, 'Don't tell me you came all the way home just to ask that.'

Joe smiled and watched as Tom moved pots around on the cooker.

# Chapter Six

Frankie was mending a fence in the high field when he saw the taxi pull up in McBride's farmyard. He stopped working as the car came to a halt, and before the taxi door opened he knew it was Joe. Frankie's mind flashed back to that morning when Joe had left, and he still remembered his heartbreak that his friend was gone for ever. Now he watched as the boy he would have laid down his life for emerged from the car. In the distance, Joe looked exactly the same, his big shoulders making him look powerful in his white shirt, the sleeves rolled up past the elbows. He still had the same shock of black hair, and his chin jutted out the way it always had, as if to challenge anyone foolish enough to think of taking a pop at him.

Despite all the inner turmoil that had been giving him sleepless nights for the past week, Frankie felt his face smile. Joe was back. And somewhere deep inside, Frankie was surprised to find that he was overjoyed. Sky stopped hammering the staples into the fence post to watch the activity down at McBride's. His face was impassive as he looked from Frankie to the yard where Tom and Joe stood locked in an embrace. Frankie glanced at Sky who smiled back.

'Tom's brother, Joe. He's been away for twenty years,' Frankie said, excitement in his voice.

Sky raised his eyebrows and smiled. They got back to work, stretching the wire tight along the posts and securing it with staples hammered into the new wood. The old, rotted posts were thrown into the back of the tractor to be taken back to the farm for firewood.

49

Frankie worked hard and fast, his mind fixed on how he would handle his first meeting with Joe. Only they knew how much history was between them. No amount of time could wipe that away. But knowing Joe, he thought, he will have convinced himself that nothing at all had happened. He pushed the thoughts away and signalled to Sky that they were finished for the day.

Kate was wringing out a cloth at the kitchen window when she saw Frankie's tractor coming into the yard. She came to the door.

'I see Joe's arrived,' Frankie chirped as he switched off the tractor engine and jumped out of the cabin. Sky began to unload the wood from the trailer. They would take a couple of hours off, then check the animals in the field later in the evening.

Kate could see the delight in Frankie's face as he walked towards her.

'You look pleased,' she said. 'I thought you'd seemed troubled all week waiting for him to come, and look at you now. What did you expect? He's just a man. He's just another guy who's gone away and come back after a lifetime. And he's your friend, Frankie. All that silly worry about what he might think. I knew as soon as he arrived you'd be made up,' Kate said, rubbing her hand over Frankie's arm.

Frankie smiled and put his arm round her.

'Well, what are you waiting for?' Kate said. 'Are you not going down to see him? Why don't you go and get shifted into some other clothes and go down and say hello.'

'Right. I'll go and invite the two of them down to the pub for an hour. Is that all right with you, sweetheart?'

'Course it is,' Kate said and Frankie disappeared inside the house.

She shook her head and smiled, wondering what kind of drunken few days were ahead as the three men caught up with all the years. Frankie was even calling her sweetheart. And even though she knew he was trying to get on her good side, she liked it just the same. She had never met Joe, but his reputation went before him in Westerbank and beyond, where he was known as a womaniser and a hellraiser who would cause a fight in an empty house.

She often wondered what Frankie had been like before she met him. Joe was gone a year by the time she had caught sight of Frankie in a pub in the town where she grew up and fell in love with him instantly. Frankie had been half drunk when he and three of his equally drunk and boisterous mates arrived in the pub. Kate was there for a retirement party for one of the teachers in the school where she taught. It had been the usual safe, boring evening with the school staff, where everyone sat sipping their drinks and talking in small groups.

Kate couldn't take her eyes off the tall, muscular stranger with the thick blond hair who was larking around at the bar with some locals. Two young girls were hanging on his every word and he seemed to be relishing the attention. When he caught sight of Kate across the room, he kept glancing over, smiling at her. She smiled back, careful not to let the rest of her party see her flirting. Her hopes of talking to him were dashed when one of his mates started a fight and they were all thrown out of the bar. She thought she would never see him again, but resolved to find out who he was.

At the end of the night, she found him sitting on the steps of the shop across the road, waiting for the pub to close so he could introduce himself. Despite the disapproving looks of the other teachers, she stayed talking to him, and he walked her home. She was completely bowled over by him and she told her mother when she got home that she had met the man she was going to marry.

Frankie was the kind of man who wanted peace at any price, and his nature seemed a million miles away from the Joe she had heard all about. She wondered how the two of them had become such close friends. Frankie didn't really speak much about Joe, and down the years it was Tom who had become such a large part of their lives. It was hard to believe that a gentle man like Tom could have a brother like Joe. And then there were the rumours about Joe's sudden departure from Westerbank.

Something about a young girl. Frankie always fobbed her off if she asked what it was all about, and he said not to listen to any of the nonsense they talked around the village. After a while, nobody mentioned Joe any more.

The sun was still strong as Frankie drove down the lane towards McBride's farm. He smiled and waved when he saw Sky sitting on a fence watching the children tear around the caravan park after a ball. Maggie was in the thick of it, chasing and harrying boys the same age as PJ, who had to keep shouting at her to stop tripping people up and playing dirty. Maggie laughed back at them, her face bursting with excitement. At first Frankie and Kate had been concerned about the way Sky seemed more comfortable around PJ and Maggie than the adults. They hadn't discovered how old he was but assumed he was in his forties, though he had an almost childlike quality and excitement about simple things. Kate thought it was because he had grown up in a mental institution and probably never had a real chance to develop his intelligence because it was assumed that since he couldn't talk, he was also stupid.

When Frankie pulled into McBride's yard, he noticed that Tom's car was gone, and his heart sank. He had psyched himself up for this moment but now it looked as though the brothers had gone out. He got out of the car and looked around the yard, but there was no sign of anybody. He stood for a moment admiring the neat and well-kept farmyard, much smarter than his own, even with Sky's extra help. He put his hands in his pockets and moved towards his car, feeling disappointed. He would come back later. As he was about to get in his car, he heard the door of Tom's house click open and a voice that stopped him dead and took him way, way back.

'Hey, Flaherty! Don't you be thinking about lifting anything around here. It's all nailed down, you know, to keep gadgies like you away!'

Frankie's heart leapt and he turned round to see a beaming Joe in the doorway, his hands stuffed in his pockets, and with the same mischievous, goading look that had got them into more scrapes than he cared to remember.

'Jesus!' Frankie said. 'Look at the nick of you, Yankee. You look as though you've never done a day's work since you left. Not that you did shag all when you were here.' He walked towards him.

'Frankie!' Joe said, taking himself out of the doorway and into the yard. 'Jesus wept, Frankie! Are you a sight for sore eyes!' Joe threw his arms round Frankie, who held him tight, feeling something close to choking rising in his chest.

'Jesus, Joe! Jesus! I thought I'd never see you again. I missed you so much. But you shouldn't have come back, Joe. You know that.' Frankie freed himself from the hug and stood holding his friend's arms, looking into his face.

'I know, Frankie. I know. But I had to come back. It was time, that's all. I wanted to come home, Frankie!' Tears streamed down Joe's face and Frankie reached out and wiped them with the palm of his hand, blinking back his own tears.

He scanned Joe's face, the lines around his eyes, the strong jaw line, slightly jowly but still youthful. His hair was thick and black, with only flecks of grey at the side, and his suntanned face was smooth and clean-shaven around his full, firm mouth. He was as handsome as ever, like a matinee idol who had grown older. But there was something in his eyes that Frankie had never seen before. It must have been his imagination, though, because Joe was never scared.

'How do you think things'll be, Frankie? It's been a long time. What do you think?' Joe said, looking his friend in the eye.

'I don't know, Joe. I just don't know. Sure, it's been a helluva long time. But around here – you know what it's like. But nobody ever knew anything, and they stopped talking after a while. I mean, Tom has never really asked anything. He just put everything down to gossip,' Frankie said. 'We'll just have to deal with whatever happens.'

# Chapter Seven

Kate looked out of the window at PJ and Maggie who were moping around the farmyard with miserable expressions. She felt bad that she had put her foot down at breakfast when they asked if they could go on a trip to the seaside with Jess and Marty and their parents. Now they were shadowing their dad, pleading with him to let them go. Kate knew Frankie would soon be buckling under the pressure, but she didn't trust this Gunboats character. News of the confrontation between him and the hippy crowd convinced her that he was a nutter.

She would have loved to allow PJ and Maggie to go on the trip but she was still haunted by the memory of losing Emily and felt over-protective of both of them. Frankie was constantly telling her to cut them some slack and allow them to spread their wings a little, but Kate couldn't bear the thought of anything happening to them. Occasionally, she allowed PJ to take the bus to the cinema ten miles away in Ayr, but she would never let Maggie go on her own with friends. Maggie had to be watched closely because of her asthma and Kate did not like her to be any distance away in case something happened to bring on an attack.

Frankie came into the kitchen and they both stood watching PJ and Maggie outside.

'Maybe we should let them go, Kate,' he said. 'I mean, it's not a million miles away.'

'I know, Frankie,' Kate said. 'But what if something happens? I don't think that family are very reliable. Especially that Gunboats character. What kind of a name is Gunboats? I think he's a head case.'

She had met Jess and Marty's parents in Mulranney's three nights ago. Gunboats McKay had said his real name was Billy, but everyone in the East End of Glasgow knew him as Gunboats. He had been in the Marines when he was younger and his claim to fame was that he had been seconded to the Special Boat Squad for a particularly dangerous mission during the Korean conflict. He said he didn't want to talk about his exploits, but that he had won medals for bravery. Kate got the feeling that the more pints he downed, the more desperate he was to relive his wartime glories. By the time she and Frankie left the pub, he was ogling her like a sailor on shore leave, and slapping Frankie on the back as if they had known each other all their lives. Kate noticed that his wife, whom he briefly introduced as Miranne, sat like a mouse, sipping a shandy and saying nothing.

'I know what you mean, Kate,' Frankie said. 'But we never get to take the kids away much, with all the work here during the summer. It wouldn't do them any harm. And I'll have a word with Gunboats so that he knows not to be doing anything stupid while they're away. What do you think?'

Kate knew that if she said no, Frankie would go along with it, but she didn't want to ruin things for PJ and Maggie who were obviously delighted with their new friends. She sensed that Frankie quite liked the cut of Gunboats because he didn't fit in with anyone else's ordered life at the caravan site; the others kind of looked down their noses at his shambolic two-berth caravan.

Kate stopped peeling the potatoes and turned on the cold tap. She looked out of the window, where Maggie and PJ were sitting on two big stones at the side of the garden. They looked as if their lives weren't worth living. Kate shook her head. She would have to give in.

'Right. OK. We'll let them go,' she said. 'But you'll have to speak to that nutcase Gunboats and make it clear that he's a dead man if anything happens to them.' Kate stood with her hands on her hips and Frankie smiled at her.

He opened the door and shouted to Maggie and PJ who looked at each other and came bounding across the yard.

'Right. You can go.' Before he could say any more, Maggie had jumped on top of him and PJ hugged his mum who was standing in the doorway, shaking her head. Then they disappeared across the field, heading for the caravan park to give Marty and Jess the good news.

The next morning when the McKays' yellow Triumph Herald duly pulled up, its horn honking, Maggie was up from the breakfast table mid-mouthful.

Outside, Gunboats got out of the car with a wide smile on his face and Miranne emerged looking happy and smart in a pink floral sundress. Kate was relieved to see that Gunboats looked clean-shaven and quite civilised. He was wearing what looked like army issue khaki shorts and a fresh white T-shirt stretched over his beer belly.

Kate helped put Maggie and PJ's duffel bags in the boot and watched as Gunboats nodded understandingly as Frankie took him to one side and explained to him how important it was that he looked after his kids who were the most precious things on earth.

'Don't you worry yourselves one wee bit,' Gunboats said. 'You know, Frankie, at one point I was responsible for a whole platoon of lads in the desert in Aden, with all these ragheads pumping bullets at us. I've never lost a soldier yet. That right, Marty? That right, Jess?' Gunboats shouted to his children, who both shouted back, 'That's right, Da.' Miranne just simpered shyly.

The car was packed up and off they went with the honking horn being outdone by the exhaust backfiring. Kate and Frankie could hear the children whooping with laughter as the car disappeared down the lane.

'Da, sing that song about the old woman and the spider. You know the one,' Jess piped up from where she was squeezed against

Maggie in the back seat. 'This is a great song. Wait till you hear this,' she whispered proudly to Maggie and PJ.

'There was an old woman who swallowed a fly. I don't know why she swallowed a fly. Perhaps she'll die.' Gunboats' voice boomed out, filling the song with as much drama as he could. 'She swallowed a spider to catch the fly. I don't know why she swallowed a fly.' After the first two lines everyone joined in the chorus, giggling as they got to the end and they couldn't remember how many things the old woman swallowed on the way back to the fly.

Gunboats belted out songs about soldiers wearing no drawers in the wars, causing hysterics in the back seat. Maggie grinned across at PJ who knew their mother wouldn't have allowed this for a second.

There were hoots of delight when they got their first glimpse of the sea, and Gunboats drove the car right up to the edge of the promenade, almost knocking over two cyclists in the process.

The beach was busy with families who had set up windbreakers to corner off little areas of the sand for themselves while they poured tea from flasks and opened baskets of sandwiches. Children queued for a ride on the donkeys who trotted along the beach, the sound of the jingling bells round their necks filling the air. The blustery breeze sent fat white clouds rushing across the bright blue sky and children chased after the shadows they made on the sand. Out across the water dozens of kids were jumping over the waves and screeching with laughter.

In jig time, Maggie and Jess were into their swimsuits and in the water, before Marty and PJ had even got undressed. Miranne spread out a tartan rug on the beach and Gunboats stood scratching his belly as he surveyed the beach like an old general looking for the enemy dug into the sand dunes.

'Your da's brilliant fun, Marty, isn't he?' PJ said, scoffing a banana sandwich as he watched Gunboats paddling at the edge of the water.

'Yeah. He's a laugh. Most of the time,' Marty said, not very convincingly.

Miranne set out the picnic for the four children and then went for a walk. They ate hungrily after swimming and running around the beach for an hour. Maggie couldn't remember having such a great time and she lay back feeling the sun warming her skin, conscious that her chest was making a wheezing noise when she breathed.

'That's funny, that noise you make, Maggie. Is it sore?' Jess asked, leaning up on one elbow so she could look at her friend.

'No. It's not sore. It's just the asthma. I can't feel it though. But I've got to watch, if I lose my breath. Because I nearly died once,' Maggie said, coughing slightly to try and get rid of the wheeze.

'Did you nearly die? What was it like?' Jess asked.

'It was terrible,' Maggie said. 'I was choking and everything. I couldn't breathe and everybody was all crying. They thought I was dead, but then I just got a bit better.'

'What makes it bad?' Jess asked, still curious.

'Don't know really. Maybe if I run too fast. Or maybe if I get too excited or scared. I've just to watch. That's what the doctor said. But I'm not a cripple or anything. I mean I'm not sick.' Maggie didn't want her friend to think she was feeble or different from anyone else. 'I'm strong, you know. Watch. I'll arm-wrestle you and I bet I win.' Maggie turned over onto her stomach and the two of them began arm-wrestling, pushing and puffing until Maggie overpowered Jess who lay back and laughed, nursing her arm.

Marty and PJ were playing football on the beach and Maggie and Jess went for a walk the length of the beach. When they returned, they saw Miranne back at their spot, standing with her hand over her eyes, as though she was searching the beach.

'Have you seen your da?' she asked Jess. 'I haven't seen him for nearly two hours. Where the hell has he gone?' She bit her lip.

Jess's expression suddenly changed. Maggie looked from one to the other.

'Maybe he's gone for a pint, Mum,' Jess ventured.

'Yeah. Maybe he's in the pub. We'll get everything together and we'll go look for him.' Miranne shook her head. 'He's some man, that Gunboats,' she said to Maggie with a smile. Jess took her hand.

They walked along the promenade, PJ and Marty marvelling at the mopeds and brightly coloured scooters that were lined up along the sea wall. Crowds of teenage boys in parka jackets and girls in tight jeans and heavy make-up and sleek, geometric hair-cuts stood around in groups, smoking and laughing.

'They're Mods. There's loads in Glasgow,' Marty said to PJ. 'I hope there's no Hell's Angels on motorbikes, otherwise there'll be a fight.'

'We've not got Mods in Westerbank,' PJ said. 'The only person I know with a scooter is Mr Mullen, one of our teachers. But he's ancient.'

Before they got to the door of the Harbour Inn, they could hear the voice of Gunboats accompanied by the rythmic twang of his banjo.

'Take off your coat and grease your throat, with a bucket o' the mountain dew. De da diddlie i dum, de da diddlie i dum, de da diddlie i diddle i de.' Gunboats was on his feet strumming the banjo with great gusto as he led the packed pub in song. People were clapping their hands in time to the music and two old men in flat caps swung each other around the floor, fags dangling from their mouths. A group of young people sat at a table laden with pints and empty glasses and stamped their feet as Gunboats leaned across to them, working the room like an old cabaret star. He was thoroughly wrapped up in the fun, but Miranne bit her lip as she pushed the kids towards where he was standing. He winked when he saw her, as though he was greeting another punter.

Maggie was thrilled at the spectacle and immediately started clapping in time to the music, joined by Jess and Marty who looked relieved that their father hadn't embarrassed them. So far, anyway.

PJ felt slightly concerned. He noticed there were at least four empty pint tumblers on the table near Gunboats, and as he watched, Gunboats drained a glass mid-song. PJ wondered how they were going to get home if Gunboats was drunk. Miranne handed him a glass of Coke and a packet of crisps and for the moment he went along with it. Deep down he felt quite excited, and when he caught Maggie's eye he thought by the look of her that she was thinking along the same lines as he was.

One after another, the people in the pub took it in turns to sing. The sun was still blazing outside and every time the door swung open, another few people squeezed into the smoky, stuffy pub, attracted by the singing.

Maggie thought it was like being in an old cowboy movie, and was thrilled to be part of it. She watched one old woman drinking what looked like brandy and was fascinated when she stuck her tongue inside the glass and licked the dregs. Suddenly she staggered to her feet and swayed towards Gunboats, shouting that it was her turn to sing.

'OK, darlin'. Give us your pleasure,' Gunboats shouted, and Miranne shot a glance at Marty. They'd both heard the slur in his voice.

'Never mind your banjo, big man. I'll do this without the orchestra,' the old woman said. She stood in front of Gunboats and he put his arm round her.

'On you go, darlin. It's all yours,' he said, playing to the gallery.

The pub fell silent as the old woman cleared her throat and started to sing 'Sailor, Stop Your Roving'. Her voice was like a foghorn and her big skirt swirled when she reached the chorus, beckoning the whole pub to join in. Everyone sang along, with Gunboats, his head thrown back, singing louder than anybody.

A roar went up when the old woman finished, and Gunboats immediately followed it up with another song.

'I wish I was in Carrickfergus, only for nights in Ballygran I would swim over the deepest ocean.' Despite his drunkenness, he sang beautifully and strummed the banjo gently, carrying the haunting tune out of the pub to the sea.

'He's great at this,' Jess whispered to Maggie who sat spellbound.

PJ shifted on his feet and looked at the pub clock ticking towards seven. He wondered again how they would get home.

No matter how often Miranne tried to get a word with Gunboats, he dismissed her with a wave of his hand, and PJ noticed that Marty and Jess were beginning to look worried. Sing-songs broke out at various tables and the atmosphere was fast becoming a rabble. PJ and the others were standing near the door when they saw Miranne take the pint out of Gunboats' hand, only for him to grab it back.

'Piss off, woman! Ya eejit!' Gunboats pushed Miranne away with one arm. She lost her balance and landed in the lap of a big, ginger-haired man who was sitting with half a dozen other men.

'Hey, you! Don't be shovin' women about like that!' the ginger-haired man snapped, steadying Miranne to her feet.

'Get yourself to fuck, carrot head!' Gunboats slurred, and sniggers broke out around the pub. There was silence as the big man stood up, his muscled chest bursting out of his vest. He seemed to be getting up for ages and was growing bigger all the time. Even the freckles on his hairy shoulders were the size of sixpences.

'Oh shit,' Marty said to PJ. 'There's going to be a rammy. Jesus. Look at the size of that guy! He'll kill my da!'

Maggie and Jess moved to the door. Maggie could feel a tightness in her chest. She coughed nervously.

'I'll rip your lungs out, ya bastard!' the ginger-haired man shouted, taking a step towards Gunboats.

'Aye. You and whose fuckin' army?' Gunboats squared up to him. 'I fought in the desert for fuckers like you! C'mon, ya freckled fucker ye! Give it your best shot!' Gunboats yelled. But by the time the last word was out, a fist to his chin sent him across a table, knocking glasses and drink everywhere. All around people jumped out of the way and held fast to their drinks as they prepared for the floor show. Like a raging bull, Gunboats was back on his feet and hurling himself at the big man, pushing him back through the swing doors and onto the street. Punches were flying and the ginger-haired man looked as if he was getting the better of

Gunboats. His friends came out and tried to hold him back, but it took three of them to drag him off Gunboats. Miranne was screaming to Gunboats to stop. Marty was comforting Jess who was in tears. Maggie watched, enthralled by it all, and PJ bit his nails, wondering how they would ever get home.

By the time they reached the car, Miranne had stopped crying. Gunboats wiped blood from his lip.

'I could have killed him, you know. If they'd left me alone,' he slurred.

Marty carried his banjo and walked with the others in silence. The promenade looked suddenly quiet and lonely; the day trippers had packed up and gone home two hours before. They all stood by the car, with Gunboats leaning on the bonnet, staring out to sea.

'You can't drive. Look at the state of you,' Miranne said, her voice shaking. 'You promised those kids' dad you would be careful. Now look at you. How are we going to get them home?' She sounded desperate.

Everyone looked at Gunboats, then at each other. Maggie and PJ looked at the ground. PJ knew there would be big trouble when they got home. If they ever got home.

'I can drive,' Marty said, standing up straight.

'What?' PJ said. 'You're only thirteen. What do you mean you can drive?' He was almost laughing at the idea. He had driven his dad's tractor in the field, but only because there was nothing else in there but open space.

'I can. I can drive. I've driven the car loads of times. Haven't I, Da?' Marty said to Gunboats.

'What?' Miranne said, incredulous. 'You've let that boy drive the car? Is there any level of eejitness you haven't reached, Billy?'

Gunboats straightened up. 'He can drive, Miranne. I've taught him how to do it. There's nothing to it. Sure I was driving when I was his age. And it's all back roads till we get to Westerbank.'

'Honest, Mum. I can do it. Just let me try. I mean, we've no option. We've got to get PJ and Maggie home or their ma and da will go mental. C'mon, Mum. I can do it. Just watch me,' Marty pleaded.

PJ looked at Maggie and smiled. He quite liked the idea. PJ had learned over the last two weeks that Marty was much smarter and more street wise than he or any of the rest of the local boys were. He wouldn't really be that surprised if Marty could drive a motor car.

They all stood around in silence. Then Miranne spoke.

'Right. Everybody in the car. We'll drive onto that back road there and see how you get on. Jesus protect us!'

They all piled into the car, and Maggie noticed that before Gunboats got into the passenger seat, Miranne gave him an almighty dig in the ribs. He groaned, but said nothing.

Maggie and PJ sat in the back and swallowed hard as Marty pulled the seat forward and started the engine. He could barely see over the bonnet. He adjusted the wing mirrors like an old hand. Then as smooth as a driver who had been doing it for years, he eased the car away from the kerb and up the back road towards Westerbank. Gunboats turned round and smiled to everyone in the back seat.

'That's my boy. That's my laddie. Eh?' he said, gently tapping Marty's knee, who ignored him and concentrated on the road.

Maggie and PJ smiled to each other as the fields and farms passed them by and they went further and further into the countryside.

'We'd better not say a word about this. All right?' PJ said to Maggie.

Now she had two secrets, if she counted the day they saw Irish Breige in Beggar's Wood kissing that man with the black hair.

# Chapter Eight

Tom hadn't dared to go back to the letters for the first few days after Joe arrived. He was afraid of what he might find in them. It was important that nobody knew what he had discovered or saw how much pain he was in. But the curiosity had been eating away at him, and every time he closed his eyes at night, he could see Maria's face, hear her voice reading the letter he had found. He waited until Joe and Frankie had gone out for an afternoon together before he decided to lift the bundle of letters he had stashed under his mattress.

Sitting on his bed, he loosened the ribbon and smoothed out the letters to see if they were in any particular order. He recognised some of the dates, remembered writing his own letters on summer's days and rainy autumn nights in the seminary in Rome. In the beginning, after Maria had returned to Scotland, they wrote to each other each week, and after his visit home when they had made love on the beach their letters became more intense. But suddenly, all communication from Maria stopped. Every week Tom wrote another letter, but still no replies came back. Now he could see why.

When he started reading, he could not stop; his eyes devoured every word. The first couple were full of the usual reports of Maria's life back home, how she missed her cousins and aunt in Rome, how that summer had changed her life for ever. Meeting Tom, she wrote, no matter what happened to them, would always be precious. Some people spent their whole lives together and never experienced what they had shared, even though it was only fleeting. From the dates, it looked as though the letters were written one every week, from the day he had kissed her goodbye at the train station. And at the end of each one, Maria asked the question, 'Why do you not answer my letters?'

After she had left Rome, Tom discovered that a rumour of his love affair had reached the ears of the spiritual director of the seminary. Tom had emphatically denied it, and he didn't even tell Maria that he had been questioned when he came home to visit her. It was only weeks after he returned to Rome that he was again summoned for an inquisition. In his despair, he confessed everything to Monsignor Quinn, how he had agonised over his vocation because he had fallen in love with a girl. The old man listened intently, his hooded eyes looking straight at Tom as though he understood. When Tom had finished, the Monsignor stood up and told him quietly to pack his bags because he was being sent on retreat to a monastery in the Tuscan hills where he would be guided in his vocation, away from such frivolous notions. He didn't have to go, the old priest told him. He could take some leave, return home and consider seriously whether in his heart he really wanted to become a priest.

'You will make a good priest, Tom. You were born for this, to lead people. It is the spirit of God inside you. You cannot run away from that because of human weakness. You must conquer it. God will guide you.'

The Monsignor left the room without another word and the next time Tom saw him was when he was standing outside the seminary waiting to get into the car that would take him to the retreat. The Monsignor's hands were warm and fleshy when he took Tom's cold hand and shook it. Tom never looked back as the car drove off to the place where he was to feel like a prisoner as he made the final preparations for his ordination.

Tom sat back on the bed, looking at the letters spread out in front of him. He recalled that he had been concerned that his letters would be intercepted at the monastery, so he had given them to the old butcher who used to deliver meat to the back door of the ancient building. How naive he had been to assume that the old man would be anything other than loyal to the brothers. He must have passed his letters straight to them. But Maria's letters. How could they have been sent to his mother? Then the penny dropped. They must have been intercepted and sent to his mother by the seminary, in the secure knowledge that she would know exactly what to do with them. It had been so logical, yet in their naivety neither he nor Maria had for a moment considered that anyone would steal their love letters.

He had tried so hard not to write to her. All the time he was on retreat he had focused on his preparations for his ordination, reading the letters from his mother saying that this would be her finest hour. He knew he could never let her down. So he tried to put the affair with Maria into perspective. He told himself that it had been an infatuation – natural for a young man – but that God would forgive him and give him the strength to forget her. But his head was filled with their conversations. He could still hear her voice, and no matter how guilty he felt, he sat down every couple of days and wrote her long, loving letters. Even on the eve of his ordination, as his mother slept in a room in the seminary close to his, Tom had sobbed into his pillow, knowing in his heart that he didn't want to be a priest.

He read another few letters, each one more agonising than the last. Then his eyes locked onto two words that made his mouth go suddenly dry: 'Your baby.' Tom felt his breath quicken. 'No,' he heard himself whisper. 'Jesus, no.' He read on, hearing Maria's voice as he did so. 'I understand, Tom. Well, I am trying to understand. But it is very, very painful. I cannot begin to describe how much I am hurting.' Tom's eyes filled with tears. 'But it is our baby. Our own gift from God. Remember how you loved my cousin's little children and you said a baby was a gift from God?'

Tom put the letter down and sat back on the bed. He closed his eyes. 'I'm sorry, Maria,' he croaked, his mind racing. Maria had been pregnant with his child, and she believed he had abandoned her. He had ruined her life. She loved him more than life itself, and he had ruined her.

He stood up on suddenly weary legs and walked across to the window. Through blurred eyes he could see Frankie's car coming up the lane with Joe in the front seat. He gathered up the letters and pushed them back under his mattress. He took a deep breath, determined to show nothing in front of his brother or Frankie. He caught sight of his face in the mirror. Dark blue eyes, tired and sad, looked back at him.

'Hi. I thought the pair of you had got lost. I was about to send out a search party round all the pubs,' Tom said as Frankie and Joe got out of the car and walked across the farmyard. 'Have you been visiting your old haunts?'

'One or two of them,' Joe said, looking at Frankie. 'We've still a lot more to get round. D'you know, we've had a great day. Haven't we, Frankie?'

'Yeah. Great,' Frankie said. 'We walked a good couple of miles back through one or two of the villages, just to show Joe how things have changed down the years – or not, in most of them.'

'See anybody you knew?' Tom asked, thinking that Joe hadn't really gone into the village much since he'd come home. He was surprised that he seemed to be quite happy just being around the farm, helping with the work and walking alone in the evenings. Tom had expected he would be back raising hell in the pubs the way he used to, but Joe told him he'd got a bit tired of that after years on the lash in New York.

'One or two,' Frankie said. 'Most people already knew Joe was home. You know what this place is like. You could hardly fart but they hear about it four miles away.'

Tom was glad to see Frankie and Joe together like the old days. He didn't want to spend the evening at home alone with Joe because his mind was so full of what he had found in the letters that he felt sure Joe would start asking him what was eating him.

'I tell you what,' Tom said. 'Let's go down to Mulranney's for a few beers. We should make a night of it.'

Joe looked at Frankie, who shrugged his shoulders and smiled.

'What the hell. Let me just nip down the road and tell Kate or she'll have my guts for garters. I've been out since twelve.'

'What's this? Henpecked? Frankie Flaherty? I never thought I'd see the day,' Joe shouted after him as he got into his car.

When the three of them walked into Mulranney's, the pub fell silent as the dozen or so customers looked round and recognised Joe McBride. Everyone in the village knew that Joe was back and had been waiting to see what he looked like after all these years. Minutes earlier, as they drove past the corner, six or seven men had eyed Frankie's car to see if Joe was inside. Frankie noticed that Joe shifted a bit in the front seat, but his face was like flint as he looked straight back at them. In his rear-view mirror, Frankie could see the men put their heads together like conspirators, passing judgement. He had felt the muscles in his stomach tighten.

Mulranney poured three pints and shook Joe's hand when Tom introduced him as his brother.

'How you doin'? I heard somebody say there was a brother back from America. Good for you, Joe,' Mulranney said, with the look of a man who genuinely knew nothing of the gossip.

Around the bar, men began to resume their conversations and one or two nodded over to Joe in a friendly way.

'How's it goin', Joe? Back from the fleshpots of New York? Aye. You can't beat Westerbank for a bit of excitement!' shouted Martin Heaney, who was a couple of years younger than Joe and had always tried to emulate him as a man about town.

'Hiya, Martin. Jesus, you've not changed much. Have you given up hard work for good?' Joe shouted back, smiling as he brought his pint to his lips.

'I gave it up years ago,' Martin retorted. 'I just make love all day now, with any widows, divorcees or single women who require my services.' The men with Martin laughed. After the coal mine closed down, Martin had set himself up as local gardener and handyman and worked in a lot of homes in and around Westerbank. His good looks and charm had got him a reputation as a womaniser and he delighted in it because it opened the bedroom doors of more women than he could sometimes manage.

Joe put his hand in his pocket and pulled out a twenty pound note. He pushed it towards Mulranney.

'Give everyone a drink on me, pal. Just for old times' sake,' Joe said, loud enough for most people to hear.

As pints were poured and set up along the bar, there were grateful noises of acknowledgement.

'On yourself, Joe! Good to see you, big man! All the best, pal!'

Then the Badger Ryan, who had been sitting at his usual perch at the bar, glowered at Joe from under his cap and said, 'I want nothing off him! I'll take no drink from him!'

The bar fell silent, and there was the sound of embarrassed shuffling of feet. The Badger finished what was left in his glass and got off the stool a little unsteadily. He had been in the pub most of the afternoon.

Frankie braced himself as he walked towards them. Joe took another swig of his beer and stood with his feet spread and his shoulders straight. It was the first time since he had come home that Frankie had seen the old Joe. He was ready to fight. The Badger stopped right beside him and stood looking Joe in the eye. Everyone in the bar held their breath.

'You've some fuckin' neck on you, Joe McBride, coming back here! Some fuckin' neck!' Ryan stabbed his finger into Joe's chest. The colour rose up Joe's neck and into his face.

'Fuck off, you old pisshead! Before I throw you out in the street,' Joe said, his eyes raging.

The Badger may have been drunk but he was old enough to remember the kind of punishment Joe McBride could mete out to anyone in a pub brawl. Frankie knew he had once been on the receiving end of Joe's wrath. He would go now. Quietly. He had probably waited twenty years to look Joe McBride in the eye and let him know that he had not forgotten. He stood staring at Joe, his mouth quivering with nerves and anger.

'Go back to America. You don't belong here.' The Badger turned and walked out of the door.

Frankie felt his face redden and the sweat break out on his back.

'What in the name of Christ was all that about?' Tom asked, bewildered.

'Nothing,' Joe said, sounding in control. 'He's just a silly old bastard.'

Joe seemed to be relaxed but Frankie noticed that his hand was trembling when he lifted his pint.

# Chapter Nine

It had been the sound of the girl whimpering that had made the Badger Ryan stop in his tracks. He was humming to himself, half drunk, as he shuffled up the narrow, blacked-out road towards his farm. In the darkness he could make out the pink flesh of what looked like a girl's leg moving as if to stand up behind the hedgerow. He stopped and peered, focusing enough to see the girl pulling up her underwear as she sniffed and sobbed. He recognised her immediately as Alice McPhee, the slow-witted only daughter of old Archie McPhee, who had been left to bring up the girl from the age of ten after his wife died. She spent nearly all her time on the farm, cooking and working for her father, after the local school suggested that she was retarded and would be better off at a special school. Old Archie, who was frail and nearly sixty when his wife died, would have none of it and kept her at home where he told everyone she did a great job and was happy as any girl in the village.

Despite her obvious slowness, she had grown into a buxom young woman with straw blonde hair and a pretty face, with pale, vacant eyes. The teenage lads who worked at the hay with Archie during the summer used to joke among themselves that Alice would let them touch her breasts for sixpence.

Now as he sat in the kitchen of his house, the Badger poured another trickle of whisky into his chipped mug and remembered that night he found her. He rolled a cigarette and lit up, took a deep breath and spat in the direction of the fireplace. Even though it was more than twenty years ago, he could still see Alice's face wet with tears as she emerged, unsteadily, from the ditch behind the hedgerow. He even remembered her words. 'It was Joe! Joe McBride! He said it wouldn't be sore! But it was sore! Don't tell my da! Will you not tell my da! He'll kill me!'

The Badger remembered wiping her tears and putting his arm round her shoulder. In his drunk, fuddled state he had been confused. Surely Joe McBride would not take advantage of a daft young girl like this. Not McBride, who could have any woman he wanted.

'Joe McBride?' the Badger said. 'Joe? Did he?' He knew little about sex and was embarrassed. He'd known only one woman and that was when he'd lost his virginity at the age of nineteen. He didn't know what to say to Alice.

'Don't tell my da!' Alice's pale blue eyes filled with tears and she suddenly pulled away from the Badger and stumbled off into the darkness. The Badger could still hear her sniffing even when she'd disappeared into the night.

He swallowed the remains of his whisky and drew on his roll-up. Five minutes before he'd spotted Alice, he'd passed Joe McBride, the only other person he'd seen on the deserted road. Joe had been walking fast and barely looked in his direction. The Badger hadn't thought much of it at the time, but after seeing Alice he understood.

It had been days later before the Badger saw Joe McBride again. The image of Alice had stayed with him, troubling him, while he worked his fields and went about his business in the town. But he had no idea what he was going to do about it. He couldn't tell Archie, who was too old and frail to do anything about it. And every time he saw Alice she fled, making it obvious that she wanted no more said about the incident. It was only when he was drunk in the pub about a week later that the Badger decided to confront Joe McBride, who was knocking back pints and holding court with half a dozen teenagers dressed for a night out.

The Badger waited until Joe had gone to the bar and was

standing by himself before he sidled up to him. Joe looked at him and quickly looked away.

'I saw you, McBride. I know. I know what you did!' the Badger whispered, his words slurred.

Joe's face flushed and he looked straight past Ryan, saying nothing.

'That poor, fuckin' half-wit lassie!' the Badger rasped.

In a flash Joe grabbed him by the shirt and almost lifted him off his feet. He dragged him away from the bar to a quieter area and pinned him against the wall. The Badger was gasping for breath.

'You shut your fuckin' mouth, Ryan! She wanted it! Now shut your fuckin' mouth about this or I'll choke the life out of you!' Joe's face was crimson.

The Badger had felt his knees go weak and he stood panting when Joe let him go. He felt like bursting into tears of humiliation and rage as he watched Joe go back to his company and say something which made them all look towards him. He had steadied himself and walked out of the bar, the sound of laughter ringing in his ears.

Now as he sat alone in his sparse, damp-smelling kitchen, the sting of humiliation returned. He could do nothing. He was no match for Joe McBride. And in any case, Alice had pleaded with him to say nothing. He wished he didn't drink so much, then maybe he would have been able to do something. Maybe he had got it all wrong anyway.

At any rate, he said not a word to anyone. And six months later when Joe McBride went away to America, still he kept quiet. It was only when Alice disappeared that the Badger began to let his story drip out gradually during drunken bouts. But by then only those who thrived on gossip, regardless of its quality, were prepared to listen to him.

# Chapter Ten

Joe opened his eyes and for a moment was surprised that he couldn't hear the ocean. He had been dreaming he was back in his house overlooking the sea on Long Island, watching the curtains billowing in the morning Atlantic breeze. Then he realised he was back in the bed and the room that had become almost a distant memory to him.

He lay with his hands clasped behind his head and looked around the room, conjuring up memories of his childhood. He had been surprised at how choked he had been when he set eyes on Tom for the first time in twenty years. They had hugged in the kind of automatic, natural way that Joe never would have believed was possible. All the way home he had been worried that his brother would be sullen and distant, but he seemed genuinely glad to see him. And Frankie. That was always going to be more difficult. He had loved him like a brother, sometimes more, it seemed. But he'd wondered whether Frankie would have turned against him after what he had dragged him into all those years ago. Frankie was understandably edgy, but Joe was pleased that the bond was still there, as strong as ever.

He thought of how he had felt getting into the car with Frankie for the first time after all these years. It was as though time had stood still as they laughed and joked, driving through the villages where they had cut a dash as handsome teenagers with nothing but fun on their minds after a hard day's work. But in reality so much had changed. The carefree boys they had been had vanished after that night in Beggar's Wood, and now that he was back home, Joe found he was even more haunted by the past. At one point when they were driving through Westerbank, a couple of men at the corner kind of glared at him, ready to rake up all the gossip. He had stared back at them defiantly, but he felt tense and he sensed that Frankie knew what was in his mind. Suddenly he found himself saying to Frankie that he always regretted not going to the police after that night. Frankie had quickly pulled the car to a stop and turned to him with a shocked expression on his face.

'You're not, for one minute, thinking that we should go to the cops now, Joe, are you?' Frankie said, looking worried. 'I mean, I haven't told a soul. Not even Kate. Everything would fall apart, for Christ's sake.'

Joe could see the panic in his eyes. Frankie had so much to lose if he went to the police. Joe realised that, but his conscience was troubling him more and more.

'No,' he said. 'I wouldn't do that. Too late now. I just wish we had, that's all.' He stared out of the window. He hated himself for having dragged Frankie into the whole mess. They drove on in silence.

Joe was thinking that in the four weeks he had been home, he had never really had a long conversation with Tom. He wanted to. He wanted to tell him so much of what life had really been like in New York and how it was nothing like the way he wrote about it in the letters to their mother. He wanted to tell him just what had been going on in his life over there, of how awful it had been for a very long time. He wanted to tell him the real reason why he came home, and that he was scared inside. Deep down he was desperate to get the truth about Alice off his chest and tell his brother. He was not surprised that Tom had turned into the decent, gentle man he was. He had always been a better person than him, and he wondered if he could sit down and tell him everything. But Tom always seemed to find something to do as soon as they were alone together. It was as though he didn't really want to know. When he lay sleepless in bed at night, Joe blamed himself. He had never treated his brother well as they grew up and had bullied and harangued him constantly. Tom had probably been glad to see the back of him.

Joe's mind drifted back to New York. When he first started out there, it was survival that drove him, but even when things were going well for him he could find no peace. He became an angry young man, first up with his fists, and gained a reputation as a hard man among the Scottish and Irish building workers. But as he grew older, he became more and more haunted by the past. The only person he had confided in was a young Irish priest last year when he had walked into an empty church in the heart of the city. At the time Joe had smiled to himself, thinking how Tom would have relished the irony of his brother turning to God for help.

Joe had poured it all out to the priest, not in confession, but in an informal conversation, and the priest had told him that God was all-forgiving, but that he must make amends for what he had done. He told him he must give the people he had hurt the dignity they deserved before it was too late. Joe had made his mind up there and then that it was time to come home. He had left his manager to run the business and look after his affairs for a few months. He had thought at first that he would be able to go back and face the truth, but as soon as he spoke to Frankie he realised he could not. Frankie had too much to lose, and so he had to make sure the secret remained where they had left it.

# Chapter Eleven

Frankie turned on his side and lay watching Kate's chest gently rise and fall as she breathed. She looked fragile, her pale skin soft and almost translucent in the moonlight. He loved to watch her sleep peacefully like this. It had always made him feel safe and secure. But ever since Joe had come home, he'd felt uneasy. His mind went back to the scene at Mulranney's when the Badger Ryan had had a go at Joe. He had forgotten that the Badger was the only other person in Westerbank who knew for sure that Joe had been involved in some way with Alice McPhee, though he didn't know the whole story. But even so, he never considered for a minute that the stupid old bastard would actually confront Joe. His world could have collapsed there and then, he thought, if Joe had lost his temper in the pub. Most people seemed to have put the incident down to the Badger being drunk again, and Tom hadn't pursued it. Even more disturbing was the fact that Joe's conscience seemed to be troubling him. Why, after all those years, did Joe have to start talking about telling the police? It didn't bear thinking about.

Frankie took a deep breath and let it out slowly in case he woke Kate. He thought of how fortunate he had been to have met a woman like Kate. He would never have believed he could attract a woman as beautiful and intelligent as she was. As a young man, Frankie had always been in the shadow of Joe; when they walked into a room, it was Joe's dark, gypsy looks that the women went for. He wondered what would have happened if Joe had still been around when he bumped into Kate that night for the first time.

He probably wouldn't have stood a chance. Kate had transformed him, organised him and made him believe he was the most important man in the world to her. Sometimes he couldn't wait until she opened her eyes in the morning so he could start talking to her. She'd always been his rock, especially when they'd lost Emily. He would never forget the way she'd tried to keep everything together, despite her sorrow. Frankie couldn't live without her.

Kate shifted in the bed a little and made a soft moaning sound as though she was dreaming. Frankie reached out and stroked her face, pushing her hair away from her eyes. He felt exhausted but sleep wouldn't come. Every time he closed his eyes his mind played out the various scenarios that could bring chaos to his life. He'd seen Billy McGowan, a local policeman, talking to the Badger Ryan outside Baldy Cassidy's bakery a couple of days ago. McGowan had grown up in Westerbank and had just been moved out of uniform into plain clothes and was now a detective in the bigger office in Ayr. He really fancied himself as some kind of Elliot Ness, always wanting to get his hands on the big case that could take him up the slippery pole in the police force. Frankie told himself he was just being paranoid worrying about McGowan chatting to the Badger. McGowan's father had known Ryan all his life and they were probably only passing the time of day, but seeing them, Frankie immediately began to think that he would be telling him about Joe McBride being back home and all the gossip that was around at the time when Alice McPhee went missing. Frankie felt so paranoid he even thought the two of them were staring at him when he drove past them in his pick-up truck. He slid his arm round Kate's waist and closed his eyes, praying for sleep to come.

# Chapter Twelve

Baldy Cassidy lay on the bed watching the naked round rump of Breige's backside as she bent over to dry her legs. He could smell the soapy freshness of her and was pleasantly surprised to feel himself getting hard again. He was definitely turning into some kind of stud, he thought to himself, licking his lips. In eighteen years of marriage to his late wife Shona he never once in his life heard her moan with pleasure while he was making love to her, never mind the screams and groans of delight that Breige made while he was rolling about the bed with her. It takes a real man to be able to satisfy a woman like that, he had told Charlie Martin the postman, the only person he confided to in lurid detail about his romps with the new wife. He had to tell somebody, because Breige had turned his life upside down since they were married two months ago; she had him thinking about sex morning, noon and night. And sometimes not just thinking about it, but actually doing it two and three times a day. Charlie had listened intently, pursing his lips, saying that he wondered what he could do in the bedroom to make Fay, his wife of twenty-two years, moan like Breige.

'You know, pet, you could come back to bed,' Baldy said, throwing back the bedclothes to reveal his growing desire. 'I think I could manage one more while the ovens are getting fired up.'

'Ah sure, and you'll have the sweat pouring out of me and me just out the bath,' Breige quipped, glancing over her shoulder at her naked husband.

'You know, Breige, you've me driven crazy for it. I never knew

79

feelings like the kind I'm getting with you. Honest to God. I could be going at it all day long.' Baldy got out of the bed and walked towards Breige. He put his arms round her from behind and ran his hands over her breasts. Breige pushed him away and gently slapped him. She turned and held on to his hands, looking him up and down.

'Now, now, Casanova. We've work to do. It's nearly half six. There's dough to be rolled.' She looked down at him. 'And that reminds me, sausage to be cooked for the pastry!' She patted his bottom and moved away from him. 'Away and get a bath. I've left the water for you.' She pulled a dress over her head and walked out of the bedroom.

When she could hear Baldy sloshing around in the bath singing, Breige slipped back into the bedroom and closed the door. She knelt down and reached below the bed. She was so practised at this now that she didn't have to look. She could just reach her hand out and feel the tin box that was her ticket to America. Breige had sex with Baldy the night he told her he kept his entire life savings in a tin box beneath the bed. He said he didn't have any truck with banks, and liked to keep his money where he felt it was safe. It was after that first night when she sneaked a peek at the box and saw the wads of money that she decided she would set her cap at Baldy and make him marry her. She would string the sex-starved old fool along, and dip into the cash box with the same enthusiasm as he dipped into her. It was perfect. And he wasn't that bad either. She had woken with worse men than him climbing all over her. If she put to the side that Baldy was a boastful, snobby gobshite of a man, she could just about live with it. Once or twice she had even nearly had an orgasm.

Baldy lay back in the bath and rubbed the big green bar of soap over his hairy chest, thinking how pleasing his life was these days. With Breige he was leading the kind of life they only do in the films. He was going for dinners and drives to the beach. And to top it all he and Breige even romped on the beach one after-noon like Burt Lancaster and Deborah Kerr in *From Here To*

*Eternity.* He knew that every man in Westerbank lusted after his young wife and he took particular delight in flaunting her in front of them down at the pub or even at Mass on a Sunday. He also knew there had been a few mutterings about Shona hardly being cold before he was jumping on some young Irish girl at least twenty years younger than he was. But he didn't care. He felt happy and young, and never in his wildest dreams had he believed sex could be this adventurous.

Baldy got out of the bath and dried himself roughly with the towel, examining his face in the mirror. He wasn't bad for forty-three, he thought, despite his shiny bald head that was now red from his recent exertions and the hot bath. It was the loss of his hair when he was a young man that probably caused him to marry Shona in the first place. He had only had sex once before he met Shona, but he really preferred not to think about that.

She had been no prize but she was mad keen on him and her family had a bit of money put by for her which helped when he inherited his father's bakery two years later and set about modernising it. Baldy knew he had always been the subject of a bit of ridicule in the village as he grew up because he was always better dressed than the rest of the lads his age, and was the first in the place to have his own car, thanks to his father's money. The Cassidys saw themselves as a cut above the rest and his father told him not to pay any attention to the runts around Westerbank because they didn't know any better. Now all they could do was look at him with his pretty wife and salivate with jealousy. He loved it.

Downstairs, Breige was puting his plate of bacon and eggs on the table as he walked through the door. She smiled widely at him and poured tea into his favourite mug.

'You know, you've me spoiled rotten, girl.' He kissed her on the cheek and sat down, admiring the neatness of the kitchen and the bright red and white chequered tablecloth with the sun streaming in the window.

Breige sipped tea and watched him wolf down the food, stabbing the yolk with a forkful of bread and bacon.

'Sometimes you look a bit tired, Brendan. It's all these early mornings. You could be doing with a couple of days' break,' she said, looking into Baldy's eyes with a concerned expression.

'It's trying to keep up with my new young wife,' Baldy said, grinning.

Breige smiled. 'You hardly ever get a game of golf in these days. Why don't you and that pal of yours, Mickey McCann, go away for a couple of days at the golf?' she said.

Baldy put his knife and fork down and slurped his tea. He had loved golf with a passion since he was a teenager, and it was always great to get away from the bakery, and from Shona, so he and Mickey could get drunk and chat up women in the bars near the golf course. But with Breige around now, he didn't feel it was right to even broach the subject, and he wasn't sure he wanted to be away from her for a couple of days.

'Oh, it's true, right enough, Breige. I love my golf, and I could do with a rest. But I wouldn't want to leave a lovely young thing like yourself around here unattended. All the randy buggers in the place would be knocking on your door.' Baldy smiled.

'Oh yeah. As if I'd be interested in any of them when I've got you, darlin',' Breige said, reaching out and touching Baldy's hand. 'No. You go if you feel like it, Brendan. Honest. I'd love you to. I'd be fine here and I could manage the bakery a day or two without you. Don't worry.' She squeezed his hand.

Baldy touched her hair and traced his finger over her mouth. 'Maybe I will. I don't know if I could do without those lips for a couple of days though.' He leaned over the table and kissed Breige on the mouth. 'We'll see. We'll see.' He looked at his watch. 'Right, pet. That's time to get moving now.' He put his plate in the sink and walked out of the kitchen, jangling the keys to the bakery next door and whistling merrily.

'I'll be through in five minutes,' Breige said. When he was gone, she sat back in the chair sipping her tea, a smile beginning to break over her face.

# Chapter Thirteen

Since he couldn't read or write, he never knew what his name looked like on paper. He had only ever heard people call him Peter when he was a boy in the children's home and later in Calvin Hospital, the asylum where he had spent most of his life. But the name didn't mean anything to him, so he was quite happy when the little girl Maggie called him Sky. It made him feel free. Sky, he thought, looking up at the endless bright blue that stretched above him and seemed to go on for ever. He smiled to himself. Sitting in the back of the trailer, Maggie caught his eye and he winked at her. She winked back, smiling.

'You look happy, Sky. Are you happy?' Maggie said, pulling a piece from an orange and handing it to him.

Sky took the fruit from her and gave her the thumbs-up. He sat back in the trailer, enjoying the sun on his face, as they trundled along the road into town, driven by Frankie and PJ up front.

As he looked out across the endless fields with farmhouses dotted across the landscape, Sky was thinking how happy he was. Nobody had ever asked him before about being happy. He had hardly ever heard the word. In the children's home he remembered laughing with other boys and girls his own age. But the nuns were always making a fool of him in the classes because he couldn't speak. He was referred to as the dummy by most of the nuns and staff at the home, so eventually the children called him that as well and he more or less forgot his name. Sometimes older kids would hold him down and torture him to see if he could scream in pain. They would take turns to pull his hair tight at the temples which brought tears to his eyes, and they used to stand in a circle and laugh at his screwed-up face and his mouth gaping open in a silent scream. Nobody ever really helped him except Molly who worked in the kitchen. She was always kind to him and when Cook wasn't watching, she gave him extra food and the odd biscuit. Molly didn't seem that much older than he was and she told him that she too had grown up in the home, and that one day she would find her parents.

One afternoon when they were in the kitchen together, she told him that she had heard the nuns talking about where he came from. His mother was a young married woman who had been made pregnant by a soldier while her husband was in the army. She was a farmer's wife and she gave him away to the Catholic church when he was born. But when the people who adopted him realised he was a mute, they put him in a home. Molly always promised him she would find out where he came from. But one day when he went into the kitchen he was told she was gone. He overheard somebody say something about her stealing money, but he didn't believe she would do that. He was devastated and cried for days, and the nuns slapped him because he couldn't tell them why he was so miserable.

He remembered every day at the children's home. Especially when he was nearly twelve and they sent him away. It was all Billy's fault. Peter had been hungry and sneaked out of the dormitory into the kitchen while everyone was asleep. He was looking in the pantry when Billy the caretaker came in, staggering and carrying a half-empty bottle of wine. Peter jumped onto a ledge and hid behind a cupboard, watching as Billy brought out a tin box with pound and ten shilling notes in it. Peter knew it was the cash box used to pay suppliers who called at the back door, because Molly had told him, and she said only Sister Theresa had a key to it. But Billy seemed to have a key and after he took some of the notes out and stuffed them into his trouser pocket, he locked it up and put the key in his jacket pocket. Peter was horrified. It must have been Billy who had stolen the money, and he let Molly take the blame.

Suddenly Peter slipped and fell to the floor. He tried to get up, but Billy was on top of him and dragged him to his feet by his hair. He started to slap him around and pull his hair, laughing and telling him it was a good job it was only the dummy who'd seen him or he would have had to kill him. He pushed Peter up against the wall and kept banging his head. Peter didn't know what made him do it, but he grabbed a knife from the shelf and stabbed Billy in the eye. The screams wakened the whole dormitory and he knew he was in for it. He was dragged away and beaten by the nuns, and left in a room by himself for the next few days. He could see the children from the windows and they waved to him forlornly. Then one morning Sister Theresa came and took him by the hand along the polished corridor to the big front door which nobody ever got to use. A woman in a black uniform came from a van outside and was handed a small brown suitcase. She took him by the hand and pushed him into the van. He remembered the wire grille on the windows and he could barely see the children in the small walled garden as the van went up the long drive. Nobody saw him go except Sister Theresa who stood on the steps of the home. He had no idea where he was going. Nobody spoke to him. He thought he must be going to jail because of what he'd done to Billy. He wished Molly would come and find him.

The journey seemed to take for ever, and Peter sat in the van staring out of the window as the green countryside gave way to villages and towns with long streets of grey and red tenements which looked dreary and sad. Finally they came to a place surrounded by fields and trees, with a high brick wall, and the van came to a stop. He was led inside and shown a small room with a bed and a table that he was told was his new home. He looked around the halls outside. There were lots of people, some sitting on chairs crying, others talking to themselves as they walked up and down. Two women were fighting and scratching each other as people stood around laughing and screaming. There didn't seem to be any children. Peter was terrified. Everywhere he went there were doors with locks on them and corridors with big burly men in white coats carrying bundles of jangling keys. He cried himself to sleep every night and barely ate any of the food that was given to him in the big canteen. Some people sat rubbing food into their hair, others guarded their plates with their arms, their eyes darting suspiciously at everyone who walked past them. Peter had no idea where he was. It was only when a young doctor examined him a few days later and told him he would be working on the hospital's farm that he understood he was in some sort of hospital. He wondered when they would let him go, so he could try to find Molly. He knew she wouldn't just desert him like that and that one day she might come to this place and find him. So he spent his days working on the farm, milking cows, and watching calves being born. The couple who ran the farm were friendly to him because he was a young boy and the old man showed him how to make little animals out of wood. After a while, Peter settled down at Calvin Hospital and stopped crying himself to sleep at night. And in time, he stopped scanning the faces of the visitors in the hope that one day Molly would come.

'C'mon, Sky.' Maggie's voice shook him from his memories. He hadn't even noticed they had arrived in the village.

Frankie and PJ were out of the car and were opening the latch to let them out of the trailer.

'OK. I'm going down to Larry's to get more nails and felt for the roof of the cow shed,' Frankie said. 'So you all behave your-selves and I'll be back in ten minutes. You're in charge, Sky.' He winked at Sky who smiled back, his arm round Maggie's shoulder.

'Can we go to the baker's and get a drink and a cake?' Maggie said.

Frankie went into his pocket and pulled out a few coins. 'That's all I've got. That'll have to do you.' He handed the money to PJ.

Inside the baker's, Baldy Cassidy used a big wide shovel to bring fresh bread out of a huge oven. Between that and the smell of newly baked pastries, Maggie's mouth was watering. She scanned the boards of chocolate éclairs and cream buns, wondering if they had enough money. In front of her, Dennis Jarvie and Micksey Larkin stood with three of their pals, pointing out cakes and buns to the woman everyone knew as Irish Breige. She was carefully placing them in white paper bags and handing them over. As he turned away from the counter with his armful of paper bags, Dennis shoved Maggie out of the way.

'Hey, you. Who you shoving?' Maggie bristled, pushing him back. She hated Dennis Jarvie. He was in the class above PJ in the school and was spoiled rotten. His father owned the local petrol station and Dennis always had loads of money for anything he wanted. He had an entourage of pals who hung around him more for the cakes and sweets than out of loyalty.

'Oh look,' Dennis said, turning round. 'It's the Flahertys and that eejit that lives with them.' Dennis was big for his age and he went up to Sky and looked into his face. 'Well? What do you have to say? Oh. I forgot. You're a dummy, aren't you?' Dennis sniggered and his friends joined in.

Sky's eyes showed his hurt and his face was pale. He looked over Dennis's head towards Maggie and motioned her to get on with buying her cakes. But Maggie's eyes blazed.

'Oh ya! Oh ya bastard!' Dennis buckled as he felt a kick on his shin.

'See you, Flaherty. You're going to get it.' His face was red and he glared at Maggie.

'Why don't you just go and get stuffed, Jarvie. We're only in here to get cakes. Piss off and leave us alone.' PJ pushed his way across to Maggie.

'You'll get it and all, if you don't watch,' Dennis said.

'Right. Right. That's enough of this nonsense,' Baldy Cassidy shouted across the counter. 'If I've to come round from this counter, I'll throw every one of you out in the street. Now behave, Jarvie. Get your arse out of here. Now!' Baldy's voice boomed.

'Stuff you, ya baldy bastard,' he said. He and his mates jostled to get out of the door first as Baldy moved to come round from the counter.

Sky shepherded Maggie and PJ towards the cake boards and they chose a cake each and asked him to point to the one he wanted.

'I would expect Frankie Flaherty's kids to know better than to rise to the bait of a little toerag like Jarvie,' Baldy said, taking the money from them and dropping it into the drawer.

Maggie said nothing but looked towards Breige who was smiling sympathetically. She looked nice, Maggie thought. With her big red lips and sticking out chest, she looked just like the women in the cowboy films who always fell in love with John Wayne or Alan Ladd. She wondered if Breige had seen them that day in Beggar's Wood. She said nothing as she backed out of the shop but looked from Breige to Baldy, wondering what on earth she could have been doing that day in the woods when she gave the man money.

Outside, they scoffed the cakes while they waited for Frankie to come back from Larry's.

'Look who's coming,' PJ said, seeing Dennis and his mates approaching.

'Just ignore them,' Maggie said. 'Here's Dad coming anyway.' She could see Frankie walking a few yards behind them.

Sky stood protectively in front of Maggie and PJ.

When Frankie arrived he loaded the felt into the back of the trailer and was about to lift Maggie in when he heard the voice of the little troublemaker everybody knew as Dennis Jarvie.

'Hey, Flaherty. Your motor's falling to bits,' Dennis shouted and his mates started to laugh. Frankie ignored him. He opened the latch and lifted Maggie in. Sky climbed in and sat down, keeping an eye on Dennis. As Frankie and PJ went into the car and started the engine, Dennis and his pals moved towards them. They still had paper bags in their hands and started to bring something out. Maggie had a feeling what was coming next.

'Look out, Sky,' she said, ducking as bits of cake and half-chewed scones came flying through the air.

A strawberry tart hit Sky on the side of his face. He looked shocked but not angry as he wiped it off. Maggie stood up and shook her fist, looking around the trailer furiously for something to throw back at them. Sky grabbed hold of her and made her sit down, then calmly licked strawberry tart from his fingers.

'I'll get him for that, Sky,' Maggie said angrily.

Sky shrugged his shoulders as if he didn't care.

# Chapter Fourteen

Tom rolled down the window of his car and sucked in the sea air as he drove along the coast road. He had made countless journeys on this road in all weathers, but on a day like this he always marvelled at the sun twinkling on the water as the waves washed over the shingle. He slowed down so he could hear the whispering sound the water made as it dragged back over the pebbles. He never tired of the sight or the sound. It always reminded him of so many years ago, of the incredible rush of happiness he had felt, and later, every time he passed the same stretch of road, the depths of sadness when it had come to an end with Maria. He drove almost at a walking pace, enjoying the sight, his mind clear for the first time in over four weeks. He had to find Maria. When he had read the last of the bundle of letters he knew in his heart that even though he had learned to live with everything that had happened, it was still not over. He had truly believed he had put it all behind him until he read her letters. Only then did he realise how raw the hurt was, and he surprised himself by the depth of his feelings. But somehow a lot of the sting had been taken out of his pain now that he knew Maria had not left him. The wasted years were painful to accept but she had loved him and that was all that mattered. He was determined to find her. He would make it up to her.

Tom had told Joe he was going to look at some machinery and would be gone for the day, and he tried to be casual when Joe offered to keep him company on the drive. He would go on his own, he told him. He had one or two other things to do and he needed some time. Joe had regarded him with some suspicion under his dark eyes and lascivious smile. He told Tom it was perfectly normal if he had a girlfriend. He wasn't a priest any more and he was entitled to get his leg over as much as the next man. But he didn't have to hide it from his brother. Tom had blushed and shaken his head. If only everything was as simple as the world his brother lived in.

After an hour's drive Tom looked out at the fishing boats in Girvan harbour, bobbing around in the soft breeze. He pulled the car into the side of the road and got out to stretch his legs. The smell of seaweed mingled with fish and diesel, the way he remembered it. The fishing village was where he and Maria had shared so many stolen moments. Her parents owned the cafe on the edge of the harbour and he squinted across the road to see if it was still open. It was. But the name over the bright red and green doorway was not Di Giacomo. He screwed up his eyes and tried to read it. It looked like Alberto's. He couldn't remember any Alberto in Maria's large family. He had never met any of them here in Scotland, as all their liaisons were secret. But Maria used to make him laugh when she rhymed off all the cousins, brothers and uncles who had left Italy before the war to make their lives in Scotland. Most of them were dotted along the Ayrshire coast, in fish and chip shops and cafes where they made their fortune and kept themselves very much to themselves among the Italian community. The Di Giacomos were strict by any family's standard, Maria had told him, and her father was determined she would marry a good Italian boy so they could produce plenty of little Italian grandchildren. If they had known that summer that their beautiful daughter who they were so proud of was in love with a young Scottish boy who was training to be a priest, the shock would have killed them. It would have been an affront to everything they had ever believed in, Maria had told Tom. They could never have held their heads up in the community again. Now, standing looking out to sea, Tom could only imagine what might have happened to Maria when she discovered she was pregnant. He felt certain she would never have aborted their baby, but he agonised over the despair she must have been in. Had she left the village altogether? The only way to find out was to go and ask.

He looked across the street at the cafe and took a deep breath. At least nobody knew who he was. He walked across the road and up to the door. He could see through the half-frosted window that only a couple of people were sitting drinking cups of tea or coffee. An older Italian man, small and balding, stood behind the counter with a white apron tied round his hefty stomach. He looked at Tom when he pushed open the door. Suddenly Tom didn't know whether just to ask his question or have a coffee. He stood, dumb for a second, while the man looked at him, curious and impatient. 'A coffee, please,' Tom finally said, pulling a wooden chair out from a table. The other two men in the cafe looked up at him, then out of the window, uninterested.

'Cappuccino? Black? White?' the man behind the counter said without changing the expression on his face.

'Cappuccino,' Tom said, remembering the steaming cups of frothy coffee he had drunk in pavement cafes in Rome with other seminarians on the rare occasions they were free from studies.

He sat down, listening to the splutters and slurps of the coffee machine. In a minute the man put a fat round cup filled with coffee in front of him.

'One cappuccino,' he said, and almost smiled.

'Thanks.' Tom searched his face to see if he seemed approachable.

The man disappeared into the kitchen and a middle-aged woman came out and gazed across the counter at Tom. She smiled with her eyes. Tom looked at her and looked away. He strained his ears to listen as she spoke in Italian to the older man. He thought he heard her say something like she didn't know, or she couldn't remember. Tom wondered if they thought they knew him or recognised him, but the only family of Maria's he had met were the ones in Rome and they had had no idea he was a student priest. He decided he was being paranoid and sipped his coffee, savouring it and the memories it brought back from what seemed like a lifetime ago. When he was finished he stood up and walked towards the counter. The old man came forward and Tom reached into his pocket and gave him a few coins. The man took the money, his expression unchanged.

'I wonder if you could help me,' Tom found himself saying.

The man turned from the cash till. The two men in the cafe leaned forward as if to strain their ears. Tom suddenly felt self-conscious and sensed his face burning. He tried to compose himself.

'I'm . . . I'm . . . Is this not the cafe that used to be owned by the Di Giacomos?' he asked, trying to sound only vaguely interested.

The old man looked him in the eye. The woman put her head round the corner from the kitchen and for a second her eyes met Tom's. He felt he should say something more.

'It's just that I remember this place years ago. Passing through. On my way to the south. I remember it used to say Di Giacomo. A big family, I seem to remember. Lots of little kids.' He felt he was on the verge of raving. He bit his tongue.

'All gone,' the old man said. 'Back home. Long time ago. All gone.' He started to wipe the top of the counter with a cloth, indicating the conversation was finished.

But Tom wanted to know more. There's no way these people know who I am, he told himself. Stop being paranoid.

'Really? All of them? Just like that? When? I've not been here for about, well, a long time. They were nice people though. Get fed up with this Scottish weather, did they?' Tom hoped he sounded as if he didn't care one way or the other, but his heart was pounding under his shirt.

The old man shrugged his shoulders and spoke in a half Scottish, half Italian accent. 'Aye. Somethin' like that. Just went back to Roma. Better for the family. Better for everyone. Lorenzo want to take his girls home to Roma. And the wee boys.' It sounded credible, but Tom saw that the woman had come out of the kitchen and was looking straight at him, as if she knew more than the old man was telling. A sharp glance from the old Italian sent her back inside the kitchen and out of sight.

'Oh well. Nice to talk to you. Great coffee. See you again. Thanks.' Tom smiled and left the cafe. Outside he felt his chest muscles relax as he let out a deep breath. For the first time in ten years he felt like having a cigarette. He walked across to his car and stood leaning against the bonnet. His heart was heavy. He was no further forward. Maria had gone back to Rome with her parents, probably because she was pregnant and couldn't face shame in the community where the Italians were regarded as the pillars of the Catholic Church. There was nobody around here he could ask, and it was clear from the attitude of the old guy in the cafe that he did not want to discuss the Di Giacomos any further. His attitude convinced Tom that the old man knew there was a hint of scandal and shame in their departure.

He began walking along the road and up the tiny side street where he remembered the old chapel was. He had sat there waiting for Maria so many times. She would come in and sit across from him, and his heart would always jump when he saw her.

Automatically, his steps took him up to the chapel and he pushed back the half-open oak door. He could smell the incense from morning benediction and he stepped softly onto the tiled floor inside the church. A stained-glass window with a dozen depictions of the Nativity dominated the wall above the altar, and in the sunshine, purple and crimson streaks of light beamed onto the white marble altar. He walked down the aisle, the sound of his shoes on the tiles echoing in the silence. He genuflected and sat in one of the pews. A sense of grief, of loss, of frustration washed through him. How empty his life was, he thought, looking at the altar, remembering himself going through the motions as a priest with his heart only barely in it. How he had betrayed God, he thought. Lied to himself. Lied to everyone. Was this his punishment for his duplicity in passing himself off as a young student priest, pure and innocent, while he broke every rule that was ever made? He let out a weary sigh. He would never find her now. He didn't know where to start. She might not even have stayed in Rome. She could be anywhere. It was over twelve years ago.

In the silence he was aware of someone coming into the chapel and he swiftly composed himself. He could hear the sound of a coin dropping into a box as whoever it was lit a candle under the statue of the Virgin Mary. Tom glanced round and his eyes met those of the woman from the cafe. She smiled. Tom nodded back and looked ahead. He could hear her tiptoeing down the aisle and was conscious of her getting into the pew behind him. He felt uneasy. He could hear himself breathe.

'You are the boy. Aren't you? You Maria's boy? Yes?' she whispered in a heavy Italian accent.

For a split second he wasn't sure if he had heard her properly. He felt light-headed. He turned round. He was inches away from the woman's face. Her sallow skin was wrinkled around the neck and mouth, but her high cheekbones and dark eyes testified to a woman who had been a striking beauty in her day. Tom didn't know what to say.

'I'm right, am I not?' Her eyes pierced him. 'You Tom. The padre?'

Tom felt his stomach fall like a lead weight. She knew everything. He opened his mouth to speak, but nothing came out.

'I saw your picture. Maria show me a long time ago. You not changed. Not much anyway.' Her eyes narrowed. 'Why you abandon her?'

'Where is she?' Tom said, his voice barely audible.

The woman's face grew dark. She shook her head. 'Why you leave Maria? Why?' she said. 'The poor girl.'

'I didn't abandon her,' Tom said. The woman sniffed as though she didn't believe him. 'Please believe me,' he said. 'Listen.' Tom told her as fast as he could about the letters and how he had agonised all these years. She sat back in the pew while he spoke, then when he had finished she closed her eyes and shook her head.

'My God,' she said, reaching out and touching his arm.

'Please,' Tom said. 'Do you know where she is?'

'I dunno,' the woman said. 'Lorenzo, her papa, he took all of them back home to Roma after . . .' She hesitated. 'After, well, you know what.'

Tom nodded. He wanted to say the baby, but the word wouldn't come. The woman seemed to sense that he was unable to speak.

'Lorenzo make all the Italians here believe I am bad, because I help his daughter. I help because I know her from she is a little girl. I'm like her auntie. She came to me when she knew she was having a baby and she didn't know what to do. All I did was take her to the doctor. I was only trying to help.' She looked frustrated.

'What happened? What about Maria and the baby?' Tom didn't want to know about family squabbles. He wanted to know where Maria was.

'I don't know. I don't know. When Lorenzo and Maria's mama find out that she is going to have a baby and the full story, about the boy priest, everything go crazy. Everything go completely crazy. They packed up and went to Roma. The whole family. Left the lawyer to sell the cafe and my Alberto bought it. Him and Lorenzo were in the army together, you know. Alberto said I never to talk about it again in my life, because now Italians say I am bad.' She looked as though she was about to cry.

'Why would they say that?' Tom asked.

'Because Maria told me months before that she had fallen in love with the young boy priest when she was in Roma for the holidays. I knew. She – I don't know how you say – she confide in me. And I didn't tell her mama. They say I'll burn in hell. Maybe I will.' Tears spilled from her eyes.

Tom touched her hand. 'I'm sorry,' he said. 'I'm sorry. It's my fault. I fell in love with Maria and I had no right to fall in love. I was to be a priest. It is all my fault.' His voice was breaking.

'She loved you,' the woman said. 'Maria loved you more than

life. I know how much she loved you and if you love someone that much you must follow your heart. I told her that. So it my fault too.'

'Have you any idea where she is now? Could I find her?' Tom said, hoping for a scrap of help.

'I don't think so. Many people here don't talk to me and Alberto would be mad if I did anything. But I will try. I will try for you. Because I see in your eyes that you love her still.'

'And the baby? Do you have any idea about the baby?' Tom said, desperate.

'I don't know,' she said. 'And that is honest truth. I know they went back to Roma and maybe they send Maria away to have the baby to stop everyone talking. I don't know. I never heard from her since the day she left. But she was so sad. So sad. I never forget that child. She was beautiful. And her eyes. Crying so hard that day.' The old woman wiped tears away from her chin. She stood up, sniffing. 'I have to go now. Alberto will be wondering where I am. He kill me if he know I was talking to you. I think he knew who you were. He kind of said to me, but I said I didn't think so. My name is Gabriella Medini. Meet me here in two weeks. Maybe I have some news.' She turned and walked away

Tom got to his feet. He wanted to run after her, ask her more questions, ask about everything that Maria had ever said to her about him. He wanted to plead with her to think hard about how he could find her. But while he stood, in the aisle of the empty church, Gabriella Medini scurried out of the oak doors and he was alone.

# Chapter Fifteen

PJ lay back against the tree chewing a blade of grass, taking it in and out of his mouth like a cigar. He had been thinking about the time they saw Irish Breige in the woods with the guy with the black hair. He'd thought about it a lot and wondered if Marty had too. He sat up and looked at Marty, Jess and Maggie who were playing some game of throwing stones in the air and catching them on the back of their hands.

'What do you think that Breige woman was doing that day in the woods?' PJ said. He was looking mainly at Marty, thinking that he would have the same idea as him.

'I think they were at it,' Marty said. 'You know. Shagging.'

Jess sniggered and Maggie looked at PJ who glanced away from her. They didn't talk like that in their house. But he quite liked it.

'Yeah,' PJ said. 'But why was she giving him money? Is it maybe Baldy's money?'

Marty stood up and walked around.

'Maybe she's having a love affair with him and they're going to murder Baldy and run off with the insurance,' he said.

PJ laughed. Marty was always coming out with fanciful ideas and stories. He had told PJ that when he grew up he was going to be a writer. Marty's imagination was brilliant, but PJ didn't think for a minute that Breige was going to murder Baldy.

'I saw it in a film once,' Marty insisted. 'It was called Double something. Double Identity. No. Double Indemnity. The man and woman fake the guy's death and get the insurance. Maybe that's what's happening.'

Maggie and Jess looked at Marty then nodded to PJ.

He shook his head. 'I don't think so,' he said. 'But something funny is going on. I don't think we should tell anybody. Let's just keep it as our secret.'

'I like secrets,' Maggie said.

'We've got a secret too, you know.' Jess turned to Maggie. Marty glared at Jess. 'See us? We're on the run. Aren't we, Marty?' Jess looked at Marty.

'Shut it, Jess,' Marty said, his face reddening under his freckles.

'It's OK, Marty. We can tell Maggie and PJ. We're like blood brothers now. Aren't we, Maggie?' Jess put her arm round Maggie's shoulder.

'Yeah. Blood brothers. And blood sisters,' Maggie said.

PJ could see Marty's distress and he stood silently for a moment.

'What is it, Marty? You can tell us. What does she mean, on the run? From who?' PJ said, his voice gentle.

Marty bit his bottom lip and looked at the ground. He bit his thumbnail.

'She's right, we're on the run,' he said. 'But she shouldn't have told you. We've got no house. We got evicted from the house in Glasgow because Da never paid the rent. He went missing for ages. Then he came back and it was too late.' His voice trailed off.

'You mean you live in that caravan all the time? Even in winter?' Maggie said.

'Don't know yet,' Marty said. 'We've only been on the run for two months. We left because the social were coming to take me and Jess away to a home because we were getting evicted and there was nowhere to stay.' Marty's voice was shaking.

'Jesus,' PJ said, trying to comprehend how that must feel.

'It's not just that,' Marty said. 'The cops are after our da. He robbed a shop and that's why he went missing. When he came back he said we had to get off our mark. Ma didn't want to go, but we were getting chipped out of the house anyway, so she had no option.'

'I never liked the house anyway,' Jess piped up. 'It was stinking, with a damp smell, and there were always rats in the close at night. I hated going out to the toilet at night. I'm glad we're on the run. It's good.' Jess jabbered on, but PJ thought her eyes told a different story.

'So what happens next?' PJ said.

'Don't know,' Marty said. 'Just keep going, I suppose. Gunboats said he'll see us through all right. He was a hero in the army, so it should be all right.'

'Yeah. Gunboats'll see everyone all right,' PJ said, not believing it any more than Marty did. 'C'mon. Let's go up to our house. I'm starved.'

They walked up the lane and into the farmyard where Kate was hanging out washing on the green.

'This is a great house,' Jess said. 'You're dead lucky.'

'That'll be right,' Maggie said. 'I wish I lived in a caravan and was on the run. It sounds brilliant.'

PJ looked at Maggie then at Marty, knowing that she was lying.

# Chapter Sixteen

'Do you fancy going over to the festival at Girvan for a couple of days?' Joe said to Tom from across the kitchen table as he buttered a slice of toast. 'You look as though you could do with the break.' He looked at his brother's face, wondering what had been going on in his mind for the last few days.

Tom had really been on edge lately. Joe didn't know how to broach the subject with him, but he felt he had been different since he'd gone to look at that machinery a couple of weeks before. At first Joe thought maybe his brother was struggling a bit after their mother's death, but he had shown no signs of it when he arrived. Indeed he got the impression, listening to Tom talk about how difficult she had been to live with, that he wasn't exactly paralysed with grief. Instinctively, Joe felt there was a woman involved, and he hoped his brother wasn't messing about with somebody's wife. In a little place like Westerbank that was never a good idea. He was dying to say that to him, but Tom was always so distant about things like that. When they were growing up and Tom was in the seminary, Joe used to be pissed off because he couldn't get talking his usual rough way about girls when Tom came home for holidays. He used to say to Frankie that Tom was a born priest. That he wouldn't know what to do if he wakened up one morning and there was a girl climbing on top of him. Now, he was sure there was a woman involved, because Tom had been mooning around like a sick calf for days, and in Joe's book that could only mean one thing.

'Yeah. Sounds fine,' Tom said, without looking at Joe. 'We could ask Frankie along. The three of us could go. Just like old times.'

Joe was pleased that Tom seemed keen. It was just what they needed. Get away from here. Joe was conscious of the whispers that had been going on since he'd come back. Every time he was in the pub, he felt there were sideways looks at him, though he knew nobody had the balls to take him on. But there was always the Badger Ryan and his big, stupid mouth. At least he had managed to stay calm when Ryan refused his drink that night in Mulranney's. But inside he had been shaking.

'What's the festival like these days?' Joe said, already looking forward to it.

'Oh, hasn't changed much. As you would expect. Cattle sales, horses, a few tinkers along the way. And the folk music. It's good fun. The bars are always stacked out and there's a lot more of a younger element. Mind you, that might just be us growing old.'

'Do you go to it much yourself?' Joe asked.

'I haven't been to the festival for a couple of years,' Tom said. 'But Frankie and me used to go and stay overnight. Just get hammered really and have a laugh with some people we hadn't seen for a while. I think Frankie will want to come. I'll go up and ask him today.'

'Great. What about that wife of his? Kate. Will she let him go? She looks to me like she has Frankie where she wants him,' Joe said, thinking of the three times he had met Kate since he'd arrived home. She was certainly a beauty, he could see that, even though she always seemed to be up to her elbows in work. There was something sensual about her, even in a baggy skirt and shirt, and he'd found that he couldn't take his eyes off her when he'd first met her. He knew she'd noticed, and once or twice she seemed to blush a bit when he spoke to her. If she'd been anybody else's wife, Joe thought, he would have bedded her by now. But he banished the thought.

'No, she hasn't got Frankie where she wants him, Joe,' Tom said, with a note of chastisement in his voice. 'She has Frankie where he wants to be. He's nuts about her. And she adores him. They're brilliant together. She doesn't boss him about or anything.'

'A woman like that,' Joe said, rubbing his chin, 'could boss me around all day long. I'd just roll over and let her scratch my belly.' He had a lewd look on his face.

'Don't even think about it,' Tom said.

'Hey! Bless me, Father, for I have sinned! But only in my mind. Only in my wildest fuckin' dreams, Father!' Joe playfully flicked a piece of toast at his brother. 'Seriously, Tom,' he said, aware that his brother didn't share his sense of humour, 'I don't fancy her at all. But she seems to be a lovely person. I'd like to get to know her more. That's all.'

'Yeah,' Tom said. 'Sure. Just keep your hands off her or you'll roast in hell.'

'There's plenty more where she came from,' Joe joked. 'All my pals will be down in hell pouring the drinks and getting the birds stripped and scrubbed waiting for my arrival!' He swaggered out of the kitchen and into his bedroom, whistling.

Tom shook his head and smiled. Same old Joe. He wondered what had made him think when he first saw him that he had changed. Though he did seem to have changed in some ways. He was more considerate now, Tom thought, and no longer treated him like the weak younger brother he used to bully. Tom had even considered sitting down with Joe and telling him all about Maria. But somehow there was still a barrier between them. When they did spend any time alone, he felt awkward because he knew if Joe questioned him closely he would just blurt everything out and he was afraid Joe would laugh at him or offer some stupid advice such as to put it all behind him and move on.

On the way to Frankie's house, Tom saw his friend on the far side of one of his fields. He was driving his tractor along the last of the line of grass he had cut for silage. Tom stopped the car and walked over to him. Frankie had been hard at it, he thought, noting the almost perfect straight lines of grass piled up from one corner of the field to the other. With the colours running like a pattern, it looked as though the field had been hand-knitted in two shades of green and pulled across the landscape. He could hear Maggie, PJ and the kids from the caravan messing around as they grabbed handfuls of freshly cut grass and threw it over each other. Maggie ran towards him when she saw him.

'Uncle Tom, hiya. We're having a grass fight,' Maggie said, her face glowing from the sun and the excitement.

'Just be careful,' Tom said, ruffling her hair. 'That fresh cut grass – could be all sorts of beasties lurking underneath it. Grass snakes even.'

Maggie's face fell and she quickly patted the grass that was stuck to her hair and clothes.

'Grass snakes?' she said, shocked.

Tom laughed and lifted her up. 'Ah-ha. That got you, didn't it?'

'No it didn't. No it didn't. I knew you were just kidding,' Maggie said, sticking her tongue out as he put her down. She ran towards the others and Tom could hear her saying something about grass snakes, which made them all stop in their tracks.

Frankie got out of the tractor and came over to Tom. Sweat trickled down his forehead and he wiped it with the back of his hand. 'Christ, it's boiling. I'm sweating like a pit pony up here.'

'You've fairly got through it, Frankie. I haven't even started mine,' Tom said, knowing that his mind had been distracted since his trip to the cafe.

'Plenty of time. If the weather holds up.' Frankie surveyed his hard work. 'Mind you, I'm glad it's over.'

'Joe was saying this morning that he fancied going over to the festival for the weekend. Just like old times. What do you think?' Tom said, hoping Frankie would say yes so that he could feel as if he was making an effort to do something with Joe.

'Yeah. Sounds great,' he said. Frankie knew he would have to persuade Kate to give him a pass for a couple of days. She seemed a bit wary of Joe, even though they'd only met a couple of times. When they were lying in bed one night, she said she wouldn't be surprised if Joe was every bit the womaniser his reputation suggested. Despite his better judgement, Frankie had been a bit irked. He knew the kind of man Joe was around women and he felt a pang of jealousy in case Kate was attracted to him. But he knew he didn't dare ask her.

'Will Kate be all right with it?' Tom asked.

'Sure she will. As long as we're not throwing loads of money around, she'll be fine,' Frankie said.

'Right. I'll give you a shout later on, and we'll make some plans. It'll be a bit of fun.'

'Yeah. We'll have a laugh. As long as your Joe doesn't get us into a fight. I'm too old for all that,' Frankie said, smiling.

'Don't worry. He's too old as well. Sometimes I can't get him out of his bed in the morning. I think he's knackered with all the work over there and now that he's relaxed he can hardly be bothered doing much.'

'Well, the break will do him good. Do us all good,' Frankie said, thinking it would be great just to get away and talk about old times. He could see himself and Joe at the festival, the way they used to lark around with the other lads and girls who were out for a wild weekend. The gossip and laughs of the festival would keep them going right through the winter months.

Back at Flahertys' farm, Joe was in the yard, surprised that Tom's car wasn't there. He had walked up from the house to join his brother and Frankie, and talk about going to the festival. But there was nobody around. The door to the kitchen was open and he could smell cooking from inside. He walked over and stood in the doorway, peering in. There was a pot on the cooker and something sizzling under the grill, but he could not see anyone. Then his eyes rested on Kate's backside as she bent over to reach inside a cupboard. He allowed himself to admire it for a moment before coughing to let her know he was there.

She was startled.

'Jesus Christ!' Kate jumped up and swung round, dropping a plate. 'God, Joe! You gave me the fright of my life!' Her face flushed.

'Sorry, Kate. I didn't mean to creep up on you. I just came to look for Tom. He was coming to see Frankie.'

'I haven't seen Tom,' she said. 'Frankie's up cutting silage in the high field. They're all up there. Kids an' all. God, the fright you gave me there.' Kate smiled, but her face was still red. She moved over to the cooker to check the grill. As she bent down, she pulled her blouse over to cover her cleavage.

Joe watched her, amused by her discomfort but struck by how lovely she was. Frankie was a lucky man, he thought. He was glad for him. He deserved a woman like this.

'Well. I'll be on my way, Kate. Sorry to have given you a fright.' He meant it. He could see that Kate was as thoroughly decent a woman as any man could meet and if he felt anything for her, it was respect.

'Do you want a cup of tea, Joe? I'm just making one before Frankie and them all come back,' Kate said.

'If you're making one then that'd be great.'

Kate brought cups to the table outside and told Joe to sit down while she brought out the teapot and a plate of biscuits. Then she sat down and crossed her slender legs.

'So how're you enjoying being back, Joe? How does it feel after all these years? It must be great,' Kate said.

'Aw, it's good to be home, Kate. Just being back in the house and stuff with Tom. And seeing Frankie. You know, Kate, Frankie was probably more of a brother to me than Tom. I was a real arse with Tom when I was young, and I hate myself for it. But Frankie, he's a match for anybody. Great pal. Coming back makes me realise just how much of a pal he was,' Joe said, looking across the fields, his mind in the past.

'So how's America? Do you have a good life there?'

'It's good enough now, but it was a struggle in the beginning. A real struggle. Many's the night I wished I was back home.'

'Why did you stay away so long then?' Kate said.

Joe was quiet for a moment and looked straight into her green eyes. He thought he could see in her expression an invitation for him to talk more. He thought there was curiosity. He wondered what kind of picture Frankie painted of him to her, if she ever asked him questions about the gossip surrounding him. In the brief conversations they had had since they met, he felt that Kate was a bright, clever woman, but also sensitive and obviously deeply in love with Frankie. He wondered if Frankie had ever considered confiding in her.

'I made the break and felt I had to stay away,' Joe said, knowing it was a lie.

They sat saying nothing, until the drone of the tractor coming up the lane broke the silence.

'Here they come,' Kate said, suddenly jumping up.

Joe waved to Frankie in the tractor. 'I was up looking for Tom,' Joe told him as he came across the yard. 'Did he get you?'

'He did,' Frankie said. 'Up in the field.' He looked from Joe to Kate. 'What's all this? The minute my back's turned you're in there chatting up my wife, you sly old bastard.' Frankie was smiling but Joe knew he was annoyed.

'I wouldn't dare. She'd slap me up and down the yard,' Joe said, smiling at Kate.

'What you up to, Joe?' Frankie said. 'Fancy a walk before I get a bite of lunch?'

Joe agreed. He didn't want to say anything about the festival until Frankie had had a chance to talk to Kate about it.

They walked beside the river where they had spent so much of their time as youngsters. Beyond the fork in the riverbank was the spot where the trees grew thicker and closer together until the light disappeared further into Beggar's Wood. Flocks of crows nested high in the sycamores and oak trees, and they both stopped at the edge of the woods, looking up as the eerie cackle of dozens of crows gave the whole place a sinister air.

'I hate these things,' Joe said. 'They give me the creeps. Remember the day we ran off and left Tom in the woods and he was terrified to move because there were hundreds of crows swooping around?' He laughed. 'Christ, he was such a timid wee thing compared to me. I wonder why that was.'

'You were a hard act to follow, I suppose,' Frankie said. He watched Joe as he looked along the road to Beggar's Wood. He knew he was remembering. They stood in silence. Then Joe spoke.

'Frankie,' he said, 'I'm worried that people might start more gossip thanks to that eejit Badger. Honest to God, I felt like knocking him clean out that night in Mulranney's.'

Frankie was glad that he hadn't. He already felt that things were catching up with them; a fight would only have made things worse.

Joe looked pensive. 'Listen. I know I've mentioned this before, but what do you think would happen if the cops found out? I mean, if we went to the police.'

Frankie felt panic rise in him and he snapped at Joe. 'Forget it. It was you who got me into this fucking mess because I covered for you. I mean I'm up to my neck in it and I've had to live with it, and now, after all these years, you want to tear down everything I've built for myself by telling the police.' Frankie struggled to control his anger. 'It's so typical of you, Joe. Only thinking of yourself. Kate would never stay with me if she knew what I'd done. It's unthinkable.'

'I'm sorry, Frankie,' Joe said. 'I know you put yourself on the line for me. I would never do anything to hurt you. Never. It's just that I'm still struggling with it. I seem to be worse now. As I get older I . . . I mean, that poor girl. I feel so responsible.'

Frankie touched his arm. 'I know, Joe,' he said, his voice calmer. 'But you just have to live with it. We both just have to live with it.'

# Chapter Seventeen

Tom was beginning to feel stupid, sitting in the church for so long. He looked at his watch. He had been here for over fifteen minutes and there was no sign of Gabriella. He shook his head. He hadn't even made a proper date with the woman, just a loose arrangement to come back two weeks later on the outside chance that she had some information about Maria. Maybe he had got the day wrong. But he was sure he hadn't. He had been counting the days from the afternoon the woman had given a glimmer of hope that he could get in touch with Maria. His head was all over the place. I must be crazy, he thought. As if I can just go back after twelve years and expect to pick up where I left off. But he couldn't ignore any chance, however slight, of learning more about Maria's situation.

When he'd left the house that morning, Joe was sitting outside staring into the middle distance. He smiled wryly when Tom told him he was going to look at some machinery again. Joe said sarcastically that he hoped she was well-oiled, for there was nothing worse than a bit of dryness to put a man off. Tom told him he had a mind like a sewer and Joe joked that he'd been swimming in the sewers most of his life and it was great fun. He shouted after Tom that he should try it some time. Tom ignored him and drove off.

When he got to the harbour, he decided that he had better not go into the cafe again, after what the old woman had told him the last time. So he went straight to the church and sat waiting and praying. The smell of floor polish mixed with incense and the silence took him back so many years. He could see himself, the young curate, smart and freshly shaved in cold water, coming in for morning Mass. He could hear his famished stomach rumbling from overnight fasting as he murmured his way through the Mass in Latin, his hands deftly mixing the water and wine. Father Tom holding up the chalice as the half dozing altar boy rang the bell.

Tom's eyes closed in fervent prayer, asking God for the strength to guide him through every lonely, miserable day. 'Lamb of God, you take away the sins of the world. Grant us peace.' But for him there was no peace. There never had been since the day he met Maria. He remembered how unhappy he had been then, and the sense of release when he finally had the courage to face up to the fact that he no longer wanted to be a priest. It was the first time in his life that he had made his mother cry and he had been riddled with guilt for a long time afterwards. But his faith in God was still deep. He had nowhere else to turn.

The sound of the church door creaking open made him turn round. His stomach churned. It was Gabriella. She nodded to him as she dipped her finger into the holy water font and blessed herself. One of her shoes squeaked as she made her way down the aisle towards him.

'Hello,' Tom said as she genuflected and sat down behind him. He turned round to face her.

Gabriella took a deep breath. 'I have some information for you. But I not sure if it is all that good. I talk to my friend on the telephone and she find some things out.' She seemed out of breath, as though she was excited or nervous.

'Thank you,' Tom said. 'Thank you so much for trying.'

'OK,' she said. 'I do it for you. And for Maria. OK. This what I find. My old friend Donatella, she lived in Roma near where Maria's family grew up and she was friends with the parents. When they moved back to Roma, Maria was, you know, with the baby. Donatella say that the mama and papa want Maria to give the baby away. You know. Adopt the bambino. But Maria would not do it. It cause many fights in the house. And then when Maria getting bigger and soon the baby being born, she is sent away to relatives. But she no come back.'

'Didn't come back?' Tom frowned. 'What do you mean? Did she run away? Where could a young girl like that go? She was only twenty-one.'

'I don't know,' Gabriella said. 'The relatives she went to stay with said one day they went to find her in the bedroom and she was gone.'

They sat in silence. Tom tried not to think of the panic and hopelessness Maria must have been feeling at the time.

Finally Gabriella spoke. 'Nobody hear from Maria for months, until she wrote to her parents telling them she had a little bambino and she was very happy. She said she was not coming back, but she loved them and wished them well.'

'Where was she?' Tom said, his heart leaping with the thought that she had kept their baby.

'A place north of Roma. I don't know if you know it. Ostia. She was working for a family as a nanny or something. Looking after their children and they give her room and board for her and the bambino. She was with them for many years, but I don't know what happened after that.' Gabriella sat back. She looked exhausted but she was smiling.

Tom looked at her inquiringly. 'How can I find her? Have you any idea?'

'I dunno. It is up to you,' she said. 'Donatella is going to make some questions and find if she is still with the family. Last time she knew she was there was about three years ago. I don't know how much more she will find. If I get the address, why not go and find her for yourself?' The woman's watery grey eyes looked almost youthful for a moment, and Tom realised that she was enjoying the adventure of the whole affair.

Tom smiled and reached over to touch the back of her wrinkled hand. 'You have no idea how much I want to do that,' he said.

'Then you must do it, my boy. You must do it.' Gabriella got up to leave. 'Two more weeks. Meet me here. I'm sure I will have an address.'

'Thank you,' Tom said.

# Chapter Eighteen

Sky loved the stillness of the woods. On a hot afternoon, after he had been doing chores on the farm, it was especially good to come into the coolness of Beggar's Wood. If he looked up he could see the sun shining above the tall trees, but down in the woods it was a different, dark world.

He walked slowly, casting his eyes carefully over the trees and the ground, searching for dead wood that would be good for carving. He had already picked up a few pieces that would be ideal for the little animals he was planning to carve. He was so happy with his new life, living with the Flahertys. It had been hard in the beginning when they all seemed to be speaking to him with raised voices because he couldn't talk. He found people always did that, forgetting that he could hear. But as the weeks had gone by, they found ways of communicating with each other. If Sky wanted to explain something difficult, he would draw it on the little notepad Kate had given him and then he would make signs with his hands to get his point across. It was amazing how well they seemed to understand each other without words. He hoped he would be able to stay with them for ever.

The sound of a branch snapping broke the silence, and Sky turned round quickly, thinking there was someone behind him. But there was no one there. Then a second later he heard the snapping sound again. He looked all around him and up at the trees.

'Jesus Christ!' a voice said. 'The fright you gave me.'

Sky turned and came face to face with Joe McBride. Sky put

his hand to his heart to indicate that he too had been startled. He smiled. But Joe wasn't smiling. He looked edgy and scared.

'What the hell are you doing here creeping about?' Joe said. 'Christ. I nearly had a heart attack.'

Sky felt himself shrink. He found he was a little afraid of Joe. The first time he'd met him at the Flahertys', Joe had looked at him as if he was nobody after Maggie had described how he had come to be at their farm. He hadn't smiled when they were introduced and Sky didn't know whether or not to put out his hand and shake Joe's. Later that evening, Joe had told him to go and get him a can of beer, and Kate had snapped at him, telling him he wasn't a servant. Sky had felt embarrassed, and he could tell that Joe was embarrassed too.

He wondered why Joe was walking in the woods and thought maybe he just wanted to get out of the sun for a while. Sky indicated that he was collecting wood for carving. He showed Joe his knife and demonstrated how he would cut the wood.

'Aye. Very good, Sky,' Joe said, not really sounding interested.

Sky didn't know whether he should try to communicate with Joe. He thought not. There was something about him that made Sky uneasy.

'I'm just out for a walk,' Joe said to him now, seeming more friendly. 'Nice and cool here.'

Sky nodded, then raised a hand to indicate he was leaving.

'Right. OK, Sky. See you,' Joe said.

Sky waved and walked away. When he looked back after a few steps, Joe was still standing at the same spot, staring at the ground.

# Chapter Nineteen

Joe brought his mug of tea outside and sat on the wooden bench beneath the kitchen window. Tom's black and white collie Rex got up from where he had been lying in the sunshine and trotted across to him, wagging his tail. As he settled down beside him, Joe ruffled the dog's head, both of them glad of the other's company in the silence of the farmyard.

'Good old Rex,' Joe said, stroking the dog who had planted a paw on his knee. 'No questions asked. No conditions. That's what's great about guys like you.'

The dog cocked his head to one side then lay down at his feet.

Somewhere in the distance Joe could hear the sound of a tractor and he thought it would be Frankie out in one of his fields, toiling away. He smiled to himself, thinking how rich his friend's life was, with his beautiful wife and delightful children. To be adored like that, Joe thought. To be loved like that. It was really all you needed. He sat back, genuinely glad his friend had found such happiness in his life. You reap what you sow, an old Irish drunk he had once shared a corner of a stinking doss house in New York with told him. You reap what you sow, he had told Joe after he came home one night with blood on his hands and a stash of money he had stolen from his former landlord whom he had left bleeding in an alleyway. Joe had shrugged and replied that it was a jungle out there, and that he would survive no matter what. When Joe woke up the next morning, freezing under the damp blanket, he could see immediately that the old man was dead. His face was blue, and his stiff, gnarled fingers were entwined round rosary beads he clutched at his chest. The icy blasts of the New York winter had finally got to the old man and his dreams of saving enough money for a passage back home to Ireland died with him, along with the shame of failure. Joe didn't move him or touch him. He simply got up, stuffed his things in a bag and walked out into the chilly dawn with the old man's words ringing in his ears. So many years ago, yet the image was still fresh.

Joe sat back on the bench and ran both hands through his hair the way he'd always done since he was a little boy. It was as though with the feel of his hair in his fingers he could somehow press out the answers that were inside his head. As though he could find the reasons that made him mess everything up. You reap what you sow, he thought.

He thought of the Badger Ryan and the disgust in his eyes that night in Mulranney's when he was buying drinks for everyone in the bar. He remembered the first time the Badger had confronted him after that night with Alice McPhee. He could have choked the life out of him because Ryan was ready to label him a rapist in front of the whole village. Joe had convinced himself that he didn't rape Alice. Sure, she wasn't the full shilling. Everyone knew that. But she was still a woman and she knew what she wanted. She had clung to him every time he was anywhere near her and always managed to turn up somewhere when he was alone, either working in the fields or in his farmyard. That afternoon she had turned up when he was eating his lunch by the side of his tractor and had plonked herself down beside him. She talked the usual rubbish, about Marilyn Monroe, how she watched all her films and could even imitate her voice. Joe had laughed as she pouted her red lips. She's off her rocker, the lads all agreed whenever Alice turned up at any function. Then to his amazement Alice opened her blouse and revealed her bra-less, plump, youthful breasts. 'Do you like them?' Alice had asked, smiling and licking her lips, as though she imagined she was some sex kitten in an old film. Joe said nothing and turned away from her in case she saw the instant bulge in his jeans. His head was swimming. 'Go away, Alice. Go home now. And stop that carry-on.' His voice was shaking. He didn't turn round again until he sensed Alice was gone and when he did, he caught sight of her walking across the field, buttoning her blouse. She looked over her shoulder and grinned at him. He couldn't get her out of his mind all day.

Later that night he and Frankie had got drunk in the village and Joe had wanted to tell his friend about the encounter with Alice. Frankie knew all about Alice and the rumours about her allowing the teenage farm boys to touch her for a few coppers. But she would never have been considered any kind of easy ride for either of them, even though they used to laugh sometimes at some of the women they ended up with from what they called the cheaper seats. But Joe didn't tell Frankie about Alice because he knew Frankie would have told him that he should have been much more sharp with her when she exposed herself like that. Frankie would have said he should have threatened to tell her dad, which would have cooled her heels a bit.

The drinks had flowed that night as they played billiards with other lads for pints of beer. When they left the bar they were singing all the way out of the village. They parted at the end of the road and went their separate ways.

Joe was strolling along the tight country lane that led to his farm when he thought he saw a figure peeking out from behind the hedge. As he got closer, the figure came into full view. It was Alice. She was smiling, with the same look on her face that she had had that afternoon.

'What the Jesus? Alice, what the hell are you doing out here at this time of night?' Joe said as he got up close to her.

'Waiting for you,' Alice said, smiling broadly, moving closer to him.

Joe stood frozen for a moment. He should tell her to go home, right now. He should take her by the hand and run her up the road to her house and not speak a single word to her. But Alice shoved her hand between his legs and all rational thoughts were gone. 'Stop it, Alice,' Joe said, but didn't remove her hand.

'I want to,' Alice said, moving her hand up and down. 'Look, Joe. It's hard.'

Had it been broad daylight and himself sober and sensible, Joe might have been able to pull back. But he was drunk and in truth the memory of Alice's breasts that afternoon had plagued him all day. His eyes scanned the immediate area, looking for somewhere to take her. Without thinking, without even considering for a second what he was doing, what the consequences might be, Joe led Alice into the field behind the hedge. She pulled at his trousers and he was on top of her on the soft grass in an instant. He shushed her when she winced with pain as he roughly entered her. He buried his face in her neck and pushed himself harder inside her. It was over in a couple of minutes and Joe was on his feet and pulling up his trousers. He was angry with himself, and also with Alice for making him do this.

'Right. Go home, Alice. You got what you wanted. Now go home. And this is our secret. If you want this again, keep it our secret. Right?' Joe said, turning away as Alice's tear-filled eyes looked up at him from the grass.

Joe walked home briskly, wiping sweat from his face and cursing himself under his breath. Why did he have to do that? He could have any woman he wanted. He felt angry and ashamed. He scurried up the road like a thief, so wrapped up in his thoughts he barely nodded to the Badger Ryan as they passed each other in the lane.

# Chapter Twenty

All the talk in the village was of the gala day that was to be held at the end of July. It was an annual event that attracted every household within ten miles of Westerbank for a full day of festivities. The Westerbank gala fell a few days after the folk festival in Girvan, so there seemed to be a kind of party atmosphere for two weekends running in the area. The gala day was Westerbank's pride and joy, and there was something for everyone. Gardens that had been planned and nurtured for months were ablaze with colour as residents fussed over their plants, hoping to win the best-kept garden competition. Tables would groan under the weight of home-baked cakes and jams, lovingly prepared by women who stood beaming by their produce. Children trained and plotted to win the races, and stood giggling later in the after-noon when their parents, some the worse for drink, made fools of themselves running in the races for mums and dads.

Invariably by the end of the day there would be a punch-up as the long day's drinking gave expression to pent-up little bitter-nesses that locals had harboured all year. But none of that mattered and it was always forgotten by the time the bunting was taken down the following day. And each year, everybody agreed that this gala day outstripped the last.

Marty and Jess were particularly excited. Coming from Glasgow they had never been to such a thing as a gala day. The only event that involved bands that they had ever known was the Orange Walk through the city centre, and Marty said that although it was quite colourful he couldn't understand why people in Scotland marched and waved flags to celebrate an ancient king called William who had beaten up the Irish. But Gunboats always took Marty and Jess anyway, because he had been in the army and said it was important they were loyal to Queen and country. He told them the Orange Walk was a way of demonstrating their loyalty to the Crown. Jess said that the men who beat the big drum actually had blood running down their wrists where the thin leather straps that held the drumsticks to their hands rubbed and broke the skin with the constant exuberant banging. But still they kept on battering the drum.

PJ and Maggie had listened fascinated and deep down wanted to go. But they knew they dare not mention it to Frankie who had once called the marchers Orange bastards.

'Dad says that some people from Westerbank walk in the march. But they never talk about it and you wouldn't know who they are unless you went there,' PJ said as they sat on the grass outside Marty and Jess's caravan.

'People march from all over the country,' Marty said.

'Dad says it's the ones that say they don't bother with the Orange Walk who are the worst, because if you went there you would see them walking with their orange sashes round their necks and their bowler hats. It's just that they don't want anybody in the village to know they're Orangemen. But he said they were Orange bastards just the same. Ooops. I didn't mean to say that swear word.' She blushed and put her hand up to her mouth. The others sniggered and PJ looked at her in disbelief.

'Are there any Orange bastards, I mean Orange bands in the gala day?' Jess asked, and they all burst out laughing.

'No,' PJ said, tittering. 'It's not like that. It's just accordions and some brass bands in the parade with the floats. It's brilliant.'

'Sounds great,' Marty said. 'I can't wait.'

The four of them were eating thick white bread sandwiches of red cheese made up by Miranne for lunch. Gunboats was pottering about under the bonnet of the car with a cigarette dangling between his lips. Maggie eyed him with renewed interest now that she knew he was a robber on the run. He was like someone from the movies. She watched his big muscular arms smudged with oil as he worked away at the engine of the car, cursing when things didn't go right. Part of Maggie relished the adventure that Marty and Jess must be having, not knowing where they would be from one month to the next, always a step ahead of the law like Jesse James. They were living like the gypsies who used to come to the village every other year, selling their wares around the farms, sharpening tools and flogging clothes pegs. Everyone said they would have stolen the eye out of your head, but Maggie was fascinated by their dark skin and rough, carefree ways. Last year when the gypsies were on the campsite for two months, their children had to go to school in the village and Maggie became besotted by a sallow-skinned boy called Pancho who had to fight a different boy in the class nearly every day until they finally stopped bullying him. Maggie went to the campsite with him after school one afternoon and sat spellbound as his old grandmother smoked a pipe and told stories of places she travelled to when she was a little girl. Then one morning when she got up and looked out of her bedroom window down to the campsite, there was no sign of the gypsies. The caravans had gone and there was only debris in the deserted field. Marty and Jess were more or less living like gypsies, and soon they would be gone too, just like Pancho.

'How long do you think you'll be staying here?' Maggie whispered, making sure Gunboats didn't hear her and discover that their secret was out.

'Don't know,' Jess said, shrugging her shoulders. 'Gunboats says maybe we'll leave after the gala day. He's working out where we'll go next. Maybe we'll get the boat to Ireland.'

'Ireland? That'd be great. Nobody would ever find you there,' PJ said, kneeling up. 'We went there once with the school on a trip and it's just miles and miles of empty countryside and wee villages. It's great. Dead quiet. You could hide there for ever.'

'And when it's safe in a while, you could write to us and we'll come and visit you,' Maggie said. She was beginning to feel sad already at the thought she would soon lose her friends. Jess was her best pal now. They shared secrets about Breige and that guy, as well as the big secret that they were on the run and that Gunboats had robbed a shop. That was more than anything she shared with other girls at school. All they did with each other was sit on the steps of the playground with their big books full of glossy pictures of little cherubs floating on clouds or animals and flowers, which they exchanged with each other. You could always tell the girls whose parents had money because they were the ones with the best scrapbook since they could afford to buy more exotic magazines. Maggie thought it was all too stupid and didn't even own a scrapbook; she would rather have played football with the boys any day. Things had been boring around Westerbank until this summer when Sky had arrived and then Marty and Jess. This was the best summer ever, Maggie thought. Yet in her heart she sensed that it was coming to an end. It couldn't last for ever.

'Let's go up and see the stuff Sky's carving to sell at the gala day. They're brilliant. Cows and horses he's made out of wood.' PJ was on his feet and the others followed him.

Outside his caravan Sky was putting the finishing touches to a clutch of wooden figures he had spread out on a small table in front of him. He looked up and beamed a smile towards the four of them, then went back to his work.

'Hi, Sky. Wow! Look at these! They're magic. Look at them, Jess.' Maggie stared wide-eyed at the perfectly carved horses, cows and sheep created by her friend.

'Look at the tail on the horse,' Marty said, running his finger along one of the horses with its rippling muscles and its tail carved into a perfect swish.

'Brilliant!' said Jess.

Sky looked up, his face showing his delight at the approval of his friends. He smiled and carried on, working expertly, his tiny brush varnishing the wooden figures, giving them an instant gleam in the sunshine.

Frankie got out of his tractor and came across the yard, accompanied by Kate. Sky had seemed to want to carve with a knife from the first time they met him, and he had managed to convey to them by signs and drawings that he had learned to carve while working on the farm at Calvin Hospital.

'These are fantastic, Sky,' Kate said. 'Look, Frankie. Look at the perfection in that. You'd think they were alive!'

Frankie watched as Sky worked silently while everyone stood by.

'You've quite a talent,' he said. 'You'll make a small fortune at the gala day. Hey, Sky. Joe, Tom and me are going over to the Girvan festival for a couple of days. Do you want to come? Get you out of here for the weekend. We used to go when we were youngsters and we always had a ball. Now that Joe's back we're going to see what it's like after all these years.'

Sky stopped varnishing for a second and sat back with the brush in his hand. He looked at Frankie, then at Kate who was smiling. Eventually he nodded his head and smiled broadly to Frankie. He looked at Maggie and she winked at him. She was thrilled that he was like part of their family now.

# Chapter Twenty-one

Sky hauled the sack of flour from the storage room into the bakery and carefully sliced it across the top before scooping it into the container. He knew Baldy Cassidy was watching him from the corner of his eye, and he wanted to do a good job. He was enjoying the tasks that Baldy had given him since Frankie had agreed to spare him for a few hours a week to help in the bakery. But it had really all been down to Kate. She had noticed that he was keen to help when he saw her baking in the kitchen and he had indicated to her that he had always been interested back in the hospital where he would watch the farmer's wife cook. Kate was impressed by the way he worked and asked Baldy if he would consider taking him on.

Sky was delighted because Baldy had said he would teach him the basics of being a baker if he wanted to learn. Sky did the donkey work for Baldy, but he didn't mind, because when Baldy was making cakes or pastries, he could watch and learn. Before long, Sky was helping with the mixtures and rolling out pastry for the sausage rolls. Baldy was a good boss and he even taught him how to make gingerbread, asking him if he knew the story about the gingerbread man. Baldy had been surprised one afternoon when he found that Sky had made a whole tray of gingerbread men and decorated them with sweets and icing. He gave Sky a friendly slap on the back and said he would make a baker out of him yet.

Although he liked the work, Sky was wary of the customers, especially kids or teenagers who sometimes laughed at him and called him the dummy. It brought back the sick feeling he had had in the children's home when the other kids taunted him. Sometimes when Baldy sent him to deliver a message in the village, kids would shout and throw stones at him. It was almost always led by Dennis Jarvie, the boy Kate had kicked in the shins that day in the bakery.

'Sky,' Baldy said, patting his apron to get the flour off his hands. He went to the till and brought out a two shilling coin. 'Would you go down to Mrs Martin at the bottom of the road and get me two jars of her raspberry jam. I need it for the cakes. She'll know who you are. I'll give you a note.' Baldy scribbled something on a piece of paper and gave it to Sky, showing him where the house was.

Sky picked up the jam from Mrs Martin who gave him a friendly smile. He put the jars in his bag and slung it over his shoulder. She waved at him, shouting her goodbyes louder than she needed to as he walked down the path and out of her gate.

On the way back, just outside Mulranney's, Dennis Jarvie and his pals were standing around, kicking a football to each other. As Sky approached, someone kicked the ball past one of the boys and it hit Sky in the face. He hadn't seen it coming and he looked around, startled.

'Oh look,' Dennis said. 'You biffed the dummy with the ball.' They all laughed.

Sky walked on slowly. He saw Joe McBride standing outside Mulranney's, watching. But Joe never acknowledged him. Sky continued up the road and through the crowd of six or seven boys.

'What've you got in the bag, dummy?' Dennis said to him, kicking the bag.

Sky heard the glass jars knock against each other. He stopped and looked inside the bag to make sure they weren't broken. He didn't see one of the boys go behind him and crouch down on all fours. Then Dennis came up close to Sky.

'Anything interesting in the bag?' He gave Sky a wicked smile and then pushed him sharply. Sky toppled backwards over the boy who was crouched behind him. Sky didn't know what hit him but he felt a searing pain in his head. He put his hand up and felt blood just above his eyebrow. He looked around, dazed, and realised he must have hit his head on the kerb. He could hear all the boys laughing, but when they noticed the blood they all ran off. Sky got to his feet and picked up his bag. The jars were smashed, and the jam was all over the bag. He felt tears come to his eyes. He looked around. Joe McBride was still standing at Mulranney's, staring at him. Then the door of the bakery opened and Baldy came rushing over.

'Jesus, Sky,' he said, dusting him down. 'Look at your head. It was that wee bastard Jarvie. I saw them all larking about but I couldn't get out in time.'

Sky bit his lip, fighting back tears. He opened the bag and Baldy could see that the jars were smashed.

'Don't worry about that, Sky. Plenty more where that came from. Come on inside. We'll get you cleaned up.'

When Sky went back to the Flahertys' in the afternoon, Kate met him in the farmyard.

'What happened, Sky?' she said. 'You're hurt.'

He shook his head as though it was nothing serious.

Maggie and PJ joined him at the kitchen table for a glass of orange squash and Maggie looked closely at Sky's cut.

'What happened, Sky?' she asked. 'Did somebody push you?'

He smiled shyly and nodded his head.

'Was it that Dennis?' PJ said.

Sky nodded.

'He's getting it,' Maggie said. PJ nodded, his lips tight with anger.

Sky waved his hand as though it was not important and smiled at Kate.

'Did nobody step in and stop them?' Kate said.

Sky thought about Joe McBride, but looked away from Kate.

'Anyway, don't worry about it,' Kate said, changing the subject. 'How are you enjoying the job at the bakery?'

His eyes lit up and he opened his bag, producing four ginger-bread men. He pointed to himself and signed that he had baked them himself.

'Wow,' Kate said. 'They look brilliant.' She caught Maggie's hand as she reached out to take one. 'Not till after dinner.'

Sky wondered why Joe McBride didn't like him. He thought it was strange that a great guy like Tom who just wanted to help people all the time could have a brother like Joe. Joe seemed the sort of person he had come across before who always picked a fight with him or wanted to hurt him in some way. He couldn't understand it but guessed it was because they felt frustrated and irritated that he couldn't communicate like others. Sky tried not to think about Joe. He was just glad to be home.

# Chapter Twenty-two

In their bedroom, Kate folded Frankie's clean, neatly ironed shirts carefully and placed them in the small holdall she was packing for him to take to the festival. She packed methodically, fresh underwear and socks for each day, as well as a casual shirt for the daytime and a more dressy number for the evening. There was his red crew-neck sweater, rolled and placed into the bag, and she pictured Frankie wearing it against the chilly sea breeze at night as he staggered back to the bed and breakfast with Tom, Joe and Sky. She knew that Frankie would have no idea what was in the bag until he opened it, and that it wouldn't matter to him because if she had packed it, everything he needed would be there. She smiled to herself, thinking how excited he had been over the last couple of days at the prospect of going off with his old pals.

Frankie came into the bedroom with a towel wrapped round his waist, running his fingers through his shock of wet blond hair. Kate felt a surge of desire as her eyes flicked over his body, still as muscular and firm as it was when she first saw it fourteen years ago.

'There you are,' Kate said, zipping up the bag. 'All you have to do now is decide what shirt to wear and when.' She lifted the bag from the bed and turned to close the chest of drawers. Frankie put his arms round her. His body felt hot from the bath and she could smell the clean scent of his hair. He pushed himself against her and fondled her breasts.

'Steady on, boy,' Kate said, feeling immediately aroused. 'You've no time for that. You've to pick up the lads in half an hour.'

'It won't take long. Count to thirty and it'll all be over.' She wriggled out of his grasp and he laughed.

'How do you think Sky will be at this little outing with you three?' Kate asked. She wished she was going with them, but she knew it was a boys' weekend. She had grown protective of Sky and enjoyed his company. She had given him a couple of shirts belonging to Frankie and he had packed them into an old canvas bag long since discarded by PJ.

'I don't know. I mean he doesn't drink, or hasn't so far, so I don't know what he'll think when we're getting wired into the beer,' Frankie said, buttoning his shirt. 'Not to worry. At least someone will be able to find their way back to the digs.'

'What did Joe say when you told him Sky was coming?' Kate asked. She thought Joe had little regard for Sky.

'He was fine. He didn't say much about it because he knows Tom and me like him a lot. He joked that we should try and get Sky laid, but Tom shot him down in flames.' Frankie laughed.

'You should leave him to his own devices. Just take him as he is. It's not anybody's business to get him a woman,' Kate said.

'I know, sweetheart. It was only a joke.' Frankie lifted his bag and Kate followed him downstairs. 'Anyway, Joe'll be too busy getting himself a woman to be bothered with anybody else.'

'It's not going to be that kind of weekend, surely,' Kate said, picturing them standing chatting up women at the bar, the way Frankie had been when she first set eyes on him.

'Don't be daft. Of course it isn't. By the time we've finished at the end of the night, none of us would be capable anyway. And why would I need a woman when I've got you?' Frankie put his arms round Kate at the bottom of the stairs and kissed her lips. 'Right. I'm for the off. I'll see you on Sunday night. I'll phone you.'

'Watch yourself,' Kate said. 'Don't be doing anything stupid. You're not nineteen now, you know.'

Frankie shook his head and went into the farmyard. He was met by Maggie who threw her arms round him. PJ stood at his side, looking awkward.

'Mind and bring me something back,' Maggie said and kissed him on the cheek.

'Don't worry, I will. And remember, PJ, make sure nothing goes wrong. You know everything that's to be done, don't you, pal?' Frankie turned to PJ and ruffled his hair.

'Don't worry, Da. I can run the show, no bother.' PJ squared his shoulders and stretched himself to his full height. He couldn't wait until he was old enough to be going off for weekends with his mates. He could only imagine the kind of fun he would have.

'In you get, Sky,' Frankie said. Sky stood, hesitantly, looking fresh and clean in one of Frankie's shirts. He smiled and got into the back seat of the car.

They drove out of the farmyard and down the lane to McBride's farm. Frankie's face broke into a smile when he saw Joe and Tom standing waiting for him with their bags by their feet. It was just like old times, he thought. He remembered picking up his best friends like this so often as they headed for unpredictable, fun weekends with not a care for the consequences.

# Chapter Twenty-three

'So how are you going to do it, Breige?' Eamon was lying back on the bed with an ashtray balanced on his bare chest. He took a long, hungry draw of his cigarette until the end of it glowed in the half darkness of the dingy hotel room. He watched as Breige pulled on her nylon stockings and hitched them to the suspenders. She looked at him.

'What d'ya mean? The money?' Breige shoved her feet into the high-heeled slingback shoes that Baldy had bought her for her birthday.

'Of course I mean the money, darlin'. How're you going to actually do it? You know. Steal it,' Eamon said, slightly irritated by how casual Breige was about the entire operation. He had built his hopes around Breige being able to pull this off. She was his meal ticket to America and everything in his life had revolved round the prospect for so long that he couldn't bear the thought of it all falling through. He had come from Dublin three months before, after Breige wrote to him and told him she had found the perfect prey for the plot they had hatched together. Now he was on the last lap.

'You leave that to me,' Breige said. 'I told you he never goes into that box very often. He keeps his weekly takings from the bakery in another place in the house, so the money beneath the bed is just for a rainy day. He's going off for a few days' golf, and once he's gone, I'll get the lot and be off my mark before he's back home. Then it's all plain sailing for us to the US of A.' Breige sat on the bed. She took the cigarette from his hand and took a drag. She blew smoke rings and watched them rise above her head.

'I'd better get some chewing gum,' she said. 'Brendan doesn't think I smoke. He says I'm his beautiful Irish princess.' She posed, pouting her lips, then lay back against Eamon and smiled. 'He thinks the sun shines out of my arse actually.' She sniggered.

'Brendan, is it?' Eamon said. 'What happened to Baldy? I hope you're not getting attached to that old fucker.'

'Oh yeah. I'm attached all right. Sure am I not married to him? That means what's his is mine and what's mine's my own.' Breige laughed.

Eamon smiled and ran the back of his hand down her arm. She was so lovely, and innocent-looking, her big blue eyes smiling back at him.

It was her eyes that had first attracted him when he spotted her waiting tables in the members' bar at the horse racing in Naas. He had watched as the rich punters with their well-fed faces, flushed with drink, leered at the pretty young girl bursting out of her black lace blouse. Eamon had been particularly bitter that rain-soaked Saturday afternoon, having spent the day chasing his money without backing a single winner. The last race had completely cleaned him out and he had barely the bus fare back home. He watched as the young girl chatted up the punters with an easy charm and stuffed the notes they gave her as tips into the pocket of her skirt. When she passed him with several glasses of champagne fizzing on a tray, he expertly lifted one off, grinned at her and said, 'Don't forget the poor.'

Breige had told him he had a cheek on him, but he could tell as soon as they made eye contact that she liked him. Hours later they were throwing each other around the bed in his digs with so much gusto and noise that the people in the room next door knocked on the wall. She was a live wire all right, this Breige. And clever too. She laughed as she showed him the wads from a wallet she had pinched from one of the punters who had pulled her onto his knee and tried to kiss her.

For the next six months they became like a drug to each other. They lived on their wits. Eamon gambled at the racetrack or played poker, and came home late at night, his pockets bulging with cash, or in a foul drunken temper because he had lost. Breige found a perfect scam, cleaning and catering in some of the better houses in Dublin, where she stole anything valuable she could get her hands on. Nine times out of ten, the man of the house was also sampling her delights and so never uttered a word against her when anything went missing.

Now and again, if Breige gave Eamon too much lip, she got a dry slap and she would fly at him, fists and legs kicking. It always ended with the two of them scrapping on the floor, then tearing each other's clothes off in violent, frenzied sex. In their more tranquil moments, they talked of their American dream, to go across the sea and make their fortune. Breige said they could make a great life over there, not like this, stealing and fleecing, but in honest decent jobs. They could have their own house with a garden and a mailbox, just like on all those American TV shows where the wife was always baking something and the husband came in from work, calling, 'Honey, I'm home.' Sometimes Eamon said the same to Breige when he came in from whatever den he had been in and they used to laugh about it.

It was Breige's idea to find a rich husband after she had read the personal ads in a Catholic monthly magazine in one of the houses she worked in. There were a lot of ads from lonely Irish farmers desperate for a wife, or from widowers who couldn't face the future with an empty bed. But the one that caught Breige's eye was from a recently widowed Scottish businessman – Brendan Cassidy. He didn't need to be stinking rich, Eamon had said, as long as there was enough to get them out of here. His advert said he was looking for someone who liked music, dancing and good food, with a view to a relationship. Breige joked with Eamon that she was up for the first three options and would deal with the relationship aspect once she found out the size of Cassidy's bank balance.

When she hugged and kissed Eamon goodbye the day she left for the boat from Belfast to Stranraer, there were tears in her eyes. For all his temper and philanderings, she loved him to death. Her plan was to go to Scotland and get a job in a bar before replying to the advert. If Cassidy proved to be easy pickings then they would be home and dry. Eamon had said they might even be in America for Thanksgiving, whatever that was.

Now Eamon got out of bed and walked across the room to see Breige off. At the door, she stood looking around at the cramped hotel room with the damp stains on the wall and the cobwebs gathering in the window corners beneath the grimy net curtain.

'This place stinks,' she said, a look of disgust on her face. 'I don't know how you can stay here.'

'It won't be for too long now, my darlin',' Eamon said, and they both looked at the pile of notes on the table by the bed.

This was the most cash Breige had taken from the tin below Baldy's bed. She hadn't counted it when she removed it while Baldy was at the pub, but when Eamon did, it seemed there was more than two thousand pounds. Breige had told him there was at least twice that amount still left. But she wouldn't remove it until Baldy left to play golf and she was ready to meet Eamon at the airport.

# Chapter Twenty-four

Maggie and Jess were the lookouts. From the tree-house window they could see across the field where Dennis Jarvie and Micksey Larkin would appear shortly. They looked at each other, their faces grim and intense. Earlier, Marty had drilled them like soldiers. He had paced up and down beneath the tree house as PJ, Jess and Maggie sat listening to his plan. This was the day Dennis Jarvie was going to get it for the way he had humiliated Sky. When PJ had told him about the incident outside the bakery, Marty was raging and said there was only one way to deal with it. Gunboats had told him there was always bullying in the army, but you had to stand up to people. You could always get them back if you bided your time. But, Marty said, it would only work if everybody did their job and followed his orders.

Marty had brought along a length of rope and a heavy rope net. He described precisely how he and PJ would attach it to two trees across the path where Dennis and Micksey were headed to Beggar's Wood to drink cheap wine. PJ couldn't quite understand how the next part of the plan would work, but Marty had assured him it would. He said it was a trap that Gunboats had learned during guerrilla warfare training. The object was to trip the enemy up, then immediately descend on them, tangle them up in the net, tie their ankles, and string them upside down from the tree. PJ told him it would never work, but Marty insisted he and his dad had once trapped a deer in the same way when they were on a camping trip up north. Marty then produced two black wool balaclavas with holes cut out for eyes and the mouth. Gunboats had kept them from his army days. These were for him and PJ, so Dennis and Micksey wouldn't recognise their attackers. PJ wondered if Gunboats had been wearing one when he robbed the shop.

Now PJ and Marty lay in wait behind a thicket.

'As soon as they fall,' Marty whispered across to PJ, 'we get right on top of them. Grab one side of the net and I'll get the other, then pull the rope tight. I'll tie their ankles, then both of us pull hard.' He looked up to where the rope was lashed to a high branch.

PJ felt his mouth go dry. He knew he could fight if he had to, and he could beat Micksey no bother, but Dennis Jarvie was fourteen and big for his age. Still, it would be great to see Dennis and Micksey dangling by the ankles. He pulled his mask over his head and waited in silence for the sign from Maggie and Jess.

The boys had taught them how to blow hard into a folded leaf to produce a high-pitched trumpet noise. They had been blue in the face before they finally got it right.

'Look,' Maggie said, peering across the field. 'Here they come.'

'Are you sure?' Jess said.

'Definitely,' Maggie said. 'That's Jarvie. And I'm sure that's Micksey with him.'

They waited until they were a little closer, then brought the leaves to their lips and blew hard. The sound carried all the way down the lane and to the start of Beggar's Wood.

'That's it,' PJ said. 'That's the signal.'

They heard it again.

Marty nodded. 'Ready?'

'Ready,' PJ said. He could barely see Marty, he was camouflaged so well in the trees. They sat perfectly still. In the distance they could hear voices laughing and joking. This was it. PJ took a deep breath. He could see Dennis Jarvie coming up the path with Micksey Larkin at his side. Dennis was carrying a bottle of cheap wine. PJ was barely breathing as he waited for the tug of the rope from Marty that was the sign for action on the count of three.

Dennis and Micksey were just a few steps away when PJ felt the pull of the rope. One, two, three, and down they went. PJ was out of his hideout as quickly as Marty and they pounced on the bewildered Dennis and Micksey.

'What the fuck?' Dennis was stunned.

'Christ, Dennis!' Micksey shouted. 'We're getting attacked! Oh fuck, Dennis, we're getting murdered!'

Marty quickly wound rope round each boy's legs in turn and then yelled, 'Pull!'

PJ was so excited, he punched Dennis in the face for good measure.

'Pull!' Marty shouted again.

PJ yanked the rope and Marty pulled as hard as he could. Dennis screamed as his body began to move off the ground. The net containing the two boys was really heavy and they had to pull with all their might.

'Let me go, ya bastards!' Dennis yelled in mid-air. 'Don't kill me! My da's got money! He'll pay you money!'

Micksey was crying. 'Mammy, Daddy!' he snivelled. 'I want my mammy!'

PJ suppressed the urge to laugh. When they had tied the rope to the tree, the two of them took a step back and watched Dennis and Micksey twist and writhe in the net. PJ couldn't remember ever being this excited in his life. Then they belted across the field.

'Jesus, Marty,' PJ panted. He thought his heart was going to burst with exhilaration. 'That was brilliant! I mean, Jesus! They didn't even have a clue!'

Marty stopped, and bent over with his hands on his thighs, trying to catch his breath. He pulled his mask back and PJ could see his face was crimson under his freckles.

'That'll teach them,' Marty said.

'What now? We can't leave them there all night.'

'No,' Marty said. 'Just as it's getting dark, we'll slip back and cut them down. By that time they should have shat their pants.'

PJ slapped his back and they both laughed as they ran back to the tree house where Maggie and Jess were jumping with excitement at their part in the successful operation.

Two hours later, after the sun had sunk behind the hills, PJ and Marty sneaked back across the field with their masks pulled over their faces. PJ was surprised to see that Marty had a pot of yellow paint and a brush. 'What's that for?' PJ said, though he had a fair idea.

'Well,' Marty said, 'they're yella. So now everybody's going to know they're yella. Let's see how they explain that to their ma and da.'

PJ sniggered. By this time the light was beginning to fade and Beggar's Wood looked dark and daunting. They crept in quietly, both of them glad they didn't have far to go. As they got closer, they could hear Micksey crying.

'What if all the blood starts to come out of our eyes and ears?' he said, his voice shaking.

'Oh, shut up,' Dennis said. 'Just keep pulling on the rope so you can lift yourself up a bit.'

'Do you know who it was, Dennis?'

'I think it was that wee Fenian bastard Flaherty,' Dennis spat. 'And that Glasgow bastard. Marty or something. Sssh. I hear somebody.'

Marty crept up first, paint pot at the ready. He gave the nod to PJ who began to release the rope suspending the nets. It was stuck. Marty put down the paint and went over to help, and slowly the bodies began to come down. A few feet before they reached the ground, they let the rope go and the boys came crashing down, groaning as they hit the ground. Marty went and stood over them. He poured yellow paint over Dennis's hair, then turned to Micksey and did the same to him.

'That's how we sort people out in Glasgow,' he said. 'You do one more thing to Sky and I'll slash your face.' He kicked Dennis in the ribs, making him gasp.

PJ and Marty watched as Dennis and Micksey untied the ropes

from their ankles, then scrambled to their feet and ran as fast as they could.

'Did you think there was a funny smell?' Marty said, giggling.

# Chapter Twenty-five

They left Sky at the horse auction where he seemed perfectly at ease among the travellers who had been rolling up with their horse boxes since before midday. Frankie, Joe and Tom had been to these auctions a hundred times over and after the initial stroll around, shaking hands and slapping the backs of old travellers they had not seen for years, they began to get bored. But Sky was happy to be surrounded by animals. He looked delighted to be in the thick of it, watching horses being traded between men who seemed to have a language all of their own and who agreed deals with a spit and handshake. One or two of the travellers were already throwing pints back at the makeshift bar on the green and their voices and curses grew louder with the draining of each glass.

'If there's not a punch-up before the afternoon's out, I'll be very surprised,' Tom said, as a couple of bruisers rolled up the sleeves of their shirts to expose arms like sides of beef and began arm-wrestling, egged on by half a dozen others.

'Yep. And I wouldn't like to be caught in the crossfire,' Frankie said.

'God, Frankie. Remember how we used to take these lads on when we were youngsters? Mind the fun it was?' Joe stood with his arms folded, watching the arm-wrestlers.

'Yeah, I remember, Joe. And I distinctly remember getting my nose busted by some eejit after you complained his brother cheated you when he beat you at arm-wrestling,' Frankie said.

'So he did cheat,' Joe said. 'He had an unfair advantage. Sure that black-eyed beauty of a sister of his was standing right in my line of vision and I couldn't concentrate.' He smiled as he recalled the moment. 'Still, I managed to sneck his sister before the day was out. So I guess I won after all.'

'Yeah. It was me who lost out, left with the bloody nose after trying to defend you, as per usual,' Frankie said. 'And the bird I ended up with had a face like a llama's arse. The things I've done for you, McBride. The bastardin' sacrifices.' Frankie laughed, but Joe looked serious for a second.

'I know, Frankie. I know.' He put his arm round Frankie's shoulder and they walked off, with Tom behind them.

Tom looked at the pair of them and shook his head. They're just the same as they ever were, he thought, feeling a little left out. You'd think they were nineteen again. No matter how close he and Frankie had become since Joe left home, it was not like this. There was something more between Frankie and Joe, always had been, and no matter how hard Tom tried to be part of the trio, he was always on the outside. Since Joe had come home it was Frankie he went for a walk with in the evenings, not him. But in truth he was glad, because he was so preoccupied with Maria he didn't think he'd be good company anyway.

'I'm choking for a pint,' Frankie said as they headed across the road to the Crown Bar.

'Me too,' said Joe. 'Let's get the first one down nice and slow, then we can get fired into the drink for the rest of the day.'

'Careful now, you two,' Tom said. 'You wouldn't want to peak too early.'

'Aw, would you listen to Father McBride,' Joe said, playfully slapping Tom on the back of the head. 'Just take the poker out of your arse and relax, for Christ's sake.'

'I am relaxed.' Tom grabbed his brother's arm. 'I'm the coolest guy here. And I bet I'm still standing while you're face down by ten o'clock tonight.'

'Well, if you are,' Joe retorted, 'get yourself a ride before the day's out. You'll be able to see things a bit more clearly then.'

Frankie and Tom looked at each other and laughed.

'Is that all you ever think about?' Frankie asked.

'It sure is. I haven't had my leg over for six months,' Joe said. 'I honestly don't know how people can go for years. I'll probably blow the semmit off the next woman who's lucky enough to shag me.'

'I thought you had plenty of women in New York,' Tom said. 'I thought it was wall-to-wall sex. Is that not what you said in one of your rare letters?'

Joe stopped outside the door of the pub and moved to the side as a young couple came squeezing through the door together, kissing as they walked. 'I did, but ever since I split with the last woman I was involved with, I've not had the same luck. Maybe I've lost my touch.'

The sound of fiddles playing spilled out into the street through the pub door.

'This is the stuff,' Tom said. 'Forget the women for the day and just enjoy this.'

They walked into the packed bar and stood for a moment in the crowd, watching the fiddlers, enjoying the skill and expertise of musicians who had never practised with each other yet were able to play as if they'd been together for years. Now and then a fiddler would leave or enter the session and not a note would be missed. Around the room, feet tapped and fingers strummed to the reels.

'Let's go into the lounge,' Frankie said. 'You can't get a blether in here.' He went to the bar and ordered three pints of Guinness, watching as the barmaid slowly poured the black liquid, waited for it to settle then topped it up with a mouth-watering creamy head. He handed over a ten shilling note.

By the third pint, the three of them were relaxed and slightly giddy. Now and then there would be raucous laughter as Joe or Frankie recalled some lark they'd got up to. Steaming bowls of soup and bread were ordered and they were glad of some solid food to soak up the drink. They had a table booked in a restaurant later in the evening, so they had promised themselves they wouldn't get wrecked in the afternoon. But the stout was slipping over slowly and the waitress arrived with another tray of pints.

'You're lookin' well,' Joe said, reaching out and holding the woman's hand as she set the drinks down. 'Does your man know you're out and all these men about?' He had already noticed she wasn't wearing a wedding ring but this was his chat-up line.

'I've no man,' the waitress said, smiling at Joe. 'He fucked off with the babysitter.'

Frankie and Tom glanced at each other. Joe never took his eyes off the woman.

'Well, that's a conversation stopper,' he said, still holding her hand.

'You did ask.' The waitress looked him in the eye. Tom thought she was about thirty-five and her expression said she had seen and heard it all before. She was pretty, in a slightly hard way, with dyed black hair cropped in the style that lots of women copied from Mia Farrow in the TV show *Peyton Place*. She pulled her hand away but it was clear that she was interested in Joe.

'C'mon, have a drink with us, pet,' Joe said.

'Can you not see I'm a wee bit busy?' The woman looked around the lounge where every table and booth was filled.

'What about later on?' Joe persisted. 'It would be nice to talk to you. I'm just over from America, visiting my brother here and my mate.' Joe flashed his most charming smile. 'This offer is for a limited period only.'

The woman smiled back, and Frankie looked at Tom. They had both seen this all before. She was being hooked in.

'Maybe later,' she said, a flush rising in her neck. She turned to walk away.

'Look forward to it,' Joe said to her back.

'You've been using the same line of patter for twenty years,' Frankie said. 'Do they actually fall for that shite in New York?'

'Not only in New York,' Joe said, sitting back triumphantly. 'As you can see.'

'Well, don't be bringing her back to the room, that's all I'm saying.' Tom smiled. 'I can really do without lying in bed listening to you grunting and panting. It was bad enough when you were fifteen and throwing one off your wrist every bloody night.' He blushed slightly when he said it, conscious that the alcohol was loosening his tongue, making him coarser than he would normally be.

Frankie burst out laughing and Joe held up his hands apologetically.

'I was just a healthy young boy,' he said. 'At least I graduated into doing it for real. Unlike yourself.'

Frankie caught Joe's eye and gave him a sharp look. Tom looked a little hurt. His face was red.

'You know nothing about me,' he said. 'Nothing at all.'

'Well, I know you were in that bloody priest college when the rest of us lads were shagging everything that moved,' Joe said.

Tom was silent. He took a long swig of his drink and wiped the froth from his mouth with the back of his hand.

'You haven't a clue, Joe.' Tom was bursting to tell the pair of them just what had happened to him while they were shagging their way around the countryside. He had been having a love affair. Not the kind of sordid encounters against a wall or in some field that was the mark of their weekends, but a real, deep and meaningful love affair with a girl who meant so much to him that he was weeping on his pillow like an eejit every night.

'I think we should close this subject,' Frankie said, putting his arm out between the brothers. 'It's got fuck all to do with you, Joe, whether Tom has had one or two hundred women. Get off his back, for Christ's sake. Come on now. Everything was going fine until women got involved. Forget the bloody women.'

Joe drained his glass and couldn't resist a pop at his old mate.

'Forget women? Yeah. Sure, Frankie. Like you never give that beautiful wife of yours a second thought. By Christ, if she was my wife, I'd be chasing her up the stairs day and night.'

'That's fuckin' enough, Joe.' Frankie grabbed him by the shirt.

'I'll have none of that. Not about my wife. Just fuckin' leave her out of it.' His eyes were blazing.

'Right, come on.' Tom reached between them and pulled Frankie's hand away. 'Just cool it, boys. We go too far back for shite like this.'

'Sorry, pal,' Joe said, grabbing Frankie's wrist. 'No offence meant. I'm sorry, truly I am. I think far too much of you to talk like that. It's just the beer.'

They sat for a moment in silence and the sound of a singer drifted in from the bar.

By the time they had visited two more bars, they decided they had had enough drink for the afternoon and sat for a while on a wall in the village square, watching the various buskers and dancers. The little town was teeming with people who made their way there every year for the three-day festival. A crowd was gathered around a skinny man in his thirties who was swallowing blazing sticks of fire. Two teenagers nearby were juggling with knives and the crowd watched enthralled. The boys always managed to catch the knives by the handles as they tumbled through the air in a blur. From the other side of the square, Tom spotted Sky walking towards them, his arms full of trinkets.

Tom stood on the wall a little unsteadily. 'Here's Sky coming. He looks as if he's cleaned them out at the fair.'

Sky was smiling broadly as he approached them. He was wearing a cowboy hat and carrying two soft toys, a goldfish in a plastic bag and two coconuts.

'Look at you, Sky. You must have been winning everything. I bet the gadgies hated you,' Frankie said. Sky held up the goldfish. 'Maggie will just love that,' he said and Sky nodded enthusiastically.

Joe looked coolly at Sky and got off the wall.

'I think I'll go back to the room for a sleep before we go out tonight,' he said.

'Good idea, Joe,' Frankie said. 'Come on, we'll go back for a kip then get changed for round two.'

145

Tom and Sky followed behind them as they walked towards the seafront to the guest house.

As they turned the corner they heard a commotion. A woman was screaming for a man to let her go, but he had her by the hair and was shouting into her face.

'You're nothing but a slut,' he spat, his face flushed with anger. 'I knew the minute my back was turned you'd be shaggin' about with him.'

'I wasn't,' the skinny woman protested. 'I was only having a carry-on. It was just kidding.'

'I'll give you kidding, ya wee whore!' The man pulled the woman's hair tighter and she shrieked with pain.

'Hey! Hey!' Joe shouted. 'That's enough, for Christ's sake!' He strode towards them, the others following behind. Frankie was telling Joe to cool it, but he wouldn't listen.

'Leave her alone!' Joe said as he approached. 'Ya cowardly bastard!' But the man pulled the woman's hair even harder. She sobbed.

Now all four of them stood close to the man who showed no signs of letting the woman go. Tom and Frankie looked at each other. Sky never took his eyes off the man.

Then suddenly Joe made a grab for the man, but he was too fast and jerked back, pulling the screaming woman with him. Joe lunged forward again, and the man quickly shoved the woman to the ground and, out of nowhere, it seemed, produced a flick knife which he jabbed at Joe, catching the back of his arm and drawing blood. Joe looked dazed, and the man jumped forward, knife raised.

'Keep your fuckin' nose out!' he shouted, his eyes burning with rage. He was about to plunge the knife into Joe when someone gripped hold of his arm from behind. It was Sky. Everyone was stunned, especially the man. He stood with the knife still in his hand but unable to move. Sky's knuckles were white as he held his arm in a vice-like grip. Joe looked at Sky, whose pale blue eyes looked straight back at him.

The man dropped the knife and Joe picked it up. Sky let his arm go. He looked at everyone, then turned and walked away.

'Did you see that? Jesus!' Joe said to Frankie and Tom's shocked expressions. He walked after Sky. 'Hey, Sky,' he called.

Sky stopped and turned round, his face pale. The two of them stood looking at each other. Joe reached out and touched Sky's shoulder, squeezing it firmly.

'Thanks, Sky,' he said. 'That could have been nasty. Thanks.'

Sky's face half smiled. He nodded and patted Joe's hand.

Frankie and Tom caught up with them.

'Well,' Frankie said, excited. 'I never had you down for a scrapper, Sky. Jesus. You're a revelation every day.' He slapped Sky on the back and all four of them headed up the road.

Within a few steps, Frankie and Joe were walking together, just ahead of the others.

'What's that guy all about, Frankie? I don't know what to make of him,' Joe said.

'He's just a kind of drifter, I think,' Frankie said. 'But he's a very hard worker. Useful around the place. Maggie and PJ think the world of him.'

'He always seemed a bit dim to me, but I'll tell you this, my guts would have been spilled on the street there if it hadn't been for him.'

Frankie agreed and told him Sky was not dim at all. 'He's actually quite clever and talented. It's just that he isn't able to speak.'

'Yeah?' Joe rubbed the blood from his arm with a handkerchief. 'Well, he saved my bacon there anyway. I'm feeling a bit ashamed at the way I've treated him. I saw him the other day when these wee bastards knocked him down outside Baldy's. And I didn't lift a finger to help him. There's something about him, his vulnerability, his eagerness to please, I don't know, it reminds me of Alice McPhee and I can't deal with it.'

Frankie didn't answer. They walked on in silence and stopped just before they got to the guest house. Joe stared into the middle distance and Frankie thought he looked empty and sad.

'What is it, Joe?' he said.

Joe stared on in silence. Eventually he spoke.

'You know, Frankie,' he said, 'I've never had a day's peace after what I did. I just wish I could somehow put things right.'

Frankie glanced over his shoulder. Tom and Sky were approaching. 'This is not the time to talk about it, Joe. The other two will be here in a minute.' He touched Joe's shoulder. 'We'll talk about it later, pal. Later tonight. I feel as if we haven't really talked about anything since you came back. It's all been everyday stuff. I want to hear about your life over there. All of it, Joe. I feel as if you've been holding back.'

Joe nodded. 'Yeah. You're right, pal. There's a lot to tell. For a long time I was so miserable over there, especially at the start. So fucking miserable. And I couldn't come home. It was years before I had any kind of decent life.' He rubbed tears from his eyes.

'Come on,' Frankie said. 'Get a grip. The boys are coming. It's the drink, Joe. You'll be fine when you get a sleep, then we'll have a few more beers. Let's go in now.'

Joe shook his head. 'I'm going to stay here and get some more air.' He sat down on a wooden bench outside the guest house and stared out to sea.

# Chapter Twenty-six

Joe felt drunk and also drained from the shock of being threatened with a knife. He was aware of Sky coming towards him and noticed how his step slowed as he approached.

'Hello, Sky.' He turned to him and smiled. 'Sit down. I want to talk to you.' He patted the bench for Sky to sit next to him. Sky looked a little apprehensive but sat down, his eyes scanning Joe's face.

'Listen, Sky,' Joe said. 'About the other day. Those kids. I'm sorry.'

Sky looked him in the eye for a moment, then nodded.

'I should have helped,' Joe said. 'I just stood there. Like you didn't matter. Like you're just the deaf guy who stupid people make fun of.' Joe's brow was wrinkled and he shook his head. 'It's not your fault. It's me. I'm just a shit.'

Sky shifted in his seat. He looked at Joe, then looked away.

Joe felt like crying. He knew it was the drink making him maudlin, but he couldn't help it. Since he'd come home he'd wanted to talk to someone, but there was nobody. Tom would be too horrified to be any help and Frankie wanted to keep everything quiet. Joe understood that he had to, but he felt more lonely now that he was home than he had in America. He leaned forward and put his head in his hands.

'I'm a bad man, Sky,' he said. 'It was a long time ago, but what I did, it was bad.'

Sky gave him a puzzled look.

Joe found he couldn't stop talking. He saw himself twenty years ago, at Frankie's door, sweating and agitated, banging with his fist until he came out.

'She's dead, Frankie! She's dead! You've got to help me!' he blurted when the door opened.

The confused look on Frankie's face. He came out of the house but had to move fast to keep up with Joe who was running towards Beggar's Wood.

'Who's dead, Joe? What the fuck's happened?' Frankie grabbed hold of his arm to slow him down.

'I never did it!' he gabbled. 'She just died, Frankie. She was dead when I got there.' He backed towards the edge of the field, panic in his eyes.

'Stop, Joe,' Frankie said, pulling Joe by the arm. 'Who's dead, for Christ's sake?'

Joe burst into tears. 'Alice', he sobbed. 'Alice McPhee! Oh shit, Frankie! She's dead! And there's a baby!'

Frankie was stunned.

'I just didn't know what to do,' Joe said desperately. 'By the time I got there she was lying on the ground and there was blood everywhere! Oh, Frankie! It's all my fucking fault!'

Frankie stared at Joe. 'Tell me you didn't take a cheap shot with Alice.'

Joe pressed his hands to his head, his lips trembling. 'I only did it once. That's all. She threw herself at me!'

'She's fucking mentally defective, Joe, for Christ's sake!' Frankie said in disbelief.

Between sobs it all came out, how Alice had met him on his way home, and about what had happened earlier the same afternoon. And then a couple of hours ago she had come to his house, crying and mumbling something about a baby. He couldn't understand it because it was only about six months since he had been with her. She seemed to be in pain and he had to take her into the barn in case his mother heard the noise. He told Alice to go up to Beggar's Wood and he would be there as soon as he could. When he got there she was dead.

Frankie had been too shocked to speak for a moment. Then he said, 'Show me.'

They went into Beggar's Wood and after a short distance Frankie could see the pale form of Alice's body lying on the ground. Her pretty face had a stunned, tormented look. Her fingers were curled round clumps of grass. There was blood on the ground and the tiny figure of a barely formed baby still attached by the cord to its mother. Its face and body were smeared with blood. Alice's eyes were wide open and her lips were blue. Frankie walked round the body, looking at Alice. Eventually he spoke.

'We'll have to bury her, Joe,' he said. 'You could swing for this if they said you killed her. What about your ma? And Tom in the priesthood?' He told Joe to run home and get two spades.

When Joe came back, the pair of them started digging. And as they did, the sky opened up and the rain came in torrents, soaking their clothes, turning the earth to mud and washing the blood off Alice's legs as she lay lifeless on the ground.

When the grave was ready, Joe dragged Alice's stiffening body into the hole. Frankie carefully lifted the little baby and laid it on top of her stomach. They covered them with dirt until nothing could be seen. Then Frankie threw his spade away, knelt down and vomited.

Joe was in tears when he stopped talking. Beside him, Sky sat on the bench, breathing softly.

Joe looked up. 'I don't know what to do,' he said. 'I didn't mean to hurt anyone. I was just a stupid boy and I didn't care about anybody except myself. I wish I could put things right somehow.'

Sky nodded and put his hand on Joe's arm.

'Now you know, Sky,' Joe said. 'Nobody knows what you know. Except Frankie.' He gripped Sky's arm. 'You won't tell anyone, will you?'

Sky shook his head.

In the small guest-house bedroom that Frankie shared with Sky, he could feel himself drowsing, partly from the drink and partly from the relaxation after working so hard all week. As he began to drift, he recalled Joe's expression when they were outside the guest house. He looked so troubled. Suddenly older somehow. As sleep overcame him, he saw himself and Joe all those years ago, laughing and joking, carefree teenagers with the world at their feet. Then he saw Joe's anguished face the afternoon he had turned up at his house in a panic. Even as Frankie slept, there was no escape. In his dream he saw Alice's body, the tiny, bloodstained baby. Then his own baby, Emily. He saw himself looking into her coffin, but seeing Alice's baby.

When Frankie woke up, his shirt was drenched in sweat. It had been years since he had dreamed like that.

The four of them went to the restaurant bar for a quick drink before dinner and Frankie was glad to throw back a couple of stiff whiskies. It helped blot out the images he had managed to suppress for so long. Now every time he looked at Joe, the familiar butterflies returned to his stomach. He noticed that both Tom and Joe were drinking as fast as he was. It was as though they all needed the alcohol to get through the night. Sky was drinking lemonade. Frankie thought how happy Sky seemed in his own world, free from the guilt that had plagued him – and Joe – for years. At least Joe seemed friendlier towards him now; he was trying to communicate with him about his childhood and Sky was drawing pictures on his pad and making signs.

In the restaurant Joe ordered a bottle of red wine to go with their steaks, saying that he never sat down to a meal in America now without a decent bottle of wine.

'Changed days,' Frankie joked. 'I remember the only wine you knew was the cheap stuff we used to knock back behind the sheds before going into the dancing.'

'That was just because you needed it to help you chat up the girls,' Joe quipped. 'Whereas I only had to turn up to be guaranteed a lumber.'

'Oh, here we go again.' Tom shook his head. 'Marlon Brando

and Errol Flynn all rolled into one. And look at you now. Just another lonely bachelor.'

Joe took the slagging in good part, but Frankie could see by his expression that he was miles away.

They had drunk the bottle of wine by the time the steaks arrived and ordered another. They tried to bring Sky into the conversation and Tom asked him how long he had been out of Calvin Castle. Sky drew a picture that looked like a winter scene. Frankie asked him where he had been from that time until Maggie found him. He drew a picture of what looked like a timber yard, then two figures hitting a man, and the man walking away. Frankie asked him if he had just been wandering since then. He nodded and shrugged. They all looked at each other, then sympathetically at Sky. But he didn't seem bothered and was more interested in eating everything on the table.

The more wine they drank, the more they talked about women.

Frankie was conscious that a woman at a nearby table kept staring over at them. She was with two men about his age and both were very drunk. All of them were dark-haired and looked Italian or Spanish. But they had Scottish accents. The restaurant was popular with the local Italian community; its food was cooked by a well-known Italian chef who had been brought up near Girvan and had returned after years in Florence. Frankie thought they were looking at Tom and whispering among themselves.

The woman got up and came across to their table. She looked a bit drunk, her dark eyes were puffy. All four of them looked up at her, but she was only interested in Tom.

'I know you from somewhere,' she said, a little slurred. Tom shrugged and shook his head, but Frankie thought he seemed a bit edgy.

'Definitely,' the woman insisted. 'I know your face. You look like somebody I met a long time ago. Were you ever in Rome?'

Tom's face reddened and Frankie felt sure he knew the woman. Joe was looking at Tom in surprise.

'I was in Rome,' Tom said dismissively. 'On and off.'

The two Italian men were following the conversation intently. The woman seemed to be searching her memory for something.

'Maria,' she said suddenly. 'Maria Di Giacomo. Do you know that name?'

Tom's face went crimson and beads of sweat appeared on his top lip. Before he had a chance to speak, the woman's face brightened.

'Tom,' she said triumphantly. 'Isn't your name Tom?'

Tom's eyes darted from her to the men she was with.

'Yes,' he said. 'My name is Tom. And yes, I know, or I knew, Maria.'

The men were getting unsteadily to their feet.

'The student priest?' the woman said with a sneer. Tom shifted uncomfortably in his seat and his eyes roamed the room as if he was looking for a way out.

'Yes,' he said softly, clearing his throat. 'That's right.'

'It's him,' the woman said as the men approached the table. 'I told you.'

Joe pushed back his plate and moved to stand up. Frankie did the same. Neither of them understood what this was about but they recognised trouble when they saw it coming. Sky stopped scraping his plate.

'Bastard,' said the fatter of the two men and grabbed Tom by the throat.

Joe was on his feet and roughly pulled the man off, while Frankie positioned himself between Tom and the other man. Two waiters arrived on the scene.

'OK, whatever this is,' one of them said, 'take it outside.' He looked at the two drunken dark-haired men and the woman. 'You lot have had too much to drink. These men have been sitting here minding their own business. So I suggest you leave before this turns ugly.'

Joe let go of his man and the waiters ushered the Italians towards the door.

At the door the fat man turned and shook his fist at Tom, and the woman shouted, 'How can you live with yourself?'

The door closed behind them.

'Well, now,' Joe said into the silence. 'Is this something you want to tell us about, Tom?'

Tom bit his lip. Frankie thought he was going to cry.

'Maria is someone I loved, Joe.' Tom's voice was faint. 'To tell you the truth, I will probably die loving her.' He rubbed his hand across his face. 'There. I've said it. I've been dying to say it out loud for years.'

Frankie had never seen Tom look so vulnerable. Everyone was stuck for words. Eventually, Frankie managed to speak.

'Do you want to tell us about it, Tom? It might help.'

Tom drained his glass. 'OK. I will,' he said softly. 'I'll tell you a story.'

He told them everything, from the day he caught sight of Maria on the Spanish Steps in Rome to the meeting with the old Italian woman, and the baby he never knew he had. He told how his mother had hidden Maria's letters and how he had discovered them only recently. He had never met any of Maria's relatives in Scotland, but had met some in Rome, which must be where the woman tonight remembered him from.

When his story was finished, Tom sat back and rubbed his eyes. The restaurant had emptied and the waiters were tidying up.

Joe sighed and shook his head. Frankie looked at Tom, seeing him with new eyes.

'You must find her,' Joe said eventually. 'No matter what else you do in your life, Tom, you must find her. Life is so short, pal. So fucking short. Don't stop until you find her.'

Frankie had never seen Joe look so sad. Sky looked at Tom and Joe, then at Frankie. He reached over and touched Tom's arm.

They left the restaurant in silence and made their way to the ceilidh in the pub at the end of the road. The place was heaving with people and the air was thick with smoke and the smell of sweat. On the dance floor, the eightsome reel was becoming boisterous but the men and women wildly throwing each other around managed to keep in step to the two accordion players and three fiddlers on the stage.

Tom squeezed his way through the crowd to the bar and ordered three lagers. By the time he came back, Joe already had his arm round the waist of the waitress who had served them in the pub earlier. He drank half his pint in one go and then disappeared into the throng on the dance floor with the woman.

Sky stood with Frankie and Tom, sipping his lemonade and taking in everything in the room. People were clapping in time to the music and Sky put his drink down on the table and joined them enthusiastically, his face bright.

'Have you never been to a ceilidh before, Sky?' Frankie asked. Sky shook his head.

'Could be an interesting night,' Tom said, moving to a corner to find a bit of space.

'Like it hasn't been so far?' Frankie asked, wondering if Tom wanted to talk further about the woman he had kept secret all these years.

Tom smiled. 'I always thought of telling you, Frankie,' he said. 'But to be honest I just didn't know where to to begin. I thought if I didn't ever talk about her, she would eventually fade from my mind. But she never did. And the past couple of weeks, now that I know she's out there somewhere, I just can't think straight at all.'

'I can imagine,' Frankie said. 'I had no idea you were going through all that shit down the years. I wish you'd told us. Kate and me would be there for you any day of the week. You know that, Tom.'

An attractive youngish woman tapped Frankie on the shoulder. 'Fancy a dance, darlin'? It's my hen party, and they've all dared me to ask a man for a dance. If you knock me back, I'll never live it down.' She put her arm round his shoulder.

'Well, since you put it like that,' he said, 'I think I can manage a dance. Just as long as they don't dare you to ask for anything else.' He smiled and took her onto the dance floor. Her friends cheered.

After two or three dances Frankie returned, sweating and flushed. To whistles and clapping from her friends, he kissed the girl's hand. Another of the girls dragged Tom onto the dance floor, and her friends roared with approval as he danced the Dashing White Sergeant like an expert. Sky was pulled up by another girl and clumped his way awkwardly around the dance floor until he got the hang of it and began swinging his partner with more gusto than direction, bumping into other dancers and laughing.

By the time the last dance was being played, Frankie, Tom and Sky had joined the women's table and were having a laugh. Joe came back from the dance floor alone and moody-looking. Frankie had seen him like this before.

'Where's the bird?' he asked. 'Don't tell us she knocked you back.'

Joe gave him a look. 'You know better than that. I'm just a bit knackered, that's all.' He brandished a piece of paper with a phone number on it. 'Let's just say she's on the back burner.'

As the crowd thinned and the room emptied, Frankie leaned over and spoke to Tom.

'We'd better get away from these women before it's too late,' he said. 'Well, I'd better. You stay if you want.'

'No', Tom said, and got up to leave.

They said their goodbyes and staggered into the street and down towards the seafront.

Joe was silent. Frankie tried to keep up the banter but he never answered. They stood at the edge of the promenade across from their guest house and watched the moonlight on the sea. Suddenly Joe spoke.

'Tom,' he said, his voice slightly slurred, 'I've got a confession to make.'

Frankie looked at him, wondering if he was going to spill everything about Alice McPhee.

'I'm not a priest now, Joe, remember? I chucked all that shite.' Tom seemed drunker in the fresh air.

'No. I know,' Joe said. 'But I'm going to confess anyway.'

Frankie braced himself.

The drink had made Tom feel light-headed, but when Joe started to speak he was suddenly sharp. His brother was telling him that he knew about the letters from Maria. He felt the colour drain from his face. Joe recounted how his mother had said a girl was writing to him while he was at the seminary and she had to intervene to put a stop to it. Joe said he didn't know much more than that. Through his trembling Tom heard him saying he was sorry, over and over again. He could feel himself losing control. And then he was on top of Joe, pushing him against the railing, his hands round his throat. Frankie and Sky moved to try and drag Tom off him.

'Tom!' Frankie said. 'Tom! Come on! He knows he was wrong. It can't be undone now. Christ Almighty, Joe! Why the fuck didn't you tell him?'

'I just put it out of my head!' Joe could barely speak from the pressure of Tom's grip. 'I thought it was just some daft infatuation.'

Tom was crying. He loosened his grip on Joe and pushed him to the side. 'You're nothing but a big-headed, selfish bastard. You always were and you'll never be anything else.' All the years of bitterness as they grew up spilled over. 'Why the fuck did you come home anyway?'

Joe pulled himself to his feet.

'I came home to die, Tom,' he said, barely audible. Tears rolled down his cheeks. He turned to Frankie. 'I'm dying, Frankie. I'm dying and I'm scared! I'm so fucking scared!' He sobbed, his head in his hands.

In the quietness, the water lapped against the shore, and somewhere in the distance they could hear the laughter and singing of the festival goers making their way home, just as they themselves had done all those years ago.

# Chapter Twenty-seven

Kate knew as soon as she set eyes on Frankie that something was very wrong. Even though he came into the yard with the car horn honking to signal his arrival and scooped Maggie up in his arms when he got out, there was no mistaking the look in his eyes. After the excitement had died down and Maggie had stopped jumping for joy at the goldfish Sky had given her, Kate went to find him in the barn. He was standing in the darkness, absently watching the two cows that PJ had penned in to prepare for their imminent calfing. Frankie didn't move when she put her arm through his.

'Hello, sweetheart,' he said, attempting a smile.

'What's wrong, Frankie?' Kate searched his face. She knew her husband better than to probe too much. She had always known there was a dark corner to him. There was a secret somewhere. And in truth she didn't really want to know about it. But she had never seen a heaviness like this hanging over him, not since Emily had died.

Kate wondered if he had fallen out with Joe. She'd sensed a tension between them, particularly that afternoon when Frankie had arrived home to find her having tea with Joe. She knew Frankie was jealous and that deep down he worried that she would be impressed with the charm of his old friend. But she wasn't. Not in the least. She'd felt the tension on a couple of other occasions too, nothing she could pin down, just a sense that things weren't as relaxed as they liked to make out. And Frankie had remarked once that he couldn't for the life of him see why Joe had come home. The way he said it had made Kate think that for some reason Frankie would have preferred it if Joe had stayed away.

In the barn, Frankie kept his eyes on the two cows. He took a deep breath and sighed.

'Joe's dying, Kate,' he said, turning towards her at last. 'Joe came home to die.'

Kate put her arms round him as he tried to fight back tears.

'What's wrong with him? Is it cancer?'

'No,' Frankie said. 'Some stupid disease. I don't even think I've heard of it. Something that wastes away the muscles and eventually eats at the brain. Motor something. Motor neuron disease. He said he could be in a wheelchair within a year or two. Can you imagine that? Joe McBride a cripple? Christ!' Frankie broke away from Kate and walked across the barn.

Kate didn't know what to say to him. In all their years together she'd always been able to comfort him. When they lost Emily, Frankie had been beside himself with grief, just as she was, and when she could she had tried to be strong. And later, when Maggie had a major asthma attack and was at death's door, Frankie nearly went to pieces but she had always known what to say to him to keep him on track. In so many ways she was the strong one. But there was something about him and Joe that seemed exclusive. She had seen it whenever they were together, and she knew that Tom noticed it as well. He had commented on it to her one evening, that even after all those years in America, the bond forged between them when they were youngsters was as strong as ever.

Kate felt sad, imagining a strapping figure like Joe with an illness that wasted away at him. 'Poor Joe. When did he tell you?'

Frankie told her how it had all come out, and that Tom had also revealed that he had been in love with a girl while he was at the seminary. And he had a baby.

Kate was at a loss for words. But she wasn't surprised to learn that Tom had been in love. There was a kind of sadness in his eyes, even when he was laughing and joking, and she had always felt that something or someone had torn the heart from him. She had thought it was something to do with Joe.

Kate took Frankie's arm and he allowed her to lead him out of the barn. He felt totally drained, and he wondered how he was going to deal with Joe now that he knew he was so ill. How he wished he could tell Kate everything. But he was terrified of losing her.

After Maggie had decanted her goldfish into a large beetroot jar, she went to bed, leaving PJ sitting down near the fireplace with his dad to report how he had managed things in his absence.

'It was no problem, Da,' PJ said, leaning back in his chair, trying to look and sound older than he was. 'Marty gave us a bit of a hand getting the cows in, and everything worked out. I wish you'd let me drive the tractor, Da. Even from here to the field. I should be driving, you know.' Marty had tried to persuade him to take the tractor up to the field to save them carrying the heavy sacks of cattle feed. But it was more than he dared do.

Frankie smiled. He was genuinely proud of how PJ had coped with the responsibility.

'You're only thirteen, PJ,' he said. 'You can't be driving just yet. Maybe next year.'

'But Marty can drive. He can drive Gunboats' motor,' PJ said, then stopped himself quickly.

'Yeah?' Frankie was surprised. 'Well, that's between him and his da. You'll be driving soon enough, PJ.' Then he leaned forward and whispered conspiratorially, so Kate wouldn't hear from the kitchen. 'Then you'll be able to chase all the young girls for miles around.'

PJ laughed and blushed at the same time. 'That'll be the stuff, Da,' he said.

After PJ went to bed, with the promise of more pocket money by way of compensation for the driving lessons, Kate took his place and listened to Frankie recount the events of the weekend. She was impressed to hear how Sky had jumped in and stopped the man stabbing Joe, and wondered at the depth of emotion that had provoked Tom to nearly kill Joe when he found out that he'd known about the letters. Frankie described how nobody knew what to say to Joe when he suddenly told them he was dying. The disease had only been diagnosed three months before after Joe went to the doctor complaining of constant tiredness and loss of balance. After blood tests confirmed he had motor neuron disease, the doc told him straight that eventually it would make him immobile and he would require help in every area of his life. At the moment the only real symptoms he felt were the fatigue, which is why he'd slept so much since he'd come home, and the occasional loss of balance which he had managed to hide from Tom.

Joe told them he had read somewhere that his brain would also go. He said he might be a gibbering wreck in a year or two. And he even joked that it wouldn't be any different from being really drunk. He felt fine just now, but it could go downhill rapidly. He admitted he had to come home because he had nobody to look after him in America, but that he had a lot of money and when things got bad he would put himself into some kind of sanatorium or nursing home so he wouldn't be a burden to anyone.

On the way home, they had made small talk and tried to lighten things up by talking about their hangovers. Joe put on a brave face and was more ebullient than any of them. He joked that he would get in touch with the waitress while he still had feeling in his extremities. It was ages before anyone brought up the subject of Tom's lost love. Tom's rage over the letters had evaporated after Joe had told them he was dying. When Joe mentioned the girl, Tom said it wasn't a priority. He apologised for the way he had behaved the night before and said that the only thing that mattered now was Joe. He would look after him. But Joe told him to forget about it. Just find your girl, he said.

Exhausted, Frankie lay back in the chair and closed his eyes. Kate went over to him and took the half-empty whisky glass out of his hand. She gently ran her fingers through his hair and stroked the fine lines around his eyes. She kissed his eyelids. He was already asleep.

# Chapter Twenty-eight

Tom walked out into the farmyard and breathed in the morning air. He could smell rain in the distance, and the slate-grey sky seemed to go perfectly with the flat, empty way he felt. He had looked in on Joe earlier and watched from the doorway as his brother slept peacefully, his face pale. They hadn't talked much about his illness or the revelations about Maria when they got home from the festival the previous night. After Frankie had dropped them off, they sat at the fireside and drank mugs of tea before Joe said he was dog tired and needed to sleep. When Tom went to bed later, he lay staring at the ceiling, thinking about Joe and everything else, and he found he was weeping, the tears running down into his ears.

Now he could see Charlie Martin the postman trundling up the lane in his dusty red van. Tom smiled to himself. It was always the same old routine with Charlie. He would get out of his van with the letters in his hand and walk slowly to the door, reading the envelopes as he came, trying to work out who they were from. When Joe was in America he would always tell Mrs McBride she had a letter from her son, before it was even in her hand. 'Looks like another letter from your Joe,' he would say, then he would stand around, hoping that she would open it and tell him what was in it. But as ever Mrs McBride would shove the letter into her apron pocket, briskly thank him and close the door. Tom's mail was always straightforward: bills or circulars from the Farmers Union, or typed letters concerning agricultural matters. There were never any juicy possibilities in his mail that Charlie could drop into conversation back at the corner in Westerbank. Tom always felt sorry for those farmers whose mail included final demands or brown packages containing porno magazines to help fill the lonely winter nights. Guaranteed, Charlie would relay it all with relish and there would be knowing nods about the bills and cackling at the thought of the hypocrites going to Holy Communion on Sunday when they'd been up all night gawping at pictures of naked women.

Charlie was walking towards Tom with two or three letters in brown envelopes in one hand and a single white envelope in the other. Tom could see he was reading the handwriting carefully.

'Usual bills, I suppose,' Tom said, wondering about the white envelope.

'Not for me to say, Tom,' Charlie said. 'How's it goin'? How's the brother? Is he enjoying his visit back among the poor?' He handed Tom the brown envelopes. 'Oh, and here's one that definitely doesn't look like a bill.' He handed over the white envelope almost reluctantly.

Tom tried to stifle a smile. If he opened the letter there and then and poured Charlie a cup of tea while he read it aloud, it would make his day.

'Thanks, Charlie,' Tom said, squinting at the letter. He didn't recognise the handwriting but noticed it had been posted in Ayrshire. His heart leapt. He hoped it was from the old Italian woman, yet he knew they hadn't arranged to write and he couldn't imagine how she would know his address.

'Oh, well,' Charlie said, seeing that Tom had no intention of sharing the letter with him. 'I'd better be off then.'

Tom smiled and turned back towards the house. He was desperate to see what was in the letter.

He sat down on the wooden bench outside his house and examined the handwriting, much as Charlie had done. It was a scrawl, and was addressed to Mr Thomas McBride, McBride's Farm, Westerbank. It was obviously from someone who didn't know the farm was called Riverside Farm. He slid his penknife across the top of the envelope and pulled out two thin sheafs of paper, his eyes immediately scanning the last page. It was signed Gabriella Medini. He turned to the start of the letter.

'Dear Tom, I hope this letter gets to you as I don't know your address, but I remember Maria saying that you had a farm in a place called Westerbank. I hope you get this letter.' Tom read quickly. She had news for him. Her cousin Donatella had made some inquiries and found out that Maria was still in Ostia. She gave the address. The man Maria worked for was a widow with two daughters. He owned a small cafe bar and had been glad to have someone like Maria living in the house and taking care of his children. Now the girls had gone away to boarding school but Maria was still living at the house and was working in the cafe. Tom turned the page.

His stomach lurched when he read that Maria had a boy aged about twelve, called Luca. My son, Tom said to himself. Luca. His mind tried to picture the child. He read on, but the letter was almost finished. The old woman said she wished him good luck and hoped he would find Maria and have the happiness he deserved in his life.

Tom folded the letter and pushed it into his jeans pocket. He felt moved by the sentiment of the old woman. During their conversations, she was one of the few people he had ever told about how he had been tormented by the memory of Maria while he was a priest and how he had always struggled with his vocation. He had even told her about his mother and how she had pushed him into it in the first place.

He got up and walked across the yard into the barn, but then walked straight back out. His mind was all over the place. How would he do it? He saw himself walking up to the address where Maria lived and knocking on the door. He imagined her face, just as it was all those years ago. What if she slammed the door on him? Should he write to her first? He walked into the yard again, lifted the brush and started sweeping furiously in no particular direction. Then he stopped. He would go and find her. He would go to Rome. He had not had a holiday in ten years and he had saved money for a rainy day. There was also the insurance money from his mother's death, which he was splitting with Joe. He could afford it. He would go. Then, whatever happened, he would live with it. He felt a rush of excitement run through his body and he smiled. He was still smiling when Joe walked out of the house and into the sunshine.

'You look pleased with yourself,' Joe said. He looked fresh and healthy, having just stepped out of the bath and put on clean clothes. Tom looked at him and his heart sank. It was hard to believe by the sight of him that he was ill. He looked great.

'I know where she is, Joe,' Tom said. 'I've got an address. The old Italian woman wrote me a letter.'

'You're kidding,' Joe said, looking genuinely pleased. 'That's brilliant, Tom. Well, that's it then. You've got to go. What the hell are you waiting for?' Joe slapped his back.

Tom laughed. He was bursting with excitement. He pulled the letter out of his pocket and began reading it aloud. He told Joe he was worried Maria would slam the door in his face.

'So what?' Joe said. 'You're never going to find out if you stand around here scratching your arse.'

'But what if she's got somebody else?' Tom said anxiously. 'What if she doesn't want me? I mean, after all these years. And the boy. He maybe doesn't even know who his father is.'

Joe shook his head. 'I always thought you were a bit of an eejit right enough. You've found the woman you've been brooding about most of your life and here you are asking yourself dumb questions. Just get in there and get your bags packed. You're going to Rome, even if I have to kick your arse up to the airport.'

Tom bit his lip and puffed. Joe looked almost as excited as he was at the prospect of finding Maria. But he was dying. How could he go off and leave him when he was ill?

'What about you?' Tom said. 'I can't just leave and you not well. I mean, anything could happen. You said so yourself.'

'You'll only be gone a few days,' Joe said. 'Forget about me. I'll be fine. I'll just get on with things my own way. Now piss off and get organised.' Joe's face was hard.

Tom hit Joe a playful punch in the shoulder and said, 'Right. I will. I'm going to find her, Joe. Jesus. My stomach's going like an engine and I haven't even booked the flight.'

Joe laughed. 'You've got it bad, pal.'

# Chapter Twenty-nine

Billy McGowan was the last customer in the bakery and Baldy wished he would stop hanging about talking. He was tired. He had been on the go since six in the morning, baking the rolls, bread and cakes, and he was about to have his busiest two days. The Westerbank gala day was a bonanza for him and he would rake in a fortune feeding the hundreds who would snack on his rolls and pastries throughout the day. Every year it was a struggle to keep up with the demand but he never complained, because at the end of the day he had wads of money stashed away. Preparation work was the most important thing, he had told Breige who was eager to get involved. Being ahead of the game was the secret. He'd also had Sky helping him to prepare for the days ahead and he was grateful for the hard work that he was putting in. Now he wanted to get some last-minute work done before he shut the shop and put his feet up for the night. But Billy McGowan clearly had nothing else to do with his time.

'You know what I was wondering,' Billy said, glancing over his shoulder and lowering his voice even though there were only the two of them in the shop. 'You know that Joe McBride. I was talking to the Badger Ryan and he kept saying he's convinced McBride had something to do with the disappearance of Alice McPhee all them years ago.'

This was a conversation Baldy definitely didn't feel like having.

'The Badger's always pissed,' he said as dismissively as he could. 'Sure you couldn't take anything he says seriously.'

Billy stroked his chin and pursed his lips. 'I was asking some of the older cops about that case, you know,' he said.

Baldy showed no interest and started counting the day's takings.

'Yeah,' Billy persisted. 'They were saying that at first people thought somebody had done her in, then that she had done a runner with that McBride. They asked a lot of questions at the time, but nobody had any idea. It's as if she just vanished into thin air.'

'Yeah,' Baldy said. 'She wasn't all there. She probably met some traveller and ran off.' He felt uncomfortable talking about Alice because he had never been honest about his involvement with her. Even when Breige asked him about the Badger getting angry with McBride in Mulranney's, he just fobbed her off. Now he was thinking he should be honest with her. He wanted no secrets between them.

'Do you know McBride well?' Billy said, walking up and down the shop.

Baldy was becoming irritated. 'What is this? An interrogation? Do you never take a day off, Billy?' He tried to smile.

'I was just asking,' Billy said.

Baldy said he knew him, that they had grown up together and that McBride was a ladies' man and a bit of a hard case. But there was no real badness in him. He seemed sound enough since he came home.

'Oh, well,' Billy said. 'I must be off.'

Baldy came out from behind the counter and let him out. He locked the door behind Billy and turned the open sign to closed. He stood for a moment with his back to the door and took a deep breath. It had been uncomfortable listening to Billy talking about Alice McPhee and he hoped the old gossip hadn't seen the heat rising in his neck. For Alice had been his only sexual experience before he married Shona. It had happened when he was delivering bread to the house she lived in with her ageing father. Alice was half daft, but Baldy couldn't help feeling aroused the way she looked at him and used to brush past him when he was carrying

ANNA SMITH

the supplies into old Archie's kitchen. One afternoon when the old man wasn't in, Alice had offered him a cold drink and to his astonishment she kissed him full on the mouth while they stood in the kitchen. She didn't object when he fondled her breasts, and Baldy couldn't help himself even though he knew he was taking advantage of her. He was twenty-two years old and he had never had sex. They did it there and then on Archie's kitchen floor.

He felt bad about it afterwards, especially when Alice used to turn up at the bakery and hang around waiting to talk to him. He was glad when she finally disappeared, though he sometimes entertained the notion that maybe she ran away because she was pregnant with his child. He never told anyone about their encounter, even when the police came inquiring after Alice went missing. Anyway, rumour had it that her disappearance was something to do with Joe McBride going to America.

He rubbed his eyes. He would tell Breige tonight.

After dinner they sat on the couch listening to Baldy's favourite Del Shannon songs on the radiogram. Baldy sipped his whisky and thought how lucky he was. Breige had her legs draped across his knee and she smiled lovingly at him. He would have to tell her about Alice.

'You know, Breige,' Baldy began, stroking her arm, 'I bet there's not too many men in the world who are as happy as me. You've changed my life so much. I wake up every day and feel glad to be alive. But I want there to be no secrets between us.'

Breige sat up with a surprised look in her eyes.

'You see, pet,' Baldy said, 'I've something to tell you. About that Alice girl you were asking about a while ago. Remember?'

Breige nodded.

He told her everything. From the first few times Alice had seemed to take an interest in him until they had sex. He confessed to her that he never told the police that he had been with her. When she asked why not, Baldy said he just didn't want to get dragged into anything.

170

'Did she go with other boys, Brendan?' Breige asked. 'I mean, she probably did.'

Baldy said he'd heard that she did but he didn't know for sure. She seemed to like the sex with him. He told Breige he had felt bad at keeping out of her way afterwards and that he had always wondered what happened to her. Breige looked at the sad expression on his face and reached out to take his hand.

'Don't worry about it, Brendan,' she said. 'It's all a long time ago. We all do things when we're young that we may feel ashamed of later on. I understand. Honest.'

Baldy stroked her hair, looking into her eyes. 'I just wanted everything to be above board with us, that's all,' he said.

'Of course.' Breige smiled. 'Everything above board.' She took his face in her hands and kissed him on the lips.

As the music played, Baldy sang along softly and Breige smiled at how pleasant his voice was. Somewhere inside, no matter how much she denied it, she was really fond of Baldy, and in truth she would not enjoy ripping him off. He trusted her so much. He had even told her his darkest secret, though she didn't really think it was that dark. But the fact that he had wanted to tell her, reveal everything to her, made her feel guilty. If Eamon knew about Alice McPhee, the first thing he would think of was blackmail. But Breige felt bad enough already without considering that. She wished Baldy was like some of the other men she'd known. They had been downright boorish and unpleasant and she'd taken great delight in fleecing them. It had always felt like a kind of justice to her and she never turned a hair, no matter how much she took. But Baldy just wanted to care for her and love her. It made her feel secure and something close to happy. Sometimes she wished she had met a man like him years ago, then maybe her life would have been so different.

She remembered their first meeting when she came to Scotland.

She had written to him and he had replied within two days, arranging to meet her at a cafe near the pier in Ayr. When she saw his ruddy cheeks and completely bald head, Breige cringed at the notion she could ever get involved with him. He was a bit boastful, but he had an easy way with him and had her laughing while they sat and drank coffee for over an hour. He didn't want to know about her background; he was only interested in who she was as a person. Breige decided he was charming, decent and generous and that he would fit the bill perfectly. They were married within three months.

But it was all going to change very soon. Eamon was exciting and daring, and once they got to America a whole new world would open up. She had phoned Eamon from the call box at the edge of the village, and he had everything in place for them to leave next week. He was getting the plane tickets for New York that day and he would meet her at Prestwick Airport. All Breige had to do was to bring the rest of the money. She wouldn't take all Baldy's money. She wasn't that much of a bastard. She would leave him plenty and he would soon get over her. She would write him a letter, and maybe he would even understand.

She took Baldy's hand in hers and pulled him up from the couch.

'Let's go to bed,' she said in her most seductive voice.

Baldy downed the last of his whisky and licked his lips.

'You temptress, you,' he said, smiling. 'I'm all yours.'

# Chapter Thirty

In the travel agent's, Eamon counted out the money to the girl behind the desk and winked at her when he put the last ten pound note down.

'Sorry, some of them are a bit wrinkled,' he said. 'I've been keeping them under the bed for years.' The girl laughed and Eamon smiled at his own brazenness. He liked to take things to the edge. That's where all the fun was.

Outside the shop he put his hand in his inside pocket and felt the remainder of the cash. He no longer had all the money Breige had given him because the temptation to gamble it on the horses had been just too strong. It had been a mistake, though, and he was now five hundred pounds light. But Breige would never know. She trusted him implicitly. And there was plenty left over for a good start in America.

As Eamon crossed the street to the cafe, he kept a careful eye out for Crusher McKenzie, the former wrestler who did all the dirty work for Jimmy Williamson, the gangster who ran the card school from the back room of a pub in the East End of Glasgow. Eamon owed him nearly fifteen hundred pounds. It was Jimmy's fault for letting the poker debt climb so high. The way he had been raising the stakes in the last couple of weeks, Jimmy must think he had plenty of cash. At least he'd been careful not to let them see all of Breige's money. His marker was good enough. Now he was hoping to be out of the country before they caught up with him. He could handle himself, but he really didn't fancy going the best of three falls with big Crusher.

He went into the cafe and slipped into the booth where a young blonde girl was waiting for him with a big smile.

Across the street, Crusher McKenzie emerged from a shop doorway and went into a telephone kiosk a few yards away. When he heard Jimmy's voice, he put sixpence in the slot.

'Hello, boss. I see him right across the road,' Crusher said into the receiver, keeping his eye on Eamon.

'What is the wee Mick bastard doing?' the voice on the other end asked.

'Chatting up some bird,' Crusher said. 'Oh, and Jimmy, he was in the travel agent's. I think he's about to do a runner.'

'Yeah? Well, it'll be hard for the fucker to do a runner if he's got no legs, won't it, Crusher?'

'Aye, Jimmy,' Crusher said. 'It will.'

'Right. Deal with it, and let me know when it's done. There's a good bonus in this one for you. Nobody pulls the wool over Jimmy Williamson's eyes, as that Irish bastard is about to find out the hard way.'

'Right, Jimmy,' Crusher said. 'No bother.'

He put the receiver down, took a cigarette from behind his ear and stuck it between two beefy fingers before lighting it and drawing deeply.

# Chapter Thirty-one

'Have you got it?' Frankie called to Joe who was standing in the middle of the stream, trying to reel in a fish. 'Do you need a hand?' Frankie watched a little nervously because the riverbed where Joe was trying to keep his balance was full of slippery pebbles.

'Since when did I ever need you to help me land a trout, Flaherty?' Joe shouted back, his eye on the straining rod. The sound of his voice echoed in the stillness of the sweltering afternoon sunshine. Not a leaf or a blade of grass stirred. Only the rush of the stream filled the perfect silence.

It was such a familiar scene, thought Frankie. The expert way Joe had cast his rod with a practised swish of his arm so the float landed perfectly, and now standing thigh-deep in the water with a struggling fish on the end of his line. They would go back home with a basket of fresh fish and a huge appetite.

Frankie opened the basket Kate had prepared for them and took out the cans of beer and sandwiches. She had been really great with Joe since she'd learned of his illness. She had gone to the library and read up on it, and had told Frankie that it seemed to be as bleak as Joe had said. It was likely he wasn't going to live long, even though at the moment he was quite strong and fit. She had put her arms round Frankie in bed one night when they were talking about it and he told her how Joe's illness had made him feel fragile. Now when Joe came to the house, Kate always made time for him and he seemed content to sit inside and talk to her when Frankie was working in the yard.

Frankie sat down and opened a can of beer, sipping it as he watched Joe reel the fish in and plop it into the net he held in his other hand. He turned to face Frankie, smiling triumphantly.

'As you can see, despite his years working in the back-breaking construction industry in New York from dawn till dusk, Joe McBride has lost none of his angling skills,' he said, as though he was narrating a documentary.

'Well done, pal. Is he a big one?' Frankie said. The fish was wriggling in the net.

'Not one I would be ashamed of. Respectable,' Joe said, picking his way gingerly out of the water and up the riverbank. 'Thirsty work, this fishing.' He flopped down beside Frankie who handed him a can of beer. He took a long swig and swirled the beer around in his mouth. Frankie handed him a ham sandwich stuffed with salad.

'I'll tell you something, Frankie,' Joe said, taking a bite. 'You've got it all. You really have. A beautiful, sexy –' he put his hand up apologetically, remembering how touchy Frankie was about Kate, and Frankie smiled – 'a beautiful, sexy wife, two great kids and a good going farm. Not to mention a dedicated farmhand who can't answer back,' Joe joked.

'Yeah,' Frankie said. 'I do appreciate it, Joe. I'm a lucky man to have met Kate. I would be nothing without her. She made everything right for me. After you left I was just pissing around, getting drunk and going a bit crazy. All that stuff with Alice was putting me off my head. But Kate just walked into my life and everything changed. I don't know where I'd be without her.' Frankie stopped, realising he was gushing, and here was Joe, not knowing whether he would be able to walk in a year's time.

They ate their sandwiches in silence for a moment, both thinking about the past.

'You know something, Frankie,' Joe said, 'I think this disease I've got is God's way of stuffing me because of Alice McPhee. Nothing ever went right for me since that day – you know, in my head. Honest to Christ, Frankie, I'm probably never going to stop paying for it.' Joe looked at Frankie and his eyes had the same pleading look they'd always had when they were teenagers and Joe was looking for Frankie's support when he had overstepped the mark again.

'Aw, that's all that Catholic shite we got in school where if you did anything bad, God was watching and he would sort you out,' Frankie said. 'I've given up on that stuff.' He lay back, his arm over his eyes, shading the sun. He wished he could turn the clock back; he knew he would do things differently. But back then they were just stupid, panic-stricken adolescents. By burying Alice it was as if they were trying to get rid of evidence of some grisly murder. He had tormented himself for years about why on earth they didn't just come clean at the time and tell the truth. They were stupid, Frankie had told himself down the years. But they weren't evil.

Joe turned on his side so he was facing Frankie.

'Since I left here that morning,' he said, 'I've never really had a day's peace. Alice McPhee followed me around from New York to Mexico and back to New Jersey. I'm telling you, Frankie, this disease is God punishing me.'

'Tell me about your life in America, Joe,' Frankie said. He wanted to stop Joe torturing himself but he also genuinely wanted to hear what he had been doing all these years. 'Tell me how it was. You only wrote about two letters in all that time and I was always dying to know what it was really like.'

In the quietness, Joe began his story, his voice soft as he recalled the day he left Westerbank and headed to England to earn enough money for a flight to America.

'I cried myself to sleep like a big wean for the first few weeks while I was in England,' he said. 'Then when I got to America I was so busy staying alive and feeding myself that I forgot to cry at night and I was asleep before my head hit the pillow.'

Joe told how he had lived in stinking, cockroach-infested hostels and rooms in New York, freezing half to death in the icy winters. He worked on a building site for an Irishman who had already made his money, and Joe had to fight somebody just about every day to prove he was a hard man from Scotland who wouldn't be messed around. He described how he robbed his landlord of a wedge of cash one night after he found out he was allowing two of his flats to be used by perverts who brought in young girls. He had beaten him up because of what he did to the girls, but as the guy lay bleeding, he decided to rob him as well. It was as if there was a craziness about him that he couldn't control. Joe said he still didn't know if he had killed the landlord, because he moved on the next day and never went back to that area of the city. He drifted across America for a couple of years, lived in Mexico for a while, working on a watermelon farm, until he was run off the land at gunpoint after he bedded the farmer's daughter. Frankie laughed and said that some things never changed.

There had been women, lots of them, young, middle-aged, and one older woman who hired him to be her driver for two years and when she died left him one thousand dollars in her will. It was enough to get him started with his own small gang of building workers. And so he made his fortune. He moved to Long Island and in the post-war boom of the fifties the construction industry took off. He made a lot of money, built his own house overlooking the bay, and instead of grafting every day he lived what seemed to be the good life. He dabbled in the stock market and made more money and he gambled at the casinos. But every night, Joe said, he had to close the door of his house and go to bed. No matter where he was, there was always a time when he had to put his head on the pillow, and when he did, he never escaped the image of the night they buried Alice McPhee. He never escaped the shame of the night he had sex with her; even though she wanted him to, he knew he'd taken advantage of her. He told Frankie that in a way he was glad when the doctor told him he had motor neuron disease. At least it was some tangible punishment for what he had done. He felt he had been waiting for it all these years.

Frankie watched Joe as he spoke, his dark eyes staring straight ahead as he unravelled the threads of his life. His face looked more at peace somehow, Frankie thought, than when they were at the festival and Joe had told them about his illness.

'That's some life, Joe,' Frankie said when he had finished, not really knowing what to say. 'You packed at least two lives in there, pal. And here was I, shovelling dung, hardly stepping foot out of Westerbank.'

'But look what you've got,' Joe said. 'I've got nothing, Frankie. I never really did have anything.'

'You've got me, Joe,' Frankie said, feeling a rush of sorrow for his friend. 'You'll always have me, no matter what happens.'

'I know, Frankie,' Joe said. 'I know. But I don't care any more what happens to me. It doesn't matter any more. It's over for me. I just want to make things up to Tom for all the shite I gave him when we were lads. I want him to be happy.'

'I know you do,' Frankie said.

The late afternoon sun was throwing shadows across the stream as they gathered their things and stood up.

'You're not a bad man, Joe,' Frankie said, looking straight at him. 'Don't ever think that.'

'Oh, but I am,' Joe said and wearily slung his haversack over his shoulder and walked on ahead.

# Chapter Twenty-two

'Well, OK. But you have to be back here in half an hour.' Kate's face was stern. 'Got that, PJ? If you're not back, then nobody goes anywhere tomorrow. No gala day. No nothing.' She looked at Maggie whose face fell at the thought of missing out on the day she had been looking forward to for weeks.

'Don't worry, Mum. It's only at the end of the road.'

Kate had come out of Mulranney's to give the children their ultimatum before they went to the fair that had arrived at the village on the eve of the gala day. All the kids in the village had been waiting since early morning for the big, garishly painted wagons to roll up and when they finally did, there was a procession of children skipping behind the trucks, pointing out the various rides. Waltzers. Chairplanes. A ghost train. The word spread around the village and by the time the rides were set up with their coloured lights blazing, there was a queue of children waiting to part with sixpence for five minutes of unbridled excitement.

Kate hated PJ and Maggie going to the fair at night because she didn't like them hanging around where the teenagers were drinking cheap wine and invariably looking for fights. But she allowed them to go as long as Sky was with them and they came straight back to Mulranney's where she and Frankie were having a quick drink with Joe and Tom. They had been out for a walk to soak in the carnival atmosphere the village took on every year at this time. The tradition had been started by the local miners' welfare group and had carried on after most of the pits had shut down. The village looked as if it was smiling, with bunting strung across the streets and fairy lights around some of the shop windows. The gala king and queen would be crowned tomorrow after the procession of coloured floats through the village. Tents had already been erected on the village green which would house the various contests, and the fairground people were building their roll-a-penny stands and coconut shies where you could win dolls and toys for threepence. All in all the place was alive with anticipation.

Inside Mulranney's, the bar was packed and Mulranney was sweating, trying to serve everyone.

The pub door opened and Gunboats came in with Miranne at his side.

'How's it goin', folks?' he said, squeezing in beside Frankie, Kate, Joe and Tom.

'Hi, Gunboats,' Frankie said. 'What you having?'

Frankie bought a pint for Gunboats and a shandy for Miranne. Gunboats had already been drinking and was full of banter. He had become a bit of a character around the village even though he had only been there for a short time. All the pubs knew that once Gunboats was in with his banjo, there would be a good sing-song before long.

At the other end of the bar, Billy McGowan drank beer with his brother. He'd come down from Ayr where he lived in digs to see his mother and have a few beers with old mates on gala day. Every now and again he glanced over at Joe McBride. He wondered if he should suggest to his bosses in Ayr that they might want to ask Joe some questions about that Alice McPhee. After all, he'd never been asked about her disappearance because he'd gone off to America for years. Then Billy's attention turned to the big guy who had just walked into the bar and joined Frankie Flaherty's crowd. Billy knew his face, but he couldn't place him.

'Who's the big duker over there with Frankie Flaherty and them?' he asked his brother Mick, interrupting his monologue about which girls were a sure thing for tomorrow night once they'd had a few vodkas. Then, remembering his detective training, Billy added quickly, 'Don't look straightaway.'

His brother casually looked around the room and saw Frankie's crowd.

'The big fella's Gunboats,' Mick said. 'That's all I know him as. He's down at the caravan site for the holidays. Big head case. But a good singer and he can fairly play the banjo.'

Gunboats, Billy thought. Gunboats McKay. His heart skipped a beat, but he tried to contain his excitement in front of his brother. Gunboats McKay was the nutter who'd held up the shop in the East End of Glasgow and left the shopkeeper with a broken arm and five hundred pounds the poorer. The police had been looking for him for nearly two months but he had vanished without trace. Billy had not been on the case but he had listened to the other guys talking about Gunboats. Details about him had come down from Glasgow.

Billy drank his pint and ordered another for himself and his brother. He must handle this very carefully, he thought. This was his big chance. He could be a sergeant by Christmas.

# Chapter Thirty-three

'God Almighty!' Frankie said when Maggie and PJ appeared at the breakfast table so early. 'Did somebody set your beds on fire?'

'Have you forgotten?' Maggie said.

'Forgotten what?' Frankie asked, winding them up.

'The gala day!' Maggie cried. 'This is it. The big day, Dad. And you're going in for the dads' race, remember. You promised.'

Kate put a plate of rashers and egg in front of Frankie. 'Let's see you get out of this one,' she whispered.

Frankie clutched his leg and groaned. 'I think it's my old football injury. My hamstring.'

'You never played football, Dad,' PJ said, amused. On the way home from the pub last night after a few pints, his father had boasted that he could beat any dad in Westerbank, no problem.

Frankie put a forkful of food into his mouth. 'We'll see,' he said. 'We'll see.'

Down at McBride's, Joe stood at the bedroom door watching Tom carefully pack shirts into his small suitcase.

'That's the fourth time you've done that this week,' Joe said, sipping from a mug of tea.

'I know,' Tom said, scratching his head. 'I just want to get it right, that's all.'

Joe walked into the room. It was as neat as it always was, everything in its proper place. He remembered how that used to drive him crazy when they were teenagers and his own room was like a bomb site. When Tom opened the wardrobe, Joe saw that his shirts were all hanging perfectly, even the ones for everyday use. Joe smiled, recalling how he would slip into his brother's room while Tom was out working in the fields and borrow his best shirt if he had a hot date. When Tom returned and noticed the missing shirt, there would be an almighty row. It seemed like a silly thing now, looking back. But Joe could still remember the tears of rage in Tom's eyes as their mother once again took her eldest son's side and Tom had to back down. Joe wished his brother had punched his face all those years ago. God knows he deserved it.

'I was a shit of a brother, wasn't I, Tom?' Joe said from the window sill.

Tom stopped packing and turned to look at him. 'You were what you were, Joe. It was a long time ago. We all had our faults. I had plenty too.'

'You had no real faults, Tom,' Joe said. 'You were the perfect son. It was me who was the reprobate. I don't know how Ma never saw that.'

'I think she probably did see it but it didn't matter because it was you,' Tom said. 'When you left I think the light went out of her life. I suppose that's one reason why she was so cantankerous and ungrateful no matter how much I did for her. I was no substitute for you. The only thing I could do right for her was be a priest. She wanted it for her. Not for me, not for God. For her.' Tom snapped the case shut.

'She was just a woman of her time, Tom,' Joe said. 'She got a real raw deal, losing Dad so young and having to bring up two daft boys like us. Can't have been easy. We never really thought of her as a woman, you know as a person, with thoughts and feelings. Or at least I didn't.'

'Yeah. Me neither,' Tom said. 'I suppose she had a rough time.' He had walked the length and breadth of his fields since he'd found the letters, trying to come to terms with what his mother had done to him. He thought he could forgive her, but in his heart he could never really feel love for her. She had killed that in him as he grew up by constantly pushing him to one side in favour of Joe.

'Why do you think she always had more time for you than me, Joe, even as a child?' Tom said. 'I never understood that.'

'I dunno. Maybe she felt that because you were going to be a priest, God would look after you. You know. You were kind of chosen. Whereas I was a handful and maybe she thought I needed more attention.' Joe shrugged. 'Anyway. It's all a long time ago. Let's not get maudlin.' Joe didn't want Tom to feel down just as he was about to go off on the biggest adventure of his life. 'Come on. Let's go and join the rest of them at the gala day.'

'OK,' said Tom. 'But I'm not going on a bender. I've a plane to catch first thing.'

Joe shook his head as they walked out of the room together.

'I know, I know,' Tom said with a laugh. 'Take the poker out of your arse, Father McBride.'

# Chapter Thirty-four

It was the hottest day of the year so far. And by mid-afternoon the village green was packed with sunburned faces. Teenage boys stripped to the waist, their shoulders scorched with the sun, tested their strength, swinging a sledgehammer on a scale, cheering lustily if the bell at the top of the column rang. Men who had spent most of the summer working peeled off shirts and sat with their milk-white skin turning pink and freckled, while wives slapped suncream and broad-brimmed hats on babies irritable in the heat. The gala queen, wanting her day to last for ever, still trailed around proudly in her royal blue satin robe, her cheeks flaming in the heat. The king had long since discarded his crown and now played football in his shorts just to prove he wasn't a cissy. Down at the edge of the park, a bunch of kids danced and sang 'Puppet On A String' along with a fat Girl Guide teacher who was playing pop records and organising a Pan's People best dancer contest for the under eights.

Frankie, Kate and Miranne sat on a tartan rug, watching Gunboats flex his muscles in a tug-of-war. When his team had pulled the others over the line, he came over and flopped down on the rug.

'This is just a brilliant day, Frankie,' he said, beads of sweat on his forehead. He opened a can of beer and drank deeply. 'This is a great place to live. I wish we could move out into the country. Don't you, Miranne?'

Miranne looked at him with the same disappointed expression she always seemed to have. 'Aye. It'd be great right enough.'

'Could you not try to get some work here?' Frankie said. 'Maybe you could put in for a house and see how it went.' Gunboats had grown on Frankie. He liked the way he blustered around and didn't really bother what anyone thought of him. He was a bit wild but he certainly wasn't the worst of them to come to Westerbank.

'I'm thinking about it,' Gunboats said. He looked at Miranne who looked away.

Across at the beer tent, they were putting out tables for later in the evening when there would be singing on the stage and a display of Irish dancers. Mulranney could be seen behind the bar, rushing around, serving the people who were beginning to filter in. In the distance, Frankie could see the Badger Ryan making his way out of the tent with a pint of beer in his hand. He already looked a little unsteady, and Frankie was thinking that he must have started very early. Maggie came up with Jess who was carrying a small trophy she had won in the sack race. Frankie felt a pang of sadness for Maggie who had come third in the race. With her asthma she could never keep up with the others, but she bravely took part in everything. Her lips were bright red from the ice jubilee she was sucking and there were streaks of cola running up her arms.

'Look at the state of you,' Kate said. 'What are you going to be like by tonight?' Maggie licked her fingers and sucked at the melting ice.

Over at the bakery, Baldy Cassidy, sweat pouring out of him with the heat of the ovens, was doing a roaring trade in pastries and cakes. Trays of gingerbread men baked by Sky were a favourite with the children who chuckled as they bit off the heads. Breige worked hard alongside Baldy, watching as the till filled up with notes. She had helped him pack his bag ready for his golf trip in the morning after the gala day. She would see him off, then spend the next few days keeping the shop open while quietly packing her own bag. She would be gone the day he arrived back. She had it planned to the last detail.

In the early evening most of the villagers went home to eat then returned for the night. Around the beer tent, the plastic tables were filling up. Frankie, Joe and Tom had been catching up with friends from other villages. Joe was often the centre of attention and Frankie was glad to hear the sound of his laughter.

'He's putting on a brave face,' Tom said.

Frankie nodded. 'Joe's not the kind of guy who will just give up.'

'He was a bit gloomy this morning. He more or less apologised for being an arse when we were young. He's all guilty now. But he shouldn't be like that. It's all in the past.'

'That's right,' Frankie said, thinking that that was the problem. Joe wanted to change the past and he couldn't; none of them could.

Joe sat down next to Kate who was watching PJ, Marty, Jess and Maggie having a laugh on the dance floor.

'You'll miss Tom when he's in Rome,' Kate said. 'You can come up to us for your dinner, you know. You don't want to be down there cooking on your own.'

'I will,' he said, and stood up. 'If you give me a dance.' He took her hand and winked at Frankie.

'Don't worry, Frankie,' Tom said, watching him. 'Joe's not going to run away with your wife.'

Frankie thought it best to laugh it off. 'You don't know him, pal,' he said.

The place was in full swing. One young woman with long blonde hair, wearing a flowing skirt and a skimpy top, was dancing on a table, cheered on by half a dozen teenage boys. Mulranney was gesturing from the bar for her to get down but nobody took any notice.

Sky was wandering around, enjoying the atmosphere. For most of the day he had been sitting behind a table, surrounded by the little animals he had carved, and it was good to stretch his legs. He'd been doing a roaring trade. Some people had gathered around the table just to see who this stranger was who had come from nowhere and couldn't talk. But when they saw how life-like his animals were they were mesmerised and, before the day was out, Sky's table was empty and he had a pocketful of money. A couple of times he'd caught a glimpse of a woman whose face he thought he knew. She seemed familiar somehow, but he couldn't remember where he'd seen her before. Now and again he would see her in the crowd, and for some reason, it made him think of his childhood. Now he watched the people on the dance floor and wished he had the nerve to get up and give it a try. He had enjoyed it at the festival in Girvan with Frankie and the boys.

He felt a hand on his shoulder, and a voice said a name that instantly jolted him back to his past.

'Peter.'

He turned round, startled. The woman with the familiar face was smiling at him.

'It is you, isn't it?' she said.

He gasped and put his hand to his mouth. It was Molly.

'Yes, it's me, Peter. Molly.' She threw her arms round him and for a second he was too shocked to move. Then he wrapped his arms round her and squeezed her tight. He let her go and looked at her face. She was crying.

'Oh Peter,' she said. 'I can't believe it's you. After all these years.' Sky wiped the tears from his own eyes and smiled. 'I tried to find you, Peter. After they got rid of me. But they said you were in a prison up north or something. It was only much later I heard you had been in Calvin Hospital all these years. After what you did to Billy.'

Sky nodded. He held her hands. Molly kept reaching out and touching his face. She asked him where he lived and Sky pointed to the table where Frankie and the others sat. He took his pad out and made a quick drawing of the caravan and the farmhouse. He drew a smiling face. Molly understood.

'You're happy, Peter. Yes, I can see that you are. God, I'm so glad we met.'

Sky pointed to Molly and touched his mouth with a finger to signal that he wanted her to talk.

'You want to know where I've been?' Molly said.

Sky nodded, and she told him her story.

After she left the children's home she got a job in a hospital in Glasgow as an auxiliary nurse. She didn't want to come back to the home at the start because she thought it might upset him, and it was only months later she learned through one of the cleaners that he had stabbed Billy. She told him Billy almost lost his eye, but he ended up being arrested for stealing and was sacked from his job as caretaker. Sky smiled and shrugged. Nobody was able or willing to tell her where they had taken Peter, and it was only years later, after she was married, that she met one of the nurses from the children's home who told her about the little mute boy who was taken to Calvin Hospital.

'By that time, I just felt it was too late,' Molly said, sighing. 'I didn't want to try and track you down there. You know. I didn't want to come back into your life and maybe unsettle you.' Her eyes filled up. 'But Peter, I never forgot you. I promise you that. I always thought of you and hoped you were coping. I missed you.'

Sky bowed his head and bit his lip. He put his hand to his heart and then stretched it out to Molly.

'I know,' Molly said. 'You missed me too.'

Sky shook his head and patted his heart again, making the same gesture with his hand outstretched. This time Molly watched his lips; they seemed to be trying to say I love you. She swallowed hard and put her arms round him.

'I should have come, Peter,' she said, hugging him. 'I should have come and found you.'

Sky's fingers touched her hair.

He took her to the table where Kate and Frankie sat with Joe and Tom. Molly introduced herself and they all sat forward, listening intently as she told them how she knew Sky. She went on to say that her husband had died two years before in a car crash and she had moved to Ayrshire to work as a nurse in the local hospital. She had always wondered what had happened to her friend Peter and in the previous few months she had contacted Calvin Castle, who had told her they had released him and he was now in the community. All they could tell her was that he had been given a job in a lumber yard somewhere on the road to Ayr, but when she got in touch with them they said he had left one day after a fight with one of the workers. They had no idea where he was. Molly said she always had a feeling that they would meet again, and something deep inside her made her believe that he wouldn't be too far away from the countryside and farms.

Kate told her how Maggie had found him and why they called him Sky. She explained that he worked with them and had become a great friend to their children, and that he also worked in the local bakery. She said he was famous for his gingerbread men. And he could also carve wooden animals which he'd sold at a stall during the gala day. Molly listened fascinated, exchanging glances every now and again with Sky, who never took his eyes off her.

Slow music again began to play, and Kate turned to Molly and said, 'You know, Molly, I hear from my husband that Sky is a fine dancer.'

Sky laughed. Molly got to her feet and grabbed him by the arm.

'Come on, Peter. Let's see if you can teach me a few dance steps.'

Joe had Maggie sitting on his knee, and he was knocking back whisky and amusing everybody with stories about the building trade in New York. Gunboats was roaring with laughter and Miranne kept a watchful eye on him.

It was Frankie who spotted the Badger first and instantly knew there would be trouble. Ryan was swaying as he approached their table from the far side of the beer tent, his face red and his mean-looking mouth tight. He was managing to hold a half-empty glass of beer without spilling it. When he reached the table he looked straight at Joe, who stopped talking and stared back at him.

'Aye. You'll tell your stories now, McBride,' the Badger slurred. 'But you'll not tell the truth, will you? You'll not tell about the kind of bastard you are.'

Joe looked at Frankie, and lifted Maggie off his knee.

'Piss off, Badger,' Frankie said. 'We're trying to enjoy ourselves here.'

'No, you piss off, Flaherty,' Ryan snarled. 'You and your old pal. No doubt you had a go at her as well, ya bastard!'

The colour drained from Frankie's face and he pushed his chair back. Kate and Tom looked at each other and then at Joe and Frankie. Joe got to his feet.

'Don't, Joe,' Frankie said, putting his hand across his friend to keep him calm. 'He's just pissed. Ignore him.'

'I might be pissed, Flaherty,' the Badger said, 'but I know what I saw, and that's all that matters.' He looked at Joe. 'You thought if you fucked off to America it would all be forgotten. But I'm still here, McBride. And I saw you.'

'What is he talking about?' Kate asked Tom.

'I dunno,' Tom said, watching Joe's expression turn to rage.

Joe slammed his glass on the table. Gunboats put his drink down and moved to stand up, but Miranne held on to him.

'I've just about heard enough from you, Ryan,' Joe said. 'Now why don't you fuck off while you still can. Because I'll swing for you, Ryan. I have nothing to lose.'

The Badger stood his ground. 'What about Alice McPhee?' he shouted, just as the music stopped. People from other tables looked round. 'Did you do her in after you had your fill of her? Did you?' His voice was almost a shriek.

Kate was looking at Frankie with a bewildered expression. He could feel her eyes on him and tried not to look at her. He was shaking inside. Kate snatched Maggie and got up from the table.

Joe lunged at the Badger and grabbed his shirt, which tore in his grip. Frankie moved swiftly between them and Gunboats was in before Tom could get out of his seat. Joe had the Badger's head in an armlock and was dragging him away from the table.

'Shut your stupid mouth, Ryan,' Joe spat with rage. He punched the Badger's face and blood spurted from his nose. 'You don't know what you're talking about. If you say that once more, I'll rip your fucking head off. I swear I will.'

'Right, come on, lads.' Gunboats was between them, holding Joe's arm, trying to prise the Badger's head out of it. Badger's face was turning purple and he couldn't speak.

'That's enough, Joe.' Frankie moved in. Joe tightened his grip. 'Stop, Joe! You're choking him!' There were tears in Frankie's eyes. Joe had lost the plot. He was going to kill the Badger. 'Stop, for Christ's sake!' he shouted again. 'Haven't you done enough?'

Silence. Everyone in the tent was watching.

Joe looked at Frankie, and for what seemed like for ever the two of them stood staring at each other. Suddenly Joe released his grip and the Badger fell, spluttering and coughing. Gunboats lifted him and dragged him away to the far side of the beer tent.

Kate stood clutching Maggie, her mind in turmoil. Whatever was going on here had shaken Frankie to the core. She had never seen him this pale or frightened. She vaguely remembered the name Alice McPhee from gossip years ago, but Frankie had dismissed it as nonsense. She could hardly remember any of the details, just that Joe McBride's name had come up. But what was more disturbing now was the terrified look on Frankie's face as he and Joe faced each other. There was something between these two. Some secret they shared that she had never been party to. She'd always felt it but had never questioned Frankie about it. Now she needed to know.

'Frankie.' Kate's voice broke the silence and he glanced over at her, a desperate look in his eyes. Kate felt her stomach turn over. 'Let's go home, Frankie.'

He turned away from Joe for the first time in his life and walked out of the tent with Kate and Maggie. PJ followed them.

As they left, the chatter slowly resumed and the music started up again.

# Chapter Thirty-five

Kate brought a mug of tea in to Frankie who was sitting staring at the empty fire. He looked different. They had walked home in silence, and Frankie barely looked at her. His shoulders drooped and she knew something awful was weighing him down. Part of her wanted to push it away and tell him that she didn't want to know, that they would just go on as before. But a part of her knew it was too late for that. She dreaded what he would tell her but there was no going back now.

'I always knew there were secrets, Frankie,' she said, without looking at him. 'I never asked. Maybe I was afraid to ask. But I always knew I never had all of you.'

'Oh, Kate,' Frankie said, looking at her. 'You do have all of me. You do. My whole life would have been for nothing if it wasn't for you.'

'I told you every single shred of my life, Frankie. You know me inside out, but I accepted there was something between Joe and you that you didn't tell me. I didn't want to know. But now I think it's time to speak.' She looked up, her eyes anguished. 'I'm scared, Frankie. I'm scared of what you're going to tell me.'

Frankie went over and knelt by her feet. He took both her hands in his.

'I'm going to tell you everything, Kate,' he said. 'God help us. I don't know what will happen after that. But I've had this inside me too long now. But please, Kate. Please try to understand. I'm so afraid of what you will do.'

Kate took a deep breath. She squeezed his hand. 'Go on,' she said.

The story unfolded slowly, and by the end Frankie was close to tears. Kate could hardly believe what he'd said.

'You buried a girl?' She shrank back from him. 'You mean you and Joe just dug a hole and put that poor girl and her dead baby in it? Jesus wept, Frankie.'

'Kate—'

'Don't.' Kate put up her hand to silence him.

She thought about their own little girl, how perfect she was as she lay in her white coffin. How broken Frankie had been as he carried it into the church that freezing winter's morning. Even through her grief, she had taken some comfort from the belief that Emily was with God. She wondered if Frankie had ever thought about Alice and her dead baby during those terrible days after Emily died. He must have been riddled with guilt, yet he couldn't tell her. Part of her felt sorry for him and she wanted to put her arms round him. But she couldn't come to terms with the fact that they had buried Alice with her baby still joined to her.

'The cold, unfeeling indignity of it,' she said, shaking her head. 'The total disregard for human decency. Mother of God, Frankie. I can't believe you did that. You're not the man I thought you were, Frankie.' Tears filled her eyes.

'What did you think you were doing?' she continued, her voice rising. 'Did you think this would just go away? Did you think you could bury somebody like a dog and just go on living? What about her father? Didn't you care about him? How dare you, Frankie! Shame on both of you! They never even got to be buried with a priest at their side. God forgive you!' Kate burst into tears. She got up and went into the kitchen. Frankie followed her.

'Please, Kate,' he pleaded. But she kept her back turned to him and he knew he daren't touch her. 'Please, try to understand. That's not who I am. I was a boy. A stupid boy of nineteen. I've lived in dread of this day since the moment I met you, Kate.'

'Why didn't you tell me before? Why didn't you tell me before things got serious between us? At least I could have made my mind up about you. At least I could have decided then if I wanted to spend the rest of my life with someone who is capable of doing what you did.'

'I was afraid I would lose you,' Frankie said barely loud enough for Kate to hear. 'I didn't want to lose you.'

She turned to face him and shook her head. 'You would have, Frankie.'

She walked past him and left the room. As she climbed the stairs, her legs felt heavy, as though the weight of Frankie's story had drained her to the bone. She stopped halfway and put her hand to her mouth, weeping softly as the disappointment, fear and disbelief overwhelmed her.

Frankie stood by the kitchen window looking out as dawn, pale and soft, spread gently across the sky.

# Chapter Thirty-six

Tom was still stunned by what Joe had told him. The image he had painted of that night in the woods had stayed with him all night as he lay in bed unable to sleep. By morning, he had more or less decided to put off his trip to Italy, but Joe had insisted. The entire journey had taken place in a kind of slow motion. Getting to the airport, handing over his tickets, boarding the plane – it was as though he was watching someone else do it.

It was only when the taxi was driving him from the airport into Rome that the sights and sounds began to sink into his fuddled, exhausted brain. And now as he sat in a pavement cafe off the Via Del Corso, he couldn't help but feel his spirits lift.

It was ten in the evening and the night was as balmy and breathless as he remembered it. He was in Rome. Part of him couldn't quite believe it as he sat in the little terrace cafe where he had so often contemplated his life. Nothing seemed to have changed. He watched families and courting couples live their lives, oblivious to the lonely figure at the tiny iron table in the corner where he always used to sit. He drank red wine from an earthen jug, relishing the taste and enjoying the way his body slowly unwound. In the jaded buildings around him lights went on in apartments and rooms as the city seemed to wake up and shake itself from the stupefying sleep of a sweltering afternoon. Shutters were thrown open, and the chattering from within mingled with the honking of horns and the buzz of scooters on the tight cobblestone streets. Tomorrow he would travel north on the bus to Ostia, and then his journey would really begin. But tonight he would simply drink in the atmosphere and remember. Tonight he would probably drink more red wine than he should so that he could go to the single bed in his pensione and blot out the last twenty-four hours.

He had sat up most of last night with Joe, listening with horror as he told the story of Alice McPhee. It was like a confession, and by the end Joe was pleading with his brother to forgive him.

'That's between you and God,' Tom said. 'I'm not a priest, it is not my place to forgive.'

'But you will always be a priest in the eyes of God,' Joe protested.

'No, Joe. I will not. Don't try and tell me who or what I am in God's eyes. I cannot absolve you of what you have done. I can barely believe it. I don't want to believe it. And you even dragged Frankie into the mess you created.' Tom was pacing the kitchen floor as he spoke. 'You actually buried a dead girl and her baby, then went on with your life as if nothing had happened! And you think I can just put on my priest's collar and forgive you? Jesus, Joe. What kind of a man are you?'

Joe had sat with his head in his hands. 'I wasn't a man, Tom, I was a stupid shit of a boy who didn't give a damn about anybody except himself.'

'You were man enough to make that poor lassie pregnant!' Tom said. As soon as he said it he was sorry, for Joe was crying. He had never in his life seen him so upset. He wanted to touch him and tell him he understood how frightened he had been. That sometimes in their recklessness people make the wrong choice and pay for it for the rest of their life. Tom wanted to tell him that God was all forgiving, that forgiveness was at the heart of everything he had learned from the day he walked into the seminary. But for too long now he had been drifting from his own faith. He still believed but he felt he was in no position to preach or to counsel his brother.

Eventually he said, 'I'm sorry, Joe, but what do you expect me to do? I'll support you, whatever happens. But I don't think you can just leave things as they are.' Despite Joe's protests, Tom told him that he and Frankie must find a way to give Alice a decent burial.

When he left in the morning, they embraced, and Joe held him tightly and for a long time.

'Good luck to you, Tom,' Joe said, his face looking suddenly older and greyer. 'I hope you find her.'

Tom smiled and touched Joe's shoulder. 'Maybe you should pray, Joe,' he said, remembering how prayer had so often pulled him through some of his worst days.

He had lifted his bag and put it into the waiting taxi.

Tom woke up with a start and for a split second had no idea where he was. The room was pitch black and it was only when his eyes focused on a chink of light coming through the high wooden shutters that he remembered he was in Rome. He'd had a fitful night's sleep when he eventually came back to the room after strolling around the city centre until the early hours. His dreams were filled with garish, twisted pictures of a girl and a baby clawing their way out of the ground. He half woke up, sweating in the stifling room, and then drifted back to sleep. When he did, he saw Joe and Frankie laughing as teenagers, dressed up on a Friday night, their hair and faces shining. Then Frankie was standing on a hillside near their farm, shouting to Joe to wait for him as Joe backed away further and further into the light and finally disappeared. Tom woke with a shiver, confused and disorientated.

He got out of bed and pulled open the shutters. The room was immediately bathed in exquisite morning sunshine. He looked down into the courtyard below, which was already buzzing with people starting their day. He resolved to try to put everything out of his mind for the next few days and concentrate on why he had come to Rome.

In the small breakfast room he was given fresh bread and coffee by the surly-looking man who had been asleep at the reception desk, an empty wine bottle beside him, when Tom had come in around two in the morning. The man was instantly more pleasant when Tom asked him a couple of questions in Italian, obviously impressed that this was not just another British tourist who expected everyone to speak English.

On the bus to Ostia, Tom settled into a seat by the window and watched the various passengers who got on and off as the bus wound its way out of the city and northwards. A priest in his black hat, who was about Tom's age, sat opposite him. His face was pale and thin but his eyes were soft and he had the look of a contented man whose life was comfortably predictable. It could easily have been him. He thought about Joe and Frankie, and what they had done. And he thought of Kate and what she would do now that Frankie had probably told her the whole story. She would feel betrayed. He wondered how she would deal with it. He hoped she didn't leave Frankie. He would die without her. It had crossed Tom's mind that they should go to the police and admit everything, but the consequences of that were dire. Who knew what would happen? They might even accuse Frankie and Joe of murder. It would have to be kept secret, just as it had always been. But things could never be the same between all of them now.

Tom studied his street map of Ostia and by the time the bus pulled into the port, he had memorised the route, from the small hotel he would stay in to the address of the cafe on the hill where he had been told Maria lived and worked. It was three in the afternoon and the restaurants and cafes around the harbour were still busy with lunchtime diners. Tom smiled to himself as he walked in the sunshine; he had forgotten what it was like to live like this. Often on weekends he and other students had taken a train or bus to another town where they ate leisurely lunches in cafes and walked in areas where few tourists ever ventured. Despite the intense studying at the seminary, it had been an idyllic life and for a long time after he came back home, he longed to go back to Italy to live. But with Joe in America and a farm to run, there was no question of leaving his mother by herself.

In the small hotel on the edge of the square near the church, Tom could see from his window the ancient church bells tumble and chime to signal four in the afternoon. He took a bath and then stood surveying the four shirts he had laid out on the bed, wondering which one to wear. Eventually he chose the pale blue one. He tucked it into his dark blue cotton trousers and looked at himself in the mirror as he combed his dark hair straight back, examining his face for lines and wrinkles. His fingers touched the flecks of grey at his temples, then the lines around his eyes. He looked tired. He took a deep breath. It was now or never. He pushed his wallet into his pocket and walked out of the room.

The streets leading up to the cafe were deserted and most of the shops were closed, with the blinds pulled down. Above him, old women sat on tiny balconies fanning themselves in the searing heat. The city was asleep. You could almost hear it snoring. In only one or two bars was there any sign of life – a few locals sat playing cards or sipping coffee and cognac. Tom felt sweat begin to trickle down his back as he climbed the cobblestone street where the cafe was. He stopped when he saw the sign hanging outside. Cafe Meridien. This was it. His chest tightened and he had trouble breathing.

Above the cafe with its dark stained-glass windows and heavy wooden frames was a small balcony which contained two wooden chairs and a large sunflower. It was a drab-looking building. Tom stared up at the balcony, trying to summon the courage to step into the cafe. He could see through the tiny windowpanes that it was empty, but the door was open. Then he looked up at the balcony again and blinked as someone walked onto it.

Tom felt dizzy for a moment and almost lost his balance. A boy was looking down at him, with no more than idle interest in the stranger who was standing in his street. He smiled briefly and Tom caught his breath. For the face smiling down at him was the image of himself in the black and white picture taken on his first day at the seminary. Tom felt his legs go weak. When he blinked again, the boy was gone.

He stood outside the cafe, trying to catch his breath, his heart thumping like a drum. When he opened the door of the cafe, he saw only the back of a woman's head. She was calling out something in Italian as she placed coffee cups on a shelf. Tom stood on the black and white tiled floor and watched her, hardly breathing. He thought the pulse in his neck was about to explode. Eventually, feeling the presence of someone in the room, she turned round with a smile on her face. That smile. That face. Those eyes. Older, but it was her. The way she used to hold her head when she was trying to figure something out, before she laughed at what a scatter-brain she was. The way her liquid eyes filled up the day he said goodbye to her. Now her mouth dropped open and she gasped. The cup she was holding shattered on the floor like a scream.

'Maria,' Tom tried to say, but it was barely a whisper.

She put her hand to her mouth. Her face was suddenly white. 'Tom,' was all she could say. 'Tom.' He thought he heard her say, 'Oh God.'

They stood staring at each other, unable to move, unable to speak.

'Maria,' Tom said, taking a step closer to the bar. 'Maria, I'm ... I'm so sorry.' He shook his head and tried to swallow the emotion rising in his throat.

Maria moved closer so that only a couple of feet of marble counter separated them. Her gaze didn't waver and Tom looked into the eyes that he had dreamed of on so many empty nights. He looked at her hair, still dark and thick and gleaming, the pale, high cheekbones, the soft neck that he longed to touch.

'You're sorry, Tom?' She looked suddenly angry. 'You're sorry?' She shook her head and her mouth tightened. 'Twelve years, Tom. Now you come? What do you want from me? My life was ruined, Tom. Ruined.' Her eyes filled up.

Tom reached out so that his hands touched the cold marble top of the bar.

'I didn't know,' he whispered. 'I didn't know about the letters,

Maria. I thought you had just stopped writing.' When he saw the confused look in her eyes he blurted out what his mother had done. They stood in silence for a moment. Then Maria looked at him, her hand on the counter top, almost touching his fingers.

'You have a son,' she said, her expression softening. 'Luca. Looks just like you.' A tear ran down her cheek and she brushed it away.

Tom bit his lip. 'I think I saw him. On the balcony. He looked down at me.'

'That's him,' she said, smiling. 'That's Luca.'

They stood looking at each other, not saying a word. Tom wanted to say all the things he had planned over and over in his mind, but no words would come.

Suddenly the boy appeared from the kitchen. He spoke in Italian to Maria, who ruffled his hair and stroked his face. Tom thought he was telling her that he'd seen this man a few minutes ago. She was smiling at him, and he in turn smiled at Tom.

'This is Tom. He's from Scotland,' she said. 'Say hello, Luca.'

Luca held out his hand, and Tom took the soft hand in his and squeezed it gently.

'Hello, Luca,' he said hesitantly.

'You like football?' the boy said, looking eagerly at Tom.

'I do,' Tom said, smiling.

'I'm going to play for Roma when I'm older,' Luca said, and for a moment his expression reminded Tom of Joe.

'Is that right? Well, you'll have to be pretty good.'

'I will be,' Luca said. He smiled and went back into the kitchen.

'He's a fine boy,' Tom said, choking. 'A fine boy, Maria. You must be proud.'

Maria watched as her son disappeared into the kitchen.

'Why have you come, Tom?' she said.

'I wanted to see you, Maria. When I found out the truth, I had to see you. I had to let you know that I didn't abandon you.' He moved his hand so their fingers touched. 'I never stopped loving you, Maria. Never.'

Maria said nothing. She didn't move her hand and they stood there with their fingertips touching on the cold marble.

'I never wanted to stop loving you, Tom,' she whispered. 'But I had to.'

They couldn't speak. In each other's eyes they could see the heartbreak that was still raw.

'Maria,' Tom said, 'is there any chance we could meet and have a talk? I want to talk to you. I have so much I want to say.'

'I don't know, Tom,' she said. 'I don't know if there's any point.'

'Listen,' he said quickly. 'There's a small cafe on the harbour. At the far side. The one with the blue umbrellas. You know it?'

Maria thought for a moment then nodded her head.

'Tonight,' Tom said. 'At seven. I'll be there. Just to talk. Please, Maria.'

Her eyes seemed to say yes, but as Tom backed out of the cafe, a man, older than him, came out of the kitchen. He gave Tom a cold look and put his arm proprietorially round Maria's shoulders. Her face flushed.

Tom's heart sank and he turned and walked out of the door.

# Chapter Thirty-seven

The aroma of bacon and sausages coming from the kitchen woke Maggie. She squinted at the sun streaking in through her bedroom window and threw back the bedclothes. Downstairs, the radio was playing 'Hey Hey We're The Monkees', and Maggie automatically glanced up at her poster of the band's lead singer Davy Jones. She hummed along with the tune as she padded out of her bedroom down the hall to the bathroom. On the way, she noticed the door to the tiny boxroom was open. The door was almost always closed because it was such a mess inside, full of stuff that ought to be thrown out. She thought she heard movement in the room and stuck her head round the door. To her surprise she saw her dad on the camp bed, fast asleep.

Why was he sleeping there? she wondered as she went to the bathroom. She remembered the silence last night as they walked home after the fight between Uncle Joe and the Badger. Dad had looked as if he was going to cry. And when they got home, Mum had sent her and PJ straight to bed. They had listened at the top of the stairs, but all they could hear were muffled voices.

Maggie crept back down the hall and into PJ's room. She climbed into bed beside him and he groaned.

'What are you doing?' he said, his eyes half open.

'Dad's sleeping in the boxroom,' she announced, a worried look on her face. 'Do you think they had a fight?'

PJ eased himself up on the bed and rubbed his eyes.

'Are you sure?' he said.

'I saw him with my own eyes. He's fast asleep.'

PJ yawned. 'It's probably nothing.' Maybe it was too hot in bed. I was roasting.'

Maggie looked at him, considering this for a moment. 'Hmm,' she said, not convinced. 'Do you think they'll get a divorce? Like Martin Shaw's mum and dad?' She remembered how confused she had felt when the parents of PJ's friend from the village split up. She had watched her own parents closely for weeks afterwards in case it happened to them.

'Don't be daft,' PJ said. 'Anyway, Catholics aren't allowed to get divorced.' He swung his legs out of bed. 'Come on. I'm starved.'

As Kate piled the dishes into the sink, she was conscious that Frankie had come into the kitchen. She was glad Maggie and PJ had gone out to play after breakfast because she didn't want them around when Frankie came downstairs. She didn't think they knew that he had slept in the boxroom, but they were obviously aware that something was wrong last night. The atmosphere on the way home and afterwards in the house had been heavy. And this morning, even though she tried to be bright and breezy, she could see Maggie eyeing her suspiciously. She was so sensitive, always terrified that something would happen to shatter her safe little world. Kate knew she could never do that, and that was part of the reason she had lain in bed tossing and turning all night. When Frankie had come to bed she was still awake, and she told him she thought he should sleep in the boxroom. It was the first time since they were married that she had asked him to do that, and she wept after he silently left the room.

Now, as he stood in the kitchen, dishevelled and lost-looking, Kate just wanted to put her arms round him. But somehow she couldn't. She went to the oven and brought out a plate of breakfast. Frankie said he wasn't hungry, but she told him he had to eat. She filled two mugs of tea and sat down at the table. Frankie sheepishly sat down beside her. She watched as he picked at his food. Eventually he pushed the plate away and sat back in the chair. He looked at her.

'Kate,' he said softly, 'you're not going to leave me, are you?' His voice was weak.

Kate reached over and touched his hand. She could not leave him. But things could never be the same.

'No, Frankie,' she said. 'I'm not going to leave you.' She took a deep breath. 'How can I leave you? You and the children. You are my whole life. Everything I do is for you. I never wanted anything else.' She stopped and turned away. She swallowed hard. 'But . . . but what you did will always be there. I don't know how I can ever put that behind me.'

Frankie sighed. 'I should have told you, long, long ago. But I can try to make it up to you.'

Kate looked at the desperation in his eyes. 'How?' she said. 'It's not me you have to make it up to, Frankie. It's that poor girl. It's not me you wronged. It was her. You and Joe. That's who you should be thinking about.'

They sat in silence. Kate didn't know where they would go from here but she knew she desperately wanted them to be together. The thought of leaving him had flitted across her mind last night but she knew deep down that she could not live without him.

'Frankie,' she said, looking into his eyes. 'You have to go to the police.'

Frankie bristled. He looked shocked, and opened his mouth to speak.

'I don't know how you should do it,' she said, 'but you and Joe have to find a way to give that poor girl and her baby the dignity they deserve. They can't lie buried like dogs for ever.'

'But Kate,' Frankie protested, 'we could end up being arrested. There would be a police investigation. Everyone would be talking and pointing fingers. What about Maggie and PJ?'

'You didn't commit any crime,' Kate said. 'You made a mistake, an error of judgement. Once they dig Alice up they'll find she died of natural causes. Then she can be buried properly.'

'But everything will come out,' Frankie said. 'You know what this place is like.'

'You and Joe,' Kate said, standing up, 'have to find a way to let the police know. Even if you send them an anonymous letter. Or a phone call or something. You could do that, couldn't you?'

Frankie sat quietly, thinking.

'I'll support you whatever you do,' Kate said. 'I love you, Frankie. No less for what you did when you were a stupid boy. We'll still be a family, whatever happens. And I'll still love you even if Alice lies buried for ever. What's done can't be undone but you can make some kind of amends.'

# Chapter Thirty-eight

Charlie Martin couldn't be a hundred per cent certain, but he was fairly sure the woman getting into the taxi was Baldy's wife Breige. He only saw her from the back, but he was positive it was her. She'd put a suitcase into the boot of the taxi before she got in. It wasn't Tommy Muldoon's taxi either, so wherever she was going, she'd got a taxi to come all the way from Ayr for her. Charlie watched from the driver's seat of his red van as the taxi pulled away and disappeared out of the village. He sniffed at the sandwiches wrapped in bread paper that his wife had made for his lunch. Cheese again, he thought, irritated. That's three times this week. He wondered what it would be like to have a woman like Breige in your bed every night. Even better if she could cook, and according to Baldy she could do that as well.

He sat back and looked out of the window, wondering where Breige could be going with a suitcase at six in the morning. He stroked his chin, his mind turning over the possibilities. Charlie had been along with Baldy the night before he left for his golf trip and he hadn't said anything about Breige going away for a couple of days. In fact she was watching the shop and had been for the last three days. Baldy was due back this evening, so where in the name of God could she be going, when Baldy was just about to arrive home? Very strange, he thought. Very strange. He drove on out of the village towards the main post office to collect his morning delivery.

In the taxi, Breige looked out at the fields, a patchwork of green and gold, and the farms dotted across the landscape like smudges from an artist's brush. It was so gentle and quiet in the early morning. She sat in the back seat, her hand firmly clutching the small leather bag that contained most of Baldy's money.

'Going somewhere nice?' the driver said, half turning his head.

Breige did not feel like making small talk with some nosy taxi driver.

'No,' she said coldly. 'Not really. Just business.'

She caught his eye when he looked in the rear-view mirror and hoped her sulky glare would keep him quiet.

It did. He just drove and said no more.

Breige had spent last night tossing and turning in bed, waking up occasionally and reaching out to feel the empty space where Baldy would normally lie, his face peaceful. She had written him a note before she went to bed, which she had agonised over. All she said in it was, 'I'm sorry, Brendan. Truly I am. You don't deserve me, and I definitely don't deserve you. There is someone else. I'm going to America where people like me either sink or swim. I'm sorry about the money, but when I get to America and make my fortune, I promise you I'll send it back. Every last penny.' She signed it Breige. This morning she'd propped it up on the mantelpiece between two of Baldy's small golfing trophies and took one last look around the living room before she left. He wasn't a bad old stick, she thought. God love him. But Eamon would be at the airport to meet her and she couldn't wait to feel his arms round her.

Baldy Cassidy was lining up his shot at the tenth hole when he thought he heard somebody call his name. He glanced at Mickey McCann who gave him a confused look. They'd been the first on the course this morning at seven and hadn't seen a soul all the way round. Baldy squared up to his shot on the green again, assessing the distance from his ball to the hole. If he put this one away, he was too far ahead for McCann to catch up with him.

That would stuff him, Baldy thought, for all his bragging at the bar last night.

'Baldy! Baldy!' The voice was closer this time.

Baldy turned round. A figure was coming over the hill. 'Is that Charlie Martin? What the hell is he wantin'?' Baldy stood with his golf club in both hands. He looked at Mickey who shrugged his shoulders. Charlie was out of breath and sweating heavily when he reached them.

'Jesus!' he spluttered. 'I've been all over the place looking for you, Baldy. I need a minute to talk to you.'

Baldy looked at him impatiently.

'It's important,' Charlie said. 'I'd say it's something you definitely need to know.'

Something fluttered in Baldy's stomach and he immediately thought of Breige.

'Give us a minute, Mickey,' he said.

He walked a couple of yards with Charlie who explained that he had seen Breige coming out of the house with a suitcase this morning and getting into a taxi. A taxi from Ayr. Baldy's face went white.

'I mean, it's none of my business, I know that, Baldy,' Charlie said apologetically. 'It's just that you didn't say that Breige was going away anywhere while you were golfing. And I thought you should know. I mean, maybe there's something wrong with her family in Ireland and she couldn't get in touch with you.'

'Did you see where the taxi was going?' Baldy said calmly.

Charlie fidgeted. 'Well, actually, when I was passing – I mean I know it's none of my business – but when I was passing the taxi office in Ayr after my round, I popped in and asked. I said someone needed to get in touch with the lady.' Charlie looked embarrassed that he had been prying.

'And?' Baldy's eyes were wild.

'Well,' Charlie said, 'they said the taxi took her to Prestwick Airport. Now it might be nothing. It might be perfectly inno—'

'Fuck!' Baldy's face was crimson now. 'Fuck!' He threw his golf club over his shoulder and Mickey McCann ducked.

Baldy turned to his golfing partner. 'Listen, Mickey, I've got to go. Urgently. I'm sorry, pal. Will you pick up my stuff? I need to go now.' He was already walking off, with Charlie trotting alongside him.

'No problem, Baldy. Just go and do whatever you need to do.' Mickey picked up the club and put it in Baldy's golf bag.

Breige's eyes scanned the people waiting outside the airport for taxis and lifts. She had hoped Eamon would be outside to meet her and felt a little disappointed. She got out and paid the driver, not making eye contact with him. She lifted her bag and struggled to a trolley.

The concourse was swarming with people and there was a long queue at the check-in desk for New York. Maybe he was in the queue, she thought, so they would get a good seat. There were couples and families with children excitedly running around, but no sign of Eamon. Breige began to feel a pang of anxiety, but she pushed it away and moved towards the cafe. He wasn't in the paper shop, or the cafe, or on any of the seats along the wall where people sat waiting for flights to be called. She looked up at the flight monitor. She still had two hours to go. He would be here soon, she told herself. She ordered a coffee and sat at a table, her eyes glued to the swing doors at the entrance. She opened her bag and put her hand inside, fingering the money. Nearly two thousand pounds. And there was still a tidy sum in Brendan's box. She hadn't cleaned him out completely. She wondered what he would do tonight when he came in and found her letter on the mantelpiece. She did her best to ignore the guilty feeling that crept over her. By that time she would be in New York.

In Westerbank Charlie's van pulled up and Baldy jumped out, key in hand, and almost burst his way through his front door.

As soon as he stepped inside the house, he could sense she

was gone. He groaned. His eyes flicked around the living room and homed in on the note on the mantelpiece. He walked towards it, feeling weak at the knees. He opened the note with trembling hands and quickly read the single page. He gasped when he got to the last sentence about the money. He crumpled the paper up.

'Fuckin' jumpin' Christ!' he yelped. 'My money.' He was out of the living room and up the stairs two at a time. He threw himself onto the bedroom floor and reached beneath the bed for the box where he had kept his savings since he was twenty years old. He had never trusted banks. He knew before he opened the box that it was almost empty.

'Aw, Breige,' he moaned. 'How could you do this, Breige? Jesus, I loved you with all my heart.' Baldy sat with the open box in his arms, tears streaming down his cheeks. He was broken, humiliated. He could imagine how they would roar with laughter in Westerbank when they heard about this. But most of all he was shattered that he had lost the woman he adored.

'Are you all right up there, Brendan?' Charlie called from the bottom of the stairs.

Baldy wiped his face and took a deep breath. He got to his feet. 'I'm fine, Charlie. I'll be all right. Just leave me here for a while now. I need to be on my own.'

'Do you want to go and get her?' Charlie asked hesitantly. 'She's maybe still at the airport. If you don't get her now, you might never see her again. And something tells me she's taken more than your heart with her.'

There was silence upstairs as Baldy stood looking at the bed where just three days ago she was telling him he was the love of her life. He'd always felt she was a vulnerable thing, because of all the stuff she had told him about her early life. He didn't want her just for the sex, no matter how great it was. He wanted to love her and make her feel happy, secure and safe. All of the things she'd never had before. He thought she'd understood that. He couldn't believe there was badness in her.

He emerged from the bedroom and stood at the top of the stairs looking at Charlie who was staring up at him with a doleful expression on his face.

'Will you take me to the airport, Charlie?' he said.

'I will,' Charlie said.

# Chapter Thirty-nine

Tom wanted to phone home and tell Joe that he had found Maria, but he decided against it; he didn't want to be phoning with all the excitement in his voice after what Joe had told him the night before he left. He would wait until he got home.

He sat for a long time on a bench in the shade of a beech tree, thinking about Maria and Luca. He assumed that the man who had come in from the kitchen was the cafe owner. It certainly looked as though he was close to Maria, the way he put his arm round her. The thought pained him, but he knew it was naive of him to think that a woman like Maria would spend her life alone.

Tom looked at his watch. It was almost seven, and he got up to make the short stroll to the cafe at the harbour. He had been praying all afternoon that Maria would come.

At the cafe with the blue umbrellas, he sat at a table near the harbour, watching fish dart around in a frenzy every time the old man at the next table tossed a piece of bread into the water. Tom drank lemonade and refused the menu the waiter offered, telling him in Italian that he was waiting for a friend. If Maria came, he hoped she would stay and have dinner with him.

It was nearly seven thirty, and the tables around him began to fill up with tourists and locals. The waiter looked at him sympathetically. She's not coming, Tom thought, and his heart was heavy. It was crazy anyway to think that anything could come of it. She had been here so long now and was settled. It was plain to see that the boy was more or less Italian. Maria had introduced

215

him as Tom from Scotland. He wondered if the boy even knew where Scotland was.

He put his hand into his pocket and fumbled for some change to pay for his drink. When he looked up, there she was. A bright blue and white dress hugged her slim body. Tom was shocked, delighted and excited all at once. He sat with his mouth open, looking at her.

'Aren't you going to ask me to sit down, Tom?' She smiled and her face lit up.

Tom jumped to his feet. 'Sorry,' he spluttered. 'God, Maria, I thought you weren't coming. I'm so glad to see you. Thanks for coming.' He was conscious that he was blabbering. She sat down. The waiter came across to them and gave Tom a knowing smile.

'Will you stay for dinner, Maria?' Tom said, feeling slightly more composed. 'Please?'

'Yes,' she replied. 'I'll stay.' She looked out across the sea. 'I talked to Fabio, the man who came in from the kitchen. We are . . .' She hesitated. 'Fabio and I, well, we're very close, Tom.'

Tom felt instantly depressed. He tried to take a deep breath to steady himself.

'He knew who you were the moment he saw the two of us. He knows everything, Tom. About you and me. I told him a long time ago.'

Tom said nothing. He watched her mouth as she spoke. How beautiful her expression was when she was serious, how she looked him straight in the eye when she talked. She hadn't changed in twelve years.

'You look exactly the same,' he said, aware that he was staring at her. 'Exactly the same.'

She smiled and his heart leapt. He had almost lost the ability to summon that smile from his memory.

'A little older, Tom.' She laughed. 'A few lines, a few grey hairs. Just like you.' She looked at his greying temples, and he touched them, smiling back at her.

They ordered the waiter's recommendation of sea bass to

share and some salad. The waiter poured them each a glass of wine. Tom took a huge gulp of his, hoping it would relax him, hoping it would help him get through dinner without making a fool of himself by doing something stupid like bursting into tears. Maria noticed him gulping the wine and he was embarrassed.

'I don't usually drink much,' he said. 'I'm just a bit nervous.'

Maria seemed much more in control than he was. He felt tongue-tied and awkward. Eventually, Maria spoke.

'Why have you come, Tom? Tell me more about the letters. I didn't quite understand today.'

Tom told her how he'd found her letters after his mother died, and that he'd gone to Girvan to try and find her.

'It is thanks to Gabriella Medini that I'm here now. She found out your address for me. I'm not here to make demands or cause you problems, Maria. I don't expect anything from you. I just had to let you know that I didn't desert you.'

Maria leaned across the table. 'Tell me about your life, Tom,' she said. 'Tell me what has happened to you since the last time we saw each other.'

Tom talked until the sun slowly slipped behind the buildings and the harbour became shrouded in darkness. Maria watched him and listened quietly until he had finished.

'Did you never meet another woman?' she asked eventually. 'I mean did you not go out with women?'

'Of course I did,' Tom said. 'I went out with a few. Had one or two relationships that could have been serious, but my heart wasn't in it. I decided it was better to be on my own.'

Maria nodded. 'I missed you, Tom,' she said. 'You know, for the first six months, while I was pregnant and being dragged back to Italy by my parents, I wanted to die. I couldn't believe you had abandoned me.'

'But I didn't,' Tom interrupted. 'I thought you had found somebody else.'

'I know that now,' Maria said. 'But for such a long time I was, well, I suppose I was grief-stricken. It was as if you had died. Something died in me as well. But I had a baby to look after.'

She told Tom how she ran away from her parents because they were determined she would have the baby adopted. She had been lucky to find Fabio, who needed help with his young children.

'Fabio is kind to me,' she said. 'Things, well, things developed. We were two people, both very lonely. There was no obligation on my part. It just kind of drifted in that direction. That's where we are now.' She sighed.

'Are you married to him?' Tom asked.

'No,' Maria said. 'He wants to marry me but I keep putting it off.'

'Why?'

'I don't know.' Maria's eyes searched Tom's face as though there was an answer there. 'I don't know.'

They were quiet for a moment, drinking their wine, both so aware of what might have been. Maria's dark eyes glistened in the soft light. He ached to be with her. He would never get over her now. He would go back home and for the rest of his life he would remember her face on this night.

'Come back home with me, Maria.' His words hung in the evening air. Maria was silent. She looked at him, then at the table, then back at him and held his gaze. Her voice was soft.

'I have dreamed of that for such a long time,' she said. 'But maybe it's too late now. Maybe it was too late a long time ago. Things are so different now. Luca's settled here. So am I. And there's Fabio. It would break his heart.'

'Do you love him?' Tom said, hoping he didn't sound as though he was pressurising her. He could feel his heart beating.

'It's a different kind of love, Tom,' she said. 'I care for him. I respect him. Yes. I probably love him but I am not in love with him. Not like – not like the way I was. I don't know that we could ever have that again.'

'We could give it a chance, Maria,' Tom said. 'We didn't choose to have things turn out the way they did. I feel I've been robbed.

Robbed of you. Of our son. Of any chance to be really happy. That wasn't my choice. Nor was it yours. Please, Maria. Please tell me you'll at least think about it.' Tom reached out and held her hand. She touched the back of his with her fingers.

'I will,' she said. 'I promise I will. I have to speak to Fabio. And to Luca.'

When they left the cafe, they walked to the edge of the harbour and along the tiny side street that led back towards Maria's home. At the end of the road they stood in the quiet street, the lights from the windows of the houses glowing in the darkness.

'I'd better be going now,' Maria said, her face turned up towards his.

He touched her hair, then her face. He took a step closer and kissed her on the lips. He could feel her return his kiss and he gently pulled her close.

'Will you meet me tomorrow night at the same cafe?' Tom said, wanting to hold her for ever.

'I'll see,' she said. 'I have a lot to think about, Tom. I just don't know.'

'I love you, Maria.'

'Don't, Tom.' Maria looked as though she was going to cry. 'You have no idea how much I've wanted to hear you say that again. But everything is so different now.' She stepped back from him and turned away, walking briskly up the road. Tom watched to see if she would look back. If she looks back, he thought, she still loves me.

Maria walked on, beyond the shops and towards the turning that led to her house. Then just before she went round the corner, she looked back briefly and Tom saw her pale face in the street lights.

# Chapter Forty

Breige watched as the queue at the check-in for New York dwindled to half a dozen, then to just four. She had been in and out of the airport constantly, peering into arriving taxis or buses, searching for Eamon. But even as she told herself he would be there any minute, the most awful, sinking feeling threatened to overwhelm her. He wasn't coming. She knew even before she made a fool of herself at the airline desk, where she asked if there was a booking in her name or Eamon's and then burst into tears when the girl told her no. Now she slowly pushed her trolley across the busy concourse, tears streaming down her face. People gave her sympathetic looks, assuming she had just said farewell to a loved one. She went into the toilet and shut herself in a cubicle where she gave way to heaving sobs.

She sat back on the seat and blew her nose. She had no idea what she was going to do now. She opened her handbag and looked at the thick wad of notes she had taken from Baldy's box. He would die when he went home tonight and discovered what she had done. She came out of the cubicle and looked at her reflection in the mirror, her puffy red eyes and blotchy face, and burst into tears again.

Eventually, Breige left the toilet and pushed her trolley aimlessly. She would have to get out of here, she thought. She would go home to Dublin. But before she did that, she would get an envelope and put most of Baldy's money in it and send it back to his house in a taxi. She would only take enough for her passage home.

She went into a shop and bought a brown envelope, then found

220

a quiet corner of the airport and stuffed most of the notes into it. She addressed it to Brendan Cassidy. She walked through the swing doors of the airport and stood waiting for a taxi, barely able to hold back the tears.

'There she is,' Charlie Martin said as he swung his van into the airport and up towards the entrance. 'Look, Brendan. She's standing with a trolley.' He pulled up at the kerb.

Baldy said nothing. He kept his eyes on Breige who seemed totally unaware that she had been spotted. He felt sick inside. Now that he was here and could see her he didn't know what he was going to do. His anguish when he had found out that she had left him had turned to anger when he realised she had all but cleaned him out. But now as he sat in the car he could see from the red puffiness about her face that she had been crying. There was no sign of the man she had said she was going to America with. Baldy wondered if she had been jilted and, despite his own hurt, he felt a rush of pity for her.

'You sit tight, Charlie,' he said, opening the car door. 'I'll deal with this.' Baldy got out of the car and realised his hands were trembling.

Breige was still facing away from him. Perhaps she was looking for her fancy man, Baldy thought. He took a deep breath and walked up to her.

'What's the matter, Breige?' he said softly, right behind her. 'Been stood up?' She turned with a look of absolute horror on her face.

'Bren – Brendan.' Her lips mouthed the name but her voice was less than a whisper. 'Oh God, Brendan.' Breige's eyes filled up and her face crumpled. 'Oh Jesus, Brendan, I'm sorry.' She burst into tears. Baldy didn't know what to do. He shifted about from one foot to the other, looking around him, then at Breige. Before he could stop himself he put an arm on her shoulder. Then he had his other arm round her and she was sobbing into his shirt.

'Hush,' Baldy said, stroking the back of her head while she sobbed and kept saying she was so sorry. He pulled her round and gently moved her towards a wooden bench beside the glass windows of the airport.

'C'mon,' he said. 'Sit down here.' He pushed the trolley over and made Breige sit down on the bench then sat beside her. She kept her head down, still crying. Then she reached into her bag and pulled out the envelope.

'Look, Brendan,' she said. 'I was going to send it back to you in a taxi. That's what I was doing right now. Looking for a taxi.' She looked into Baldy's eyes and burst into tears again. 'Oh, I'm so sorry. How could I have done this to you?' She pushed the envelope towards him, but he didn't take it.

'And where were you going, Breige?' Baldy asked.

'I – I was going back home. To Dublin,' she said. 'I've done enough damage here.' She rubbed her eyes. The two of them looked away from each other, then Baldy took her face in his hands.

'I take it this fella – where is he anyway? Has he gone off already with some of my money? Or is it all here?' He looked at the envelope.

Breige wiped her tears. 'I'm so ashamed,' she said. 'It was all a scam, Brendan. It's just that – it's just that I didn't bank on you being a good man. I didn't bank on liking you.'

'What do you mean a scam?' Baldy asked, though he thought he already knew the answer.

He sat kneading the palms of his big soft hands as though they were dough, while Breige told him the whole sordid tale. She spared him no details. She saw him wince when she told him that she had already given Eamon a lot of his money and that he was supposed to buy the tickets to New York. It was all organised. But he hadn't turned up. She should have realised, she told Baldy. And now she deserved all she got.

'If you want to get the police,' she said, 'I'll face the conse-quences. You gave me a chance, Brendan, but I was so wrapped up in that shite Eamon that I couldn't see that I would have been better off with you.' She burst into tears again. 'Oh Brendan,' she sobbed. 'Why couldn't I have met a man like you years ago, then maybe I wouldn't be such a bad lot.'

Baldy rubbed his face with his hands and shook his head. He fought back his own tears.

'You know, Breige,' he said, his voice quivering, 'when I met you, I thought sure you had been sent by God himself. You were everything I ever wanted in a woman. When I closed my eyes on that pillow at night I couldn't wait to wake up in the morning so I could see your lovely face again.' He sniffed. 'Oh, I knew you were far from perfect. I always thought you were hiding things from your past, but I didn't give a damn. All that mattered was that you were with me, Breige. I never thought you could do this to me. I mean, the whole of Westerbank will be splitting their sides with laughter.' He wiped his eyes. 'Stupid Baldy. Throwing himself at that young woman, and her taking him for the ride of his life. What an eejit. But you know something, Breige. I don't give a twopenny shite for what anybody says about me. Because the only thing that matters to me is that you're not going to be there any more when I wake up in the morning. That's the pain, Breige. Nothing else.' He turned his head away so she wouldn't see his tears.

They sat, not looking at each other and not speaking. Taxis came and went. People passed with luggage and trolleys, laughing and talking. Eventually Baldy spoke.

'What will you do?' he asked.

Breige swallowed and sniffed. 'Go home,' she said. 'Go back to Dublin. Get a job. Try to see if there ever comes a time when I can look at myself in the mirror again. I'm sorry, Brendan. I wasn't always bad.'

She handed him the envelope. He took it and held it as if it didn't belong to him. He didn't say anything. He stood up, his heart aching. He wanted to put his arms round her and take her home with him. But how could he ever trust her again? He would say goodbye to her and forgive her, then he would go back to Westerbank and put on a brave face. But when he opened his mouth, none of that came out.

'It doesn't have to be like this, Breige,' he heard himself say. She looked up at him, rubbing her swollen eyes.

'What do you mean?' she said.

'You could come home,' Baldy said, thinking he could be making the biggest eejit of himself in the history of the world. 'We could start again. Maybe one day you could really love me.' His throat tightened and he struggled to say the last words. Breige looked at him in disbelief.

'Oh Brendan,' she said. 'You mean it? Even after all I've done? You would actually take me back?' She was overwhelmed.

Baldy nodded. They stood looking at each other. Then he put his arms round her and held her tight. She squeezed him and he could feel her body heaving as she sobbed.

He released her and lifted her bag off the trolley. They walked towards the van where Charlie Martin sat staring at them, his mouth opening and shutting.

'In the name of Christ!' he muttered.

# Chapter Forty-one

'Gunboats says we're leaving in a couple of days.' When Marty said it, PJ understood why he had been so glum all morning. The two of them were sitting in the tree house, attempting to carve animals from pieces of wood the way that Sky had shown them. Marty's efforts were looking better than PJ's.

'Leaving?' PJ said. 'Where are you going?' He had known all summer that Marty and Jess would be on the move eventually, but he still felt rotten inside. Marty was just about the best mate he'd ever had. He was a lot different from the rest of the lads in Westerbank. He was smart and tough. He was never scared of anybody or anything and PJ would have loved him to be around when they were older. He knew stuff about girls as well; he said he'd felt a girl's breasts through her blouse behind the smoking sheds at school in Glasgow. PJ was awestruck; he could only imagine what that must be like.

Marty stood up and looked out of the tree-house window at Maggie and Jess who were making daisy chains on the grass below.

'Gunboats says we'll probably get a ferry to Ireland where Miranne has cousins.'

'That'll be good,' PJ said, trying to sound cheery. 'If you stay there, you'll maybe go to school and have a laugh. Irish guys are a good laugh. Mind I told you we were on that camping trip? They were great fun.'

Marty looked at PJ and then back out of the window.

'I suppose so,' he said. 'But I like it here. I mean, we have a laugh. I wish we could just settle here and go to school and stuff. But it's because Gunboats did that robbery.'

'Yeah,' PJ said, feeling funny talking casually about a robbery as if it was no more than going to the shops. 'But we can still keep in touch. I mean you can send postcards and letters. We can be penpals. Once you get sorted.' PJ didn't want to admit that he was wondering how this would be possible if they were moving around in a caravan.

'Yeah,' Marty said, his face sullen. He slumped back down and they carved in silence for a while, not knowing what to say to each other. Then Marty put his wood on the floor. 'I'm bored with this now.' To keep upsides with him, PJ put his wood down too.

'Yeah. Me too,' he said. They both got up and stood looking down at Maggie and Jess.

'Tell you what,' Marty said. 'I could teach you to drive before I go.' He folded his arms and stretched himself up straight. PJ thought he looked just like Gunboats.

'Drive?' PJ said. 'How?'

'Gunboats' car,' Marty said. 'He's up helping your da in the field this morning. They'll not be back for at least a couple of hours. And Ma's gone into the village.'

PJ looked at Marty in disbelief. 'Do you mean just take your da's car and drive it down the road? You're kidding! My da would kill me stone dead.'

Marty shrugged and shoved his hands in his jeans pocket. 'How's he going to know? Sure we'd only be out for twenty minutes and straight back. We could go down by the woods where the road is dead quiet. C'mon, PJ. Do you want to drive or not? You said you were dying to drive. Then, when you're older, you can always say I taught you,' he joked.

PJ shuffled his feet and looked at the floor. Nothing would thrill him more than to get behind the wheel of a car. He had never stopped fantasising about it since the day Marty drove them all home from the beach. It didn't look that hard, if you took your time. And he had imagined himself doing it so much. He thought of his dad. There would be hell to pay if he ever found out. But if they were quick, nobody would find out and it would be their secret. He looked at Marty and both their faces broke into a smile.

'Right,' PJ said, excited. 'OK.'

'We'll tell Jess and Maggie we're going for a walk and they can't come.' Marty climbed out of the tree-house window and grabbed the rope. When they were both on the ground, they moved to walk away from Maggie and Jess.

'Where're you going, PJ?' Maggie said, getting up and putting her daisy chain round her neck. Jess got up beside her and they both started after the boys.

Marty turned round.

'You can't come,' he told them. 'This is not for girls. Just wait. We'll be back in a wee while.'

'But where're you going?' Jess persisted. 'We want to come too. We can do anything boys can do. Can't we, Maggie?'

PJ looked at Marty and shrugged.

'OK,' Marty said. 'But the two of you better keep your traps shut about this. Right?'

Both girls nodded and followed on behind as they walked briskly up to the caravan site.

In the police station, DC Billy McGowan listened intently to the DCI's instructions. The chief introduced the officers from Glasgow to the small team that had been chosen to assist in the arrest of Gunboats McKay. They would make their way down to the caravan site where intelligence had told them he was living in some caravan that was falling to bits. It wouldn't be hard to spot. But nobody must make a move until Gunboats had been identified and the team from Glasgow was ready to pounce. It was all going to be precision stuff.

'Are we all clear now, lads?' DCI Galloway addressed the gathering.

'Yessir,' came the collective reply.

'Right. Let's get cracking.'

Everyone left the room, adrenaline pumping. But nobody was more excited than Billy McGowan. He had already been congratulated by the boss of the Glasgow operation, who said that once he got a bit of experience under his belt, there would be no stopping a guy like him. And his own boss had been interested when he suggested that it might be worth having a chat with that Joe McBride who was back from America all these years after Alice McPhee went missing.

At McBride's farm, Joe sat outside with a mug of tea, trying to make up his mind what to do. He hadn't slept a wink since Tom had gone off to Rome two days before and he was more exhausted than he could ever remember. He had been told by the motor neuron specialist that chronic fatigue was one of the early symptoms of his illness, and that within a few months he would feel more and more tired. He had been thinking long and hard as he lay awake at night, wondering how he would manage when he became really ill. He had thought about looking into nursing homes near Westerbank so he could be close to Tom and Frankie. He didn't want to be a burden to anyone. In the end he had made up his mind to go back to America before Tom came home. He had plenty of money and could be cared for just as well over there, for the short time he had left.

During his soul-searching since he had come home, Joe felt that he had screwed up so many people's lives. There was nothing for him here. Tom would hopefully find his girl and maybe there was a future in it for him. Whatever. There was really no place for him in any of their lives. The Badger was right about that. The final straw had been the expression on Frankie's face the other night when the Badger came out with all that stuff about Alice McPhee. That and the look on Kate's face. Tom was right. He had messed up everything for them. There was nothing he could do about it now, but it broke his heart to see how he had hurt the friend he used to weep over because he missed him so much during those early days in America. And the worst thing was, he couldn't make it right now. It was too late.

He decided that one way open for him was to write a letter to the police in Ayr and post it on the day he left for America, telling them all about Alice. He would state his case sincerely, telling the truth, but he would not mention that Frankie had helped him. He would say he had done it all by himself and tell them the exact spot where she was buried. He could see it in his mind and remembered how edgy he had felt standing at the spot that afternoon when Sky had suddenly appeared beside him.

He sat down and wrote the letter. When he finished it, he sealed the envelope and addressed it to the chief of police in Ayr. He left it on his bedside table. Then he wandered around the house not knowing what to do next. He went back outside and walked the length and breadth of the yard. He would go for a walk along the river, gather his thoughts, then he would go and tell Frankie about the letter and that he was going back to America.

Kate worked furiously in the house, scrubbing worktops, washing windows and tidying out drawers. Cleaning up and putting things in their place helped her sort the events of the last couple of days in her mind. Frankie had come back to their bed after that first night, but they both lay awake half the night, unable to sleep. She hadn't reached across the bed to hold him, even though she knew how much pain he was in. She lay there, trying to work out how they could get on with their lives from here. Waves of anxiety swept over her. Frankie was her rock. She relied on him for absolutely everything. Without him she didn't feel secure. But now when she looked at him she felt she didn't really know who he was. She couldn't believe that the man she loved could ever have been capable of doing something like that. She just didn't know how to deal with it. She had wept in bed, distraught that this shadow would hang over them for the rest of their lives. But she knew she couldn't leave him. And she could never leave the children or take them away from Frankie. She was stuck with it, and she would have to find a way to live with it. Frankie, too, was miserable, but she didn't know what to say to him. But she had to try. She would talk it through with him tonight.

'The keys are here,' Marty said from the driver's seat, and he pulled the keys out of the ignition and jangled them in front of PJ.

PJ smiled, but it was more a kind of grimace. He was excited and terrified at the same time. He felt his mouth go dry. He glanced at Maggie who looked shocked.

'Quick,' Marty said. 'Get in before anybody sees us.'

PJ glanced around the caravan site. It was quiet. An old couple sat dozing on deckchairs outside their caravan at the far side, but most of the other campers had gone out for the morning. He jumped into the passenger seat. Maggie and Jess got in the back and sat rigid with excitement and fear.

Marty turned the key and the engine spluttered to a start. He smiled confidently at PJ, winked and turned the steering wheel.

He drove out of the site and onto the village road.

'We'll turn up here.' He pulled into the first fork which took them by the river that ran alongside Beggar's Wood. 'The road here's like a dirt track, but cars still use it. It's where we saw that Irish woman shagging the guy.' He laughed.

PJ smiled. He hoped Marty couldn't see the terror in his eyes. Maggie's face in the rear-view mirror was white and she was clutching Jess's hand. He wanted to tell Marty that he had changed his mind, that this was stupid. It wasn't that he was afraid of driving. He was nearly sure he could do it, no problem. It was the thought of his dad finding out. He would kill him. Especially with Maggie in the car. But he had to go through with it now. It would make him and Marty like blood brothers.

Marty pulled the car into the side of the track and jumped out. 'In you get,' he said to PJ, who slid over to the driver's seat.

PJ said he knew about the gears, and Marty explained to him how to gently let the clutch out at the same time as he leaned on the accelerator. That was the secret.

PJ tried it, concentrating as he let the clutch out, but the car jolted and lurched forward two or three times.

'You're full of kangaroo petrol,' Marty said with a chuckle. 'Just take your time, PJ. Come on, man. You can do it.'

PJ tried again, his tongue sticking out as he tried to get the co-ordination right. To his amazement the car pulled away smoothly and they were off. He glanced quickly at Marty, hardly able to believe it.

'We're moving, Marty,' he said, gripping the steering wheel, his knuckles white. 'I'm driving.' He looked into the mirror and Maggie was smiling.

'Keep your eye on the road,' Marty said. 'Keep concentrating. That's the most important thing. Gunboats said so when he took me for my first lesson last year.'

A few miles before Westerbank, Charlie Martin noticed the lorries had arrived and the navvies were starting to dig up the road.

'Shit.' He turned to Baldy. 'There's roadworks on the cut-off back to Westerbank. I think I'll come off here and go along the river. It seems a bit longer, but we'll be quicker in the end. What do you think, Brendan?'

'Fine,' Baldy said. He glanced back at Breige and smiled. She gave him a sheepish smile back. 'You all right back there, Breige?' he said, putting out his hand to pat her knee. She nodded.

PJ kept the car straight and on the narrow path, driving slowly. It felt fantastic. He was actually driving and he wasn't even frightened any more, as long as his dad didn't find out. 'This is brilliant,' he said, smiling, his face flushed with excitement. 'It's magic, Marty. What do you think, Maggie?'

'Brilliant,' Maggie said, sounding a little wheezy.

They drove on for another half a mile. This is what it would be like in just a few years, PJ was thinking. He imagined himself getting dressed on a Friday night and going out in his dad's car to pick up his mates, then going off to find some girlfriends. His dad used to tell him of the great nights he and Joe had when they were young men, before Joe went off to America. It would be just like that for him, PJ thought. If only Marty wasn't going away. They could have been just like his dad and Joe had been.

'Watch out here,' Marty said. 'It gets a bit narrower. Just be careful.'

PJ managed to change down a gear and drove even more slowly. He was thrilled with himself, the way he changed the gear so smoothly. But suddenly a car appeared round the bend in the river, coming in the opposite direction. There wasn't enough room for two cars to pass. PJ froze.

'Shit!' Marty said. 'Brake, PJ! Brake! Oh shit!'

There was no time to brake. And even if PJ had, it would have made no difference. The other car was going at a pace and it smashed into them head on, knocking their car off the road. PJ's head hit the windscreen. He saw it happening, as though he was above the car, watching it from the outside. He touched his head and felt blood. He thought he heard Maggie scream. Everything went slowly, like a dream. He looked briefly at Marty as the car shot off the road. Then they heard a splash and PJ thought he could see the car hitting the river. Maybe he was dreaming. Splash. It was dark in here. And quiet. Down and down it went, and it got darker until PJ couldn't see anything. He turned to where he thought Marty was, but he felt his eyes beginning to roll. He looked in the back and saw Maggie and Jess huddled together. Their eyes were closed. PJ felt water at his feet, then his knees. His pants were wet. Maybe he had peed himself. He felt a punch on his arm. He thought he heard Marty saying to open the door. He tried, but he couldn't. He was tired. Then the water was up over his waist and filling the car. Marty shouted again to open the door. PJ pushed the door and it opened. He opened the back door and dragged Maggie out. Then they were floating somewhere in the darkness, but he didn't know where. It must be a dream. Where was Marty? PJ felt sleepy. He was floating away. He tried to hold Maggie but he could feel her slipping from his grasp.

Baldy felt his head smash against the windscreen and he was aware of shards of glass in his face. He could hear Breige screaming, and when he looked round, Charlie was half out of the shattered windscreen. There was blood everywhere.

'Jesus, Mary and Joseph! Breige! Breige! Are you hurt?'

'No,' she said. 'Oh Brendan! Your face! You're covered in blood.'

Brendan moved and pushed the door open. 'It's OK, Breige. I'm fine. Jesus! Charlie? Charlie?' Charlie was half in and half out of the car. Baldy could hear him moaning.

Baldy got out of the car and leaned over the bonnet. 'Can you hear me, Charlie?'

Charlie opened his eyes and groaned. There was blood on his head and his hands were cut. Breige staggered towards Baldy, who took her in his arms.

'Where's the other car?' he said, looking around.

'Jesus!' Breige said, staring at the river where a car was disappearing under the water. 'Brendan, look! Jesus, Brendan, it's sinking!'

Joe heard the bang as he walked along the riverbank. He had just waved to Charlie Martin who had driven past him with Baldy in the front of his van and what looked like Breige in the back. They must have hit something. He quickened his step round the bend and stopped dead when he saw what he thought looked like the top of Gunboats' car disappear beneath the water. Charlie's van was almost on its side at the edge of the bank, and he was pulling himself out of the passenger door. Baldy and Breige were staring at the river. Breige was getting hysterical, saying that it was all her fault.

'Jesus!' Joe said. 'Who's in that other car?'

'I don't know!' Baldy said.

'It's PJ,' Charlie said, leaning against the van. 'And that wee laddie, Gunboats' boy!'

'Oh Christ!' Baldy said.

'Quick, Breige. Run up to the Flahertys' farm,' Joe said, taking off his shoes. 'Run and get Frankie. And phone for an ambulance.' He pushed Breige in the direction of the farm and then dived into the river.

As Breige ran, she saw a tractor turn into a farm road. She recognised the driver as Frankie Flaherty; two other men were on the trailer. 'Frankie!' she called. 'There's a car in the water! Joe's trying to get them out!'

In an instant Frankie was out of the tractor and Gunboats and Sky leapt out of the trailer. All three of them ran down towards the river.

'In there, Frankie!' Baldy shouted when they arrived. 'Joe's already in the water. I think the two boys are in the car, maybe some people in the back. I don't know.'

Frankie couldn't speak. PJ and Maggie were in the car. He knew it. He just knew it.

Sky was already out of his shoes and had dived into the water. It was black and cloudy. He held his breath and swam hard under water. There was a car in the distance. He swam towards it. One car door was open and there was nobody in the driver's seat. But he could see someone in the passenger seat. He wormed his way in through the open door and grabbed hold of the figure, a boy, and managed to get him out of the car. Jess was in the back. Lungs bursting, he seized her with one hand and dragged her out, then he kicked his legs as hard as he could towards the light.

He broke the surface gasping. His vision was blurred but he could make out figures on the riverbank. He kicked hard again towards the bank.

'I've got you, Sky. Come on, son.' It was Gunboats, in the water up to his waist. Suddenly he recognised who Sky was clutching.

'Aw, no,' Gunboats wailed. 'Aw God, no! My boy! Jess! Marty, I'm here.' He grabbed hold of the three of them, and dragged them out to the soft earth. Sky choked and coughed, then collapsed face down into the mud. Gunboats turned Jess on her back and shook her. She spluttered and coughed. He knelt by Marty and did the same, pushing at his back, but there was no response.

'Come on, son,' he said, kneeling in the mud, his face contorted. 'Aw please, son. Come on. Please don't be dead,' he sobbed. He turned Marty round, covered his mouth with his own and breathed. But Marty didn't stir. Gunboats stopped. Through his tears he saw the blue of Marty's lips, the pallor of his face. He was gone. Gunboats had seen enough dead bodies in his day to know that. His roar of pain and grief was heard by Miranne who was running to the river, along with half the village, having been alerted by Breige that there had been a car crash involving two boys.

Frankie was frantically running up and down the edge of the river, shouting for PJ and Maggie, and for Joe. But he could see nothing. He ran further and further down, following the current. He was numb with fear. Suddenly he saw something moving down-river with the current. Two figures, maybe three. Frankie dived into the water and swam towards them. It was Joe. He was holding PJ and Maggie, trying to keep their heads above water. But PJ wasn't moving and neither was Maggie.

'I'm coming, Joe!' Frankie shouted. 'Hang on, I'm coming!'

Finally he was close enough to grab hold of Joe's hand. But it slipped out of his grasp. He grabbed Joe's hand again.

'Hold on to me, Joe!' he shouted. 'Don't let go, please! I've got you, Joe! Hold on!'

Frankie felt Joe grip his hand and he swam with all his might to the edge of the river. He dragged himself out and pulled Joe and PJ after him. Maggie almost slipped away again but he managed to grab her and pull her back. Her eyes were closed and her face was white. She looked just as she had when she had almost died from asthma five years ago. Frankie heard himself let out a yell. He looked around frantically and saw Kate and several other people from the village racing towards him.

'Get an ambulance,' he screamed. 'Somebody get an ambulance.'

One of the villagers told him it was on its way. He turned to

PJ, who wasn't moving either. There was a gash on his forehead oozing blood. Frankie turned him over and slapped his back, again and again.

'Come on, son,' he whispered. 'Come on, PJ! You can do it! Come on, pal! You can't die! You can't!' Suddenly water spurted out of PJ's mouth and nose and he made a groaning noise. He started to breathe.

'That's it, son,' Frankie said, tears running down his face. 'That's it.'

PJ gasped then began to breathe fast, his eyes flickering.

Frankie jumped across to Joe, who was lying very still, hardly breathing. He looked up at Frankie and slowly smiled. His fingers tightened round Frankie's hand. Then his grip relaxed.

'Joe!' Frankie said. 'Joe! Come on, Joe!' He knelt down and gently slapped Joe's face, but there was no response. He held his head and put his mouth over Joe's and began to breathe. Joe's body felt limp and lifeless; his eyes were still half open.

A hand touched Frankie's shoulder and a voice said, 'He's gone, Frankie.' It was Michael Jamieson, the local policeman at Westerbank.

Frankie knelt back on his heels, his head in his hands.

'Come on now, Frankie,' Jamieson said. 'Your family needs you.'

Kate was kneeling over Maggie, clasping her body. She looked up at Frankie, her face an agony of despair.

'Oh no, Frankie,' she wept. 'Oh please, no.'

On the road into Westerbank, the convoy of three police cars on their way to arrest Gunboats McKay slowed to a halt in the main street as word came over the radio that a car had gone into the river and two were reported dead. A man and a boy. It might be the son of Gunboats McKay. They were told to use a bit of discretion.

In Rome, Tom was getting ready to go out and meet Maria. There was a sharp knock on his bedroom door.

'*Prego, Signor. Telefono. Urgente.*'

Tom felt his stomach turn over. Something bad had happened. He had left the number of his hotel at home but had never expected anybody to phone him. He rushed downstairs to the phone in the hallway.

'Tom?'

'Frankie,' Tom said, feeling his knees go weak. 'What's wrong?'

'It's Joe, Tom.' Frankie was sobbing. 'Joe's dead. There's been a terrible accident. And Maggie. Maggie's . . . Oh, Tom. Come home.'

# Chapter Forty-two

In the small hospital room, Frankie and Kate sat silently watching Maggie's pale face as she breathed through the oxygen mask.

Frankie had barely been able to speak since they'd arrived in the ambulance hours earlier. He couldn't begin to imagine how he and Kate would cope if Maggie didn't survive. And PJ would never get over it. He couldn't stop sobbing and kept blaming himself. Finally Sky took him outside. Sky himself was barely able to stand after his ordeal trying to rescue Marty and Jess. The moments by the riverbank after it all happened were something of a blur now to Frankie, but as he got into the ambulance, the last face he saw was Sky's. He had looked so lost and alone, with tears running down his cheeks. The doctors had told Frankie and Kate that they would have to wait until Maggie came round to see if the few minutes she had been starved of oxygen had caused any brain damage. If she didn't come round soon, they would do some tests on the brain. Frankie had held Kate as she wept, but he couldn't find any words.

He could hear the hand of the clock on the wall click forward every minute. He wondered if Tom was on his way home. He would be distraught about Joe, but Frankie had hardly taken in that Joe was dead; all he could think about was Maggie.

'Kate,' he said, 'I feel so responsible for all of this. I'll never live with myself if anything happens to Maggie.'

She looked at him, then reached over and held his hand.

'Don't, Frankie,' she said. 'It's not your fault. I don't know why these things happen. But it's not going to help if you blame yourself.'

Frankie shook his head. 'Maybe it's all punishment. You know. For what Joe and me did.'

Kate squeezed his hand and shook her head. 'Don't even think it. There's too much at stake here. What about PJ? Can you imagine what he's going through? He needs you, Frankie. He needs you to be strong.' She looked at him, his eyes red and puffy from crying. 'And I need you. Now more than ever, Frankie.'

The door opened and PJ came in with Sky.

'You look terrible, Sky,' Kate said. 'You should be resting.'

Sky shook his head.

'Dad,' PJ said. 'Tom's out at reception. I saw him come in.'

Frankie got to his feet. 'I'd better go see him.'

Tom was standing with his back to him in the empty corridor. He turned when he heard Frankie's footsteps. Frankie was struck by how pale and drawn Tom looked. He stopped so that they were only a foot apart.

'I'm sorry, Tom,' he said. 'Jesus. I'm so sorry.' He put his arms round Tom and held him as he sobbed into his shoulder.

'Why couldn't I have been here, Frankie?' he said. 'I didn't even get a chance to say goodbye to him.'

After a moment Tom wiped his eyes and tried to compose himself. 'What about Maggie? Is she going to be all right?'

'We don't know, Tom,' Frankie said. 'We can only pray.'

The two of them walked into Maggie's room. Kate got to her feet and hugged Tom, and then Tom embraced a tearful PJ and squeezed Sky's arm.

They all watched Maggie who lay motionless on the bed. Sky reached over and touched her arm.

She blinked a couple of times and everyone held their breath. Then Maggie opened her eyes and looked around at all the faces staring down at her.

'Hello, Sky,' she said, a half smile coming to her lips.

Kate and Frankie burst into tears and hugged each other, and Tom rushed out to get the doctor.

Maggie looked at PJ who was in tears at her side.

'Are you all right, PJ?' Her voice was barely audible. 'Where's Marty and Jess?'

'Sssh, now,' Kate said. 'The doctor said you've to rest.'

# Chapter Forty-three

Tom watched the colours change in the autumn sky. A perfect amber sunset. The weeks drifted by and soon the talk would be of winter. A heaviness had hung over the village since the tragedy, and Tom rarely went out because he couldn't face the sympathetic faces all around him. Joe was considered a hero who had died to save PJ and Maggie. That was how they would always remember him in Westerbank, no matter what the Badger Ryan said.

They would also remember the day of Joe's funeral, for on the same day they dug up Alice McPhee from Beggar's Wood. Only Tom, Frankie and Kate knew how the police finally managed to solve the mystery of Alice. Tom had found the letter Joe had written, and the three of them decided that it should be passed to the police. They had opened it first and Frankie was moved to tears when he found that Joe had left his name out of everything. When they dug Alice up, the press and TV cameras were there, hoping for a murder story. But her post mortem established that she had died from complications relating to premature childbirth. The police made no mention of Joe McBride's letter, so how she came to be buried in the woods in the first place remained a mystery to the villagers. People would speculate about it for generations. The Badger Ryan was seen talking to reporters and hinted to them that Joe McBride might have had something to do with it, but nobody took him seriously.

At Joe's funeral, Baldy Cassidy, still traumatised from the crash and drinking whisky to steady his nerves, confessed to Frankie

241

and Tom that he had had sex with Alice McPhee months before she died. He said he thought a couple of other lads had been there too, and that there had probably been a few guilty consciences in the village when she went missing. Frankie and Tom showed the right amount of interest but made no comment.

Alice and her baby were buried in a quiet ceremony four days later in the cemetery beside her father. Only a handful of villagers turned up, and Kate was one of them; Frankie was working in his fields.

Gunboats and Miranne were arrested, and welfare workers came and took Jess away. She screamed and clung to her mother when the police arrested her parents, and neither Frankie nor Kate could bring themselves to tell Maggie the full story yet.

Sky moved in with Molly, and when Breige became pregnant he went to work full time for Baldy. He was a real stalwart to both PJ and Maggie, and never failed to visit them at least once a week when he finished work at the bakery. He was held in high regard in the village after his heroic efforts to save Marty.

Tom felt that sometimes he and Frankie didn't know what to say to each other on the rare occasions the two of them sat together drinking tea late into the night. After the funeral they had got very drunk and Frankie had said that he thought all of this was punishment from God because of Alice McPhee, but that maybe he had been given a second chance because PJ and Maggie had been allowed to live and Kate had not left him.

Tom had been so intent on trying to put Maria out of his mind that he hadn't even told Frankie what had happened in Rome. It would anyway have sounded cold and selfish to say that any chance he had had of getting back together with Maria had been ruined by the phone call telling him Joe was dead. But time and again as he sat in his kitchen at night he tormented himself by wondering whether Maria had been waiting for him at the cafe that night. Now he would never know. Before leaving Rome he had tried to phone the cafe where Maria worked but there was no answer, and he hadn't had time to go there. He'd simply thrown his things into his suitcase and headed straight for the airport. He should have gone to the cafe, he told himself during sleepless nights. He had asked the man in reception to take a message to Maria's home, but he had no idea if she ever received it. When he called the hotel a few days after Joe's funeral, he was told that the man on reception had been fired for being drunk on duty. Nobody knew anything about his note to Maria. After much agonising, Tom wrote to her, but he received no reply.

So he learned to live with it, just as he had done before. He walked in his fields every night, checking on his cattle. But mostly he just walked and walked to get the evening in. Tonight as he trudged home his heart felt heavier than ever. Maybe he would go up and see Frankie and they could go to Mulranney's for a pint. He couldn't live like this for ever.

As he got nearer his house he saw Frankie's car in the yard; maybe he had had the same idea and was up for a pint, Tom thought, and quickened his pace. We just have to get on with things, he told himself.

When he climbed the fence into his yard, Frankie was standing beside his car with a smile on his face. Tom hadn't seen that in a long time and smiled back automatically.

'How's it goin', Frankie?' he asked. 'I was just going to come up and see if you fancied a pint. I can't stand the house much longer.'

'I might,' Frankie said, still smiling. 'But you won't.'

Tom looked at him, confused.

'Somebody's looking for you,' Frankie said. 'The taxi dropped them at my house by mistake.'

As he said it, Tom felt his head swim, for just at that moment the back door opened and Maria, smiling, got out of the car, followed by Luca who dragged out a battered old suitcase and dropped it onto the ground.